HISTORY A̶ ̶L̶̶I̶̶B̶̶R̶̶A̶̶R̶̶Y̶ CENT

Books should be returned or renewed by the
last date stamped above

CUSTOMER SERVICE EXCELLENCE

Libraries & Archives

Kent
County
Council

00884\DTP\RN\04.05   LIB 7

Raider Publishing International

New York   London   Cape Town

C155223017

© 2011 Stephen Cheshire

All rights reserved. No part of this book may be reproduced stored in a retrieval system or transmitted in any form by any means with out the prior written permission of the publisher, except by a reviewer who may quote brief passages in a review to be printed in a newspaper, magazine or journal.

First Printing

The views, content and descriptions in this book do not represent the views of Raider Publishing International. Some of the content may be offensive to some readers and they are to be advised. Objections to the content in this book should be directed towards the author and owner of the intellectual property rights as registered with their local government.

All characters portrayed in this book are fictitious and any resemblance to persons living or dead is purely coincidental.

Cover Images Courtesy of iStockPhoto.com

ISBN: 978-1-61667-308-6

Published By Raider Publishing International
www.RaiderPublishing.com
New York London Cape Town
Printed in the United States of America and the United Kingdom

For
Grandma, Grandpa,
Grandad Terry, Ann
And all my family
"Your love is my strength"

THE FIELD TRIP

Stephen Cheshire

It has been a myth to many people that there is life outside the current universe. But people have claimed to have had experiences with extra terrestrials. When you look up at the night sky and you see the stars glisten down on you, what do you think? I can remember a film I saw when I was younger, in which each star represented a loved one that had been lost and they were looking down on you. Now that is quite a nice way to picture it, but the big question a lot of people would ask as they look up at them is, "What is beyond the galaxy? Another time? Other forms of life?"

Who knows? Taking into consideration our knowledge of the solar system, there are approximately one hundred billion stars in our Milky Way Galaxy. That is quite a lot. The likeness of parallel universes and the possibility of life on other planets has been expanded quite a bit. Our universe is believed to be one thousand trillion, trillion (1,000,000,000,000,000,000, 000, 000, 000) meters away from planet Earth Should Planet Earth be found in the vastness of possibilities, how would we be reached from outer space? Aliens from another universe or planet within our solar system and galaxy will have a lot of searching to do for the beautiful planet we call home.

But what would be the reason for an alien kind to invade us? Over population or lack of resources on their planet perhaps; anything which we have and they have not got or want could encourage them to do this. You always hear on the TV and the news about the sightings of UFOs.

In 1942, during the Second World War a bomber squadron was on its way to Germany to carry out a bombing raid and return to the UK. During the flight, one of the gunmen witnessed a small yellow glow by one of his fellow comrades. He looked at it through his heavy machine gun to see it swiftly moving round the craft. Just picture it like this: You know those bright blue lights you put up in restaurants and cafes? You see the flies zapping around them. It was just like that. But during the Second World War, if they told the command that they had witnessed something like a UFO, or anything suspicious, pilots would be grounded and sent for psychiatric assessment because some of them made up strange excuses so they wouldn't have to bomb or attack the other countries. Because of this the pilots and engineers were reluctant to say anything. But the day following the mentioned sighting, a Wing Commander of the RAF witnessed the same sort of light and movement, although it was of a different color.

During the Second World War the Nazis were doing some research into anti gravitas machines. Then there was something being developed called 'the Bell' right through the course of the Second World War.

The Bell was said to be an experiment carried out by Third Reich scientists working for the SS in a German facility known as Der Riese (The Giant) near the Wenceslaus mine. The mine was located around fifty kms away from Breslau a little north of the village of Ludwikowice Kilodkzie which was formerly known as Ludwigsdorf. This village was close to the Czech border.

The device was described as metallic, approximately nine feet wide and twelve to fifteen feet high, with a shape similar to that of a bell. It contained two counter-rotating cylinders filled with a substance that was similar to Mercury that glowed violet when activated. This is known as Xerum five two five today. It has been described as Red Mercury. When the Bell was active, it would emit strong radio active waves which led to the death of several scientists and various plant and animal test subjects. The

Bell was considered so important to the Nazis that they killed sixty scientists that worked on the project and buried them in a mass grave so no one would ever know of it. The only reason we know about the Bell is because of SS General Jakob Sporrenberg's testimony. He was charged with the murders. Sporrenberg was tried after the war by the Polish War Crimes court for the murder of his own people on what subsequently became Polish soil. But the thing is, would that have happened if the bell did not exist? Whether it had been evacuated out of Germany is unknown.

What does the word 'Roswell' mean to you? The Roswell UFO incident involved the alleged recovery of extra terrestrial debris including alien corpses, from an object that crashed near Roswell, New Mexico, USA, in July 1947. Since the late 1970s the incident has been the subject of a controversy and the subject of conspiracy theories around the true nature of what crashed in Roswell. The US military maintains that what was actually recovered was debris from an experimental high altitude surveillance balloon belonging to a classified program named Mogul. However, many UFO proponents maintain that a crashed alien craft and alien bodies were in fact recovered, and that the military then engaged in a cover up. Since then, Roswell became so widely known that when the name Roswell is heard either on the TV, radio, or elsewhere, people are automatically reminded of the UFO incident.

My story begins with an Armazoid spacecraft approaching a planet not even known to Earth, Planet Geneson. Geneson is approximately eight point nine trillion miles away from Planet Earth, way beyond the galaxy we are currently in. Small groups of Armazoids have been sent by there from their home planet, Armazon, to investigate the production of nuclear weapons capable of destroying planets with one strike. So you can guess from this that the Armazoids were very paranoid.

I want you to picture their small spaceship. It had a slightly pointed nose with two atomic engines at the back. The ship was capable of holding six Armazoids and had its crew quarters in the rear. Let me tell you a bit about the Armazoids. The Armazoids are way ahead of our time. We couldn't catch up with them even if we tried. It is absolutely out of the question. The Armazoids have a number of powers even the world's leading physicians couldn't claim. They have the power to change the size of anything, so if one of them is five foot six, they can shrink him down to nothing when they have the energy. The Armazoids are generally five foot six, with a short, stumpy body. The body is covered with a green skin. Like us, they have two eyes and a heart- nothing special.

*   *   *   *

Gremlon looked out of his window onto the huge, green planet as the small orange clouds gently passed over the islands.

"There it is" he said. "Planet Geneson. The place every one has been talking about."

"Do you think these people are developing weapons of mass destruction?" Comlon asked.

"Well, that's what we are here to find out" Gremlon said soberly.

The medium sized craft gently hovered above the planet. There was no sun like we have, to help generate food. A few moons circled the planet. The three Armazoids switched on their computers and looked at their digital screens as a small antenna came out and pointed down onto the Geneson Military Centre. The three Armazoids looked on as the high tech computers on board gathered the data in readiness to send it to the mother ship in a short while. The craft slowed down, orbiting the planet. Gremlon, the leader of the group, got out of his seat and looked down onto the huge green and red planet as Comlon, his colleague who he had known for all his life, looked down at his computer. The antenna pointed down onto the group of tiny islands as the orange looking clouds floated along. The enhanced computer slowly started scanning the ground below them as the spacecraft's retro rocket fired, keeping it in its orbit above the planet.

"Anything?" Gremlon asked.

"Nothing yet" Comlon replied.

The huge computer continued scanning the planet. Gremlon slowly turned his head to the left looking at the on board radar as it scanned for thousands of miles around him. He was feeling drowsy after all the traveling they had done from Armazon and the ship, but something made him jump. He slowly turned his head and looked at the black and green screen in front of him. He looked at the small, yellow blips conning towards their ship.

"Oh shit," he said. "We've got company."

Gremlon jumped up out of his seat and sat in the left-hand control seat of the ship. He pushed the tiny red button down folding the antenna away so he could power up the engines and return to the mother ship. He waited anxiously for the giant doors on the top of the ship to fold away and close as the yellow blips got closer to them by the second. He started up the engines as the crafts started to pull out of the orbit above the planet. He pushed the two throttles to the maximum. The two atomic engines at the back glowed a light yellow, propelling the ship along.

"Get the burners on" Comlon yelled. "They are right behind us."

"Won't be a minute" Gremlon said.

Gremlon looked down onto the computer screen. The rays from the chasing Gemlon ships fired onto them as they powered away from the planet.

"Ready!" Gremlon yelled

But before he could activate them, one of the rays hit the engines. There was a small explosion at the back. Gremlon looked down at his screen as the afterburners continued to fire up. He pushed the two power levers forward. The blue ray zoomed from the back, blasting the ship forward. The Gemlon space ships watched as the Armazoid's craft disappeared.

Gremlon lay back in his seat as the silver light of the passing stars passed the main front window. "That was close," he said. "You guys ok?"

The two Armazoids nodded, stunned by the sudden fire fight they had just got into.

"Let's assess the damage," Gremlon ordered.

He got up, looking down at the two control sticks as they continued blasting through the universe back to the mother ship. A short time elapsed.

"It should be ok until we get back to the ship," Gremlon said.

He sat down in the front seat of the craft and continued to look out as they sped through the galaxy. He looked at the huge yellow star as it shone in the center of the galaxy they were in.

"How far have we traveled?" he asked.

"About three point nine trillion," Comlon replied.

The ship went quiet as the other Armazoids assessed the data they had picked up from Planet Geneson. Gremlon suddenly jumped, as there was a sudden explosion. "Oh shit! Now what?" he went.

Gremlon looked down at his computer. He watched as the left atomic engine started to shut down. Light smoke started entering the cabin of the ship. There was a sudden surge. He continued looking at his computer as both the engines flared up. The ship started to slow down as he switched on the radio. On the main ship, Circo, the

Armazoid leader stood in the control room as they stood parked out trillions of miles away from the galaxy.

"This is Gremlon," the radio mumbled.

Circo slowly walked over to it.

"Gremlon, this is Circo. Can you hear me?" he asked. There was a short break.

"Yes, only just," Gremlon said. "We have been hit."

Circo stood looking down onto the radio. It went completely dead. "Gremlon," Circo said.

Gremlon looked up as the ship started to fill up with more smoke. He scanned the area around him looking for a place or a planet to ditch the craft. The sparks flew out of the radio. But something caught Gremlon's eye as the ship banked to the left. He saw a medium sized planet coming into view. He stared at the lumps of blue and a funny looking green color.

"There," he went.

Gremlon was pointing at Planet Earth. He looked at the huge, round planet as it slowly got closer and closer to them. He slowly turned the ship and headed towards it. Sparks continued to rain down onto them from the ceiling above as the instruments and system gauges started to fail. The planet grew bigger and bigger. The nose of the ship started to heat up. Gremlon pulled the control stick back, straining the craft's hydraulic system. The two other Armazoids could only sit and watch as the flames sped over the ship adding to the heat from the burning engines, and the craft gently rocked from side to side. The orange flames and plasma trails disappeared from the ship. Dense, jet black smoke poured from the back of the engine. Gremlon looked out of the window as they continued quickly dropping from the sky.

"What is this place?" Comlon asked.

"I, I don't know," Gremlon replied.

"How high are we?" Comlon asked.

"We are one five thousand feet above it. We've got maybe two minutes of glide time before we crash," Gremlon said.

Something else caught Gremlon's eye. He looked to his left to see two black jets pulling up next to him as they continued dropping towards the ground.

"What the hell are they?" Gremlon asked.

The two other Armazoids walked up to the window and looked out as the ground continued to get closer and closer.

One of the black jets pulled in front of the alien space craft, gently rocking its wings. Gremlon followed the black jet over the land. No one was about apart from them and the two jets. The craft continued slowly descending towards the planet. The last of the cockpit computer and gauges shut down one after the other blacking out, but there were a few still running at the back. He looked out to see a long strip in front of them, approaching as they passed through five thousand feet.

"Sit down," Gremlon ordered. "Now."

The two other Armazoids sat down as Gremlon reached out and pulled down the landing gear lever. The landing gear came down as the airstrip came closer and closer to them. The two black jets continued accompanying them towards the threshold of the runway. The extra drag from the landing gear helped slow the spacecraft down for a landing. Gremlon grasped hold of the control stick and pulled the nose up as the back gear slammed into the ground. The black fumes continued piling out of the aircraft. The speed brakes opened as the nose gear slammed down onto the runway of the huge military airstrip. The spacecraft started to slow down. Gremlon felt the nose wheel starting to creak. He held on tight as it touched ground, skidding along the rest of the runway.

The onlookers at the military air base watched as the

craft slowly came to a stop. The smell of the burning engines and landing gear wafted up their noses. Gremlon slowly looked up as he peeked out of the window. The alien life forms slowly started walking forward towards them. Gremlon looked at their grey uniforms and wide hats. The weather outside was freezing.

Time slowly went by for the Armazoids as they prepared to leave the ship. They were now completely surrounded. Gremlon looked down at his computer. He pushed the tiny emergency button. On his doing this it would signal their location to the mother ship. He also took the time to assess the area outside him. The computers read very high levels of carbon dioxide.

"Suits," he ordered. "Carbon Dioxide out there, and lots of it."

The group got into their suits, looking at one another as they prepared to go outside. They armed themselves, ready to fight till the death. Gremlon looked at his two comrades as he pulled the red lever. The back door opened leading through to the cargo bay. The two back doors slowly opened one after the other. The smoke poured in from the outside.

Gremlon walked out, looking at the group of men as they stood looking at them. There was another group turning up near them dressed all in white.

"What do we do?" Comlon whispered to Gremlon.

Gremlon didn't say a word.

The group of people slowly walked up to the aliens. Comlon swiped his sidearm. The group of people in front of him pointed their weapons at them.

"Now," Gremlon yelled.

He fired onto the men. The purple rays zapped through the air slamming into one of the men dressed in grey. The men in gray swiped their firearms, firing back at the Armazoids.

"Shit," Gremlon said as he dove to the floor.

He fired back and watched as Comlon and the other Armazoid fell to the ground. He knew he would have to surrender but the fate of Planet Armazon rested in his hands and on that ship.

Gremlon dropped his weapon onto the floor. He stood up slowly, looking at the group of alien life forms as they walked slowly towards him, clutching their weapons. Two of the alien life forms placed him in a strong, plastic bag. Gremlon felt his body being tightly compressed as he was lifted and placed on a metal table. He struggled to get out but the straps were too tight. He trembled as he wondered where on earth he was going. All he could see was the color black.

If you haven't already guessed, the craft had crash landed in Russia. Now a bit of history on Russia before we continue with the story. I promise it won't be long and the whole book is not on history. Russian history begins with that of the East Slavs. The East Slavs are a Slavic Ethnic group formerly the main population of the medieval state of Kievan Rus. They are the speakers of the East Slavic language. By the seventh century they had evolved into the Russian, Ukrainian, Belarusian peoples. The first East Slavic state, Kievan Rus adopted Christianity from the Byzantine Empire in 988. After the 13th century, Moscow slowly and gradually came to dominate the formal cultural centre. By the 18th Century the Grand Duchy of Moscow had become the huge Russian Empire, stretching eastward from Poland towards the Pacific Ocean. Expansion in the western direction sharpened Russia's awareness of its separation from much of the rest of Europe and shattered the isolation in which the initial stages of expansion had occurred. Succeeding regimes of the 19th Century responded to such pressures with a combination of half-hearted reform and repression. Russian serfdom was abolished in the year 1861, but its abolition was achieved on terms unfavorable to the peasants and only served to increase revolutionary pressures. Between the abolition of serfdom and the beginning of World War I in 1914, the Stolypin reforms, the constitution of 1906 and State Duma introduced notable changes to the economy and politics of Russia, but the tsars were still not willing to relinquish autocratic rule, or share their power.

The history of the Russian Federation is brief. It dates back to the collapse of the Soviet Union late in 1991. The Soviet Union Republics (USSR) was a socialist state that existed in Eurasia from the years 1922 to 1991. The Soviet Union emerged in the wake of World War I. That was when the Russian Empire collapsed during the Russian Revolution. The Russian Revolution is the collective term for the series of revolutions in Russia in the year of 1917, which destroyed the Tsarist autocracy and led to the creation of the Soviet Union. In the first revolution of February 1917 (March in the Gregorian calendar) the Tsar was deposed and replaced by a Provisional Government. In the second revolution during October, the Provisional Government was removed and replaced with a Bolshevik (BINFO) (Communist) government. The February Revolution of 9 March 1917 was a revolution focused around the city of St Petersburg. In the chaos, members of the Imperial Parliament or Duma assumed control of the country which then led to the formation of the Russian Provisional Government. *RGIN). The army leadership felt they did not have the means to suppress the revolution and Tsar Nicholas II of Russia, the last Tsar of Russia, abdicated, effectively leaving the Provisional Government in control of the country. The Soviet workers' councils, which were led by more radical socialist factions, initially permitted the Provisional government to rule Russia, but insisted on a prerogative to influence the government and control various militias. The February Revolution took place in the context of heavy military setbacks during the First World War, which left much of the army in a state of mutiny. After a chaotic period known as the Russian Civil War, Vladimir Lenin, a Bolshevik gained power over most of the Russian Empire. After Lenin's death the power of the Empire was handed over to Josef Stalin, who with command, economy and brutal methods got the country through to a very large scale industrialization. The USSR followed an aggressive and expansionist foreign policy and attacked a number of countries. After the USSR had attacked Poland, Finland and some of the Baltic countries in 1939-40 the union itself was attacked in the year of 1941 by Germany, a country the Soviet Union had a non – aggression pact and shared Poland with. After four tense years of war the Soviet Union once again emerged as one of the world's superpowers and occupied most of Eastern Europe, and installed totalitarian, Soviet loyal dictatorship there. The post war period was marked by the Cold War, an ideological and political struggle between the USSR and the communist countries on the one side and the United States and much of the west on the other side. In the year of 1980 and after that it became apparent that the Soviet block had lost this fight and when Mikhail Gorbachev took power in the Soviet Union in 1985, it was very clear that reforms in the social stricture were necessary.

Now Russia, sometimes known as the Russian Federation in this day and age is a country in northern Eurasia. It is a federal semi-presidential republic, which is comprised of eighty three federal subjects. Russia shares borders with the following countries: Norway, Finland, Estonia, Latvia, Lithuania, Poland, Belarus, Ukraine, Georgia, Azerbaijan, Kazakhstan, China, Mongolia and North Korea. Russia also has maritime borders with other countries like Japan and the USA. With an area of

17,075,400 square kilometers or 6, 592, 800 square miles Russia is the largest country in the world and covers more than a ninth of the entire planet's land area. It goes all across the top of the Asian continent and over forty percent of Europe. Russia is the ninth most populated country in the world with a population of one hundred and forty-two million people. It also has the world's largest supply of mineral and energy resources, including major deposits of: timber, petrol, natural gas, coal and ores and is considered an emergency super power. It also has the world's largest forest reserves and its lakes contain approximately one quarter of the world's fresh water supply. Russia has forty national parks and over one hundred nature reserves. Most of Russia consists of vast stretches of plains that are mainly steppe to the south and heavily forested to the north of the country. The mountain ranges are found along the southern borders, such as Caucasus in which is Mount Elbrus. Elbrus stands at a height of eighteen thousand five hundred and ten feet. It is the highest point in both Russia and Europe. The Ural Mountains are rich in mineral resources, and form the north-south range that divides Europe and Asia. Russia has an extensive coastline of over thirty seven thousand km which is along the Arctic and the Pacific Oceans, as well as along the Baltic Sea, Sea of Azov and Black and Caspian seas.

The climate of the Russian Federation is under the influence of several determining factors. The enormous size of the country and the remoteness of many areas from the sea result in the dominance of the humid continental and sub-arctic climate, which is prevalent in European and Asian Russia except for the Tundra and the extreme southeast. The mountains in the south obstruct the flow of warm air masses from the Indian Ocean, whilst the plain of the west and north leave the country open to Arctic and Atlantic influences. Throughout much of the year Russia has only two distinct seasons. Winter, summer and autumn are mainly brief periods throughout the year. The coldest month is January, mainly on the sea fronts. But it can get warm in July.

Tourism in Russia, first local and then international, has seen a rapid growth of late. Its rich cultural heritage and great natural variety place Russia among the most popular tourist destinations in the world. The most popular tourist destinations in Russia are Moscow and St Petersburg the current and the former capitals of the country and great cultural centers, which are recognized as world cities. Moscow and St Petersburg feature such world-renowned museums as Tretykaov Gallery and Hermitage. So there you are; you now know a bit about Russia and how it began. (I promised you this book isn't all history.)

1

Helsalorf Gerserfty the Russian President, woke to a knocking on his door. His eyes slowly opened to the heavy knocks. His head burned from the warmth of the heaters. He sat up slowly and rubbed his eyes. Then he got out of the bed and walked across the red carpet towards the front door of his room. He found himself looking at his assistant, Jersalorf.

"Sorry to wake you sir, but there has been an incident," Jersalorf said quietly.

Helsalorf didn't say a word at first. Then he spoke. "Ok. A minute."

He dressed slowly and as he got into his suit he wondered what on earth had happened for him to be woken up so early in the morning. The sun had started to come up over the horizon of Moscow. Helsalorf walked out of his bedroom down to his office. He sat down as three of his military top generals stood waiting to speak to him. He looked at his white coffee cup on his desk as he sat down.

"Ok, bring me up to speed," Helsalorf said.

One of the generals stepped forward. "Sir," he said quietly, "an alien spacecraft has crashed here."

Helsalorf didn't say a word. He wondered if he was still asleep and if this was just a dream running through his head.

"An alien spacecraft," he repeated. "Any survivors?"

"Yes, sir. Crash landed a few hours ago. We only just

got the message," his general said.

There was a silence in his office. He looked up at the clock.

"Did anyone see the ship crash?" he asked.

"No, sir," his general said. "It flew in from the north, over the Yenisey and crashed at our air force base there. We managed to guide it in."

"Did any living thing emerge from the craft?" Helsalorf asked.

"Yes sir," the general replied. "Three of them."

"Did they offer any resistance?" Helsalorf asked.

"Yes. Two were shot and we got one at area fifty two," the general said.

"Has he tried any type of communication with you?" Helsalorf asked.

"No sir," his general replied, "but we are working at it."

"Ok," Helsalorf said. "I want a media blackout on this. No one is to know- only us."

"Yes sir," his general said.

It was a little while before Helsalorf could think straight again. He knew Russia was in a terrible state financially and the country was on the brink of going bankrupt. He knows this could be the start of a new beginning for the state of Russia. The morning seemed to go very slow for Helsalorf. Every few minutes he found himself looking up at the clock.

2

Three Months Later:

New Haven, USA. It had been a very long day on the other side of the planet. The afternoon in New Haven City slowly came to an end. The sun shone down on the busy city as Bradley Harrison, a seventeen-year old student, stared out of his classroom window at the golden statue of the high school founder. The reflection of the sun on the golden statue glistened in his eyes. He felt his hair itching from the hot sticky heat burning his head. The hanging baskets by the main entrance gentle blew in the afternoon breeze as the sun beamed down on the busy city. Bradley looked at Mr. Knightsbridge, his physics teacher. The thirty seven year old bachelor stood up straight, looking at the group as he felt his pens in his top pocket. Bradley looked at his new suit jacket as his short, dark hair stood up. He stood in front of the digital computer board as the huge map of New York City stood out.

The bell rang as the clock struck three. Home time. The group slowly got up as the bell continued ringing and the burning sun shone in through the window onto the group.

"Ok, New York, here we come. I am sure it is going to be the best field trip we have been on this year, so half past eight, bang on, please," Mr. Knightsbridge said. "Oh yeah, and don't forget your homework for next Monday. I want to see at least two thousand words on what the effects of an electromagnetic pulse are and how it could wipe out a country."

Bradley looked disappointed as he knew the whole of his weekend after New York was going to be spent writing about the EMP. "It goes bang and anything electric is fried," he said walking towards the room door.

"I'll need just a bit more, Bradley, my friend," Mr. Knightsbridge said.

Bradley looked over at Kevin. He threw his new gray rucksack over his shoulder. The breeze from the open window gently blew through his short, spiked hair.

"We going straight to the gym?" Kevin asked.

"Yep" Bradley replied.

"Safe," Kevin replied.

Bradley and Kevin slowly walked through the busy corridors towards the exit of the school. They walked out of the main entrance into the clean, cool air.

"New York tomorrow," Kevin said.

"Yep. But sadly it's a day with Ms. Javies," Bradley replied. "What's the bet she puts us all in different groups."

"That most possibly will be true," Kevin replied. "You know what she is like."

Bradley and Kevin continued walking through the busy corridors. They looked up at Max and Eric who stood by the main entrance of the school, ready to leave. Their bags were slung over their shoulders rammed to the full with schoolwork and folders.

"Hey guys," said Kevin.

"Hi," Max went. "Are we shooting?"

"Yep," Bradley replied. "I am." He pushed the door open and felt the hot air blow onto his face from the sub. He looked over at Kate and Jane, as they got into their friend's car, ready to go home. Bradley pointed over at them. "Here, watch this," he said.

He took a deep breath looking over at the two blond

girls.

"Alright, short skirt, fancy coming out with me?" Bradley yelled. "I'm free tonight." He watched as Kate looked over her shoulder at him.

"Get real, freak," she yelled.

"Euggggh," Bradley went.

Kate looked at him in disgust. Bradley laughed as he continued towards the exit of the school. "Bloody hell, it's hot."

"Yep, most probably the same in New York tomorrow," Kevin replied. "All day long."

"Lovely. A whole day without course work," Bradley replied.

"Have you get your science project done on EMP?" Max asked Bradley.

"Na, almost done," Bradley went. "You?"

"Yep, I'm done," Max went.

"Nerd," Bradley joked. "I mean, big deal. It pulses out, all electric fried. Merry Christmas." He made a left turn and walked onto the quiet street looking at the cars as they drove past them.

"Have you heard from Queen's Gate College yet, Kev?" Bradley asked.

"No, not yet. I'll let you know when I do," Kevin replied. "You?"

"Same," Bradley replied. "I'm debating whether to join the police or the military."

"Me, I'm applying for the NYPD," Kevin went. "Just think -patrolling them streets. They say it's a different story everyday."

"Suppose it would be a laugh," Bradley went.

The group approached the crossroads.

"Ok, shall we meet at my house same time as usual? Four?" Bradley asked.

The group nodded as they set off in different directions.

The sun slowly started descending below the horizon. The trees moved gently in the breeze as the leaves dropped onto the road. The air slowly started to get cooler and cooler as the afternoon turned to evening. Bradley turned up the swept path as he looked down at the well kept flowerbeds. He pulled the post out of the small post box and he reached into his pocket pulling out the shiny set of keys. He walked up the clean steps holding onto his keys. He slipped them into the locks. He turned the golden handle and walked into the house.

"Hey mum," he went.

"Oh, hi, Bradley. How was your day at school?" she asked him.

"Fine. Glad it's over," Bradley replied.

"Did you have Ms. Javies?" she asked.

"No. Not today. But sadly I have her all day tomorrow when I am in the Empire State," Bradley said, rubbing his hands together. "Might have some fun with her."

"Oh, dear! Never mind. You will be finished there in just under a year's time and then you can go to college," his mum said. "It's a lot better and you won't have Ms. Javies there."

"Yeah, I suppose that is a benefit," Bradley replied. "Right, I have got to get ready. Kung Fu isn't on this afternoon so I am going straight to the club."

Bradley rose from the dining room chair. He ran up the well-hoovered stairs towards his bedroom and pushed the door slowly open. His window was wide open and a soft breeze was blowing in. He entered the room, got out of his school clothes and chucked them down on the floor. He quickly dressed in his clean clothes and looked for his small string bag. He reached into his pockets and pulled out the old tatty brown wallet as he looked at his bag hanging up behind the door. His mum had obviously hung it there when she has cleaned his room out.

"Women!" he said, smiling.

Bradley walked out of his room. He clicked his knuckles as his string bag gently rubbed up and down on his back. The floorboards creaked as he walked along.

"Right, I am off," Bradley went. "Time to kick some ass."

"Oh, see ya, Bradley. Be good," his mum yelled.

"I will," he replied. "I always am."

Bradley walked out the front door of his house. He pulled it shut as he stepped down on to the newly laid pathway.

"Come on, let's go," Bradley said.

Bradley, Kevin, Max and Eric slowly walked along the busy street. Bradley looked down the street as the busy city came into view.

"So, we're Kung Fuing this afternoon, are we?" Kevin asked.

"Na. The lesson is off. Alex is ill. Oh well, more time on the shooting range. I can't be bothered to gym," Bradley replied.

"Me, neither," Max went. "Too knackered. Got a long day tomorrow."

The group continued along the road. Cars zoomed by as they approached the high street gun club. Bradley looked up at the huge magnum weapon on the top of the old building. The group approached the entrance. He pushed the door open and slowly walked in. He smelt the gunpowder as Barry, the shop manager, stood behind the counter and polished his Winchester shotgun.

"Hey, Brad," he went.

Bradley looked at him. "Oh, hi Barry. I see the old Winchester is looking good" Bradley replied.

"Yep, it's my pride and joy. I was out last Saturday with the wife, clay pigeon shooting," Barry said rubbing his weapon and continuing to polish it.

"You popping a few rounds?" Barry asked.

"I'd love to," Eric went.

"Me, too," Max replied.

Barry looked up at the clock as the shooters in the club slowly walked through the metal door, back into the shop after their round.

"Right. In you go, boys. Have fun" Barry went. "As I always say - be safe."

"When can I have a go on that?" Eric asked.

Barry looked at Eric as Bradley looked over his shoulder at Barry.

"You?" Barry said."Never."

"Oh," Eric went.

The group slowly walked through the metal door as they looked down at the weapons stacked up on the table. Bradley leant down and picked up a handgun from the table. He slipped the magazine into the slot below, cocking the top back and forward. The golden bullets were loaded into the chambers and the gray door was locked into place. Bradley placed the ear muffs over his ears as he looked through the small gray plastic goggles. He stared through the scope and flicked off the safety switch. He pulled the trigger and launched a bullet through the air. The golden bullet slammed into the cardboard cutout at the end of the range.

"Bulls eye," Bradley went. He continued shooting at the targets as Eric sat next to him.

"You miss all the time," Bradley remarked.

"Oh no, I don't" Eric replied.

Time went by. Bradley looked down at his watch as he walked out of the shooting range. "Right. I need to get home. I am very tired. Didn't sleep well last night," Bradley went.

"Me too," Kevin replied.

The group slowly walked to the exit of the store. The

strain of schoolwork slowly lifted off their backs as the prospect of New York came closer. Bradley looked across the busy street to see Kate and Jane slowly walking out of the clothes store across the street.

"Look," he said. He looked again at the two girls as they walked up the quiet side street. "Hello again," he yelled.

The two girls continued walking up the street looking at Bradley as they held onto the small cardboard bags full of clothes after the afternoon shopping spree.

"What did you buy?" Bradley yelled.

Kate and Jane looked away from Bradley as they walked up the street.

"I don't think she likes you," Eric said in a sarcastic voice.

Bradley didn't answer. He watched as the two girls slowly walked away and up the street, heading for home. Bradley smiled.

"Right, I'm off," Kevin said. "Ill see you lot in the morning."

"Me, too," Bradley replied. "I'll see you tomorrow."

He walked off, heading towards his home. He watched the quiet street slowly start to come into view. He watched as the trucks headed off to their destinations in the distance. Bradley turned up the pathway towards the front door of his house. Walking up to the wooden front door, he pulled out his key. He admired the shiny lock as he placed his key in it. The lock slowly pulled back, letting him open the door which swung open. Bradley smelt the strong aroma of food and he saw his dad sitting down at the dinner table.

"Hey, Brad," he went.

"Hey," Bradley said.

Bradley put his bag down onto the floor. Slowly slipping of his shoes, he walked into the sitting room. He smelt the food still wafting around the well-kept dining room.

"Did you have fun?" his mum asked.

"Yep, was brill," Bradley said as he sat down on a chair, listening to the squeak of the wood running along the floor. He started to eat his dinner and felt the warm food running down the back of his throat.

"So, New York tomorrow?" his dad asked. "You got enough money?"

"Yep," Bradley replied. "Can't wait. I think it's going to be an exciting day."

"I'm sure it will," his dad replied. "That's where I met your mums."

"As you keep saying," Bradley replied. The time went by slowly for Bradley. The sun had finished going down and the night sky had turned dark. He looked up at the clock as it struck nine-o clock.

"Right I'm off," he said. "Busy day tomorrow."

"If I don't see you in the morning, have a good time," his dad said.

"Cheers. Don't be late for work," Bradley replied.

"I'm never late," his dad replied. "You know me."

Bradley walked up the stairs into his bedroom. He looked out of the window onto the roads. They were now devoid of commuters and workers. He turned around flinging his quilt back over his body. He got into bed feeling the cool air coming in through the window. He gently closed his eyes thinking of the day ahead.

3

You may find it hard to believe that it was an Italian who was the first European to explore New York Harbor. In the New World Di Verrazano met Native American tribes such as Le nape, Manhattans and Raritan. However, though Verrazano was the first explorer to visit New York City, it is in fact Dutch explorer, Henry Hudson, who has been credited with bringing the Big Apple to Europe. After many attempts to find a Northeast Passage to Asia, Henry Hudson received funding from the Dutch East India Company, a very popular tea production firm, to explore the world in the year 1609. Within 20 years many Dutch settled down into New York City and called it New Amsterdam. Many of the migrants saw New York as a place of religious freedom. The Dutch continued to settle down in New Amsterdam until the year 1664 when the British took control of the island from the then Governor Peter Stuyvesant.

Despite losing the island to the British and with no or little resistance Stuyvesant had prepared for an invasion for many years. He asked the Dutch West India Trump Building on Wall Street for money to build a 2,400 foot wall with lethal spikes across the northern end of the populated part of the island. This part of the island is called Wall Street.

The British conquered Manhattan easily with an attack from the ocean and not on foot. The United Kingdom

renamed New Amsterdam as New York after James the
Duke of York. Until the Revolutionary war, New York City
was one of the most important places in North America due
to its outstanding location and for trading. The British
Troops fought off any opposition from the colonists on the
island, and even took control of the New York
Revolutionary War.

In the year 1783 the British soldiers and loyalists left
New York City. Six years later President George
Washington was elected President of The United States at
Federal Hall on Wall Street, and the capital of the New
Country was now New York City. In the early beginning of
the 18th century New York City flourished due to economic
power. The state of New York soon acquired the nickname
the Empire State. A few months before the start of the 19th
century the New York Stock Exchange was opened with
great success at the place called Wall Street, in the south of
Manhattan.   In 1825 the Erie Canal was completed to
provide boats a gateway to the Atlantic Ocean. The
economic impact of the Erie Canal on the state of New
York was tremendous. Businessmen were able to ship
many goods and services in and out of the city through this
man made river. New York City's ports were some of the
busiest in the world at that time.

But before New Yorkers celebrated Christmas and New
Year's Eve in 1834 a devastating fire engulfed many stores
and churches in Canal Street. Store owners lost thousands
of dollars.

The mid 18th Century was plagued by diseases, intense
immigration, a weak economy and political corruption. The
Civil War did not help matters in the city. New York was a
focal point of the Draft Riots in 1863. Very young men
were drafted to fight in the ongoing American Civil War by
Congress. There were several days of riots in protest of the
drafts and the improving black economy and increasing

black political and social power. According to many publications the riots claimed over a million dollars in damages and more than 100 people lost their lives.

Also, in the mid 18th century, New York was prone to local gangs in the five boroughs. William Marcy Tweed also known as Boss Tweed was the most famous political boss in New York City's history. Behind closed doors at Tammany Hall, Tweed made illegal deals with gangs and crooked politicians from Brooklyn, Queens and Manhattans in the 1860's and 70's. Tweed was eventually exposed when one of his former associates ratted on him out to the New York Times because the illegal funds he gave the man were not sufficient.

New York City of the 19th century was mostly remembered for its prosperity and skyscrapers. Grand Central Station, the biggest train station in New York City with lines leading all over the United States, was opened in 1903. But early in the 20th century more than 140 women and workers died in the 1911 Triangle Factory Fire. Also, there was a boating accident which claimed many lives.

New York is now the most populous city in the United States of America and is in the center of the New York metropolitan area. As a leading global city, New York exerts a powerful influence over worldwide: commerce, entertainment and fashion. The city is often referred to as New York City to prevent it from being confused with New York State of which it is a part. New York City is located on a large natural harbor on the Atlantic Ocean's North East coast between Boston and Washington DC. The Hudson River runs between New York City and New Jersey separating them. New York City has five boroughs: which constitute the Bronx, Brooklyn, Manhattan, Queens and Staten Island.

The city population is estimated at 8.3 million and with a land area of 305 square miles (790-KM) New York City

is the most densely populated city in the USA. The
population of the whole of the New York Metropolitan area
is estimated at 18.8 million people over the 6,720 square
miles or 17,400 km. The population of Greater New York
was estimated at 22.155 million people in 2008.

New York has been listed as the one of the American
cities with an extreme use of mass transit, which runs 24
hours a day, and for the overall density and diversity of its
population. In the year 2005 nearly 170 languages were
spoken throughout the city and 36% of the population was
born outside of the United States. New York is sometimes
referred to as The City that Never Sleeps, The Big Apple as
well as The Capital of the world.

So in New York City, the sun slowly went down over
Manhattan Island. The tourists watched out over the city as
the orange sun slowly disappeared and cargo ships headed
off into the Atlantic Ocean for destinations all over the
planet. The horn from the ships echoed as the evening sun
shone down red on the Hudson River. The evening tugboats
chugged up the dirty old river, the ripples from behind
interfering with the reflection of the sunlight on it. The
lights in the skyscrapers started to switch on and light up
the evening sky. People, smartly dressed in their suits and
carrying their briefcases, left their offices with the new
documents of the day locked and sealed inside them, and
the evening cleaners started their night shifts. The smell of
toilet disinfectant permeated the air as the old ladies
sprayed the windows with their old yellow shammy cloths
and window sprays. The afternoon taxi drivers went home
after their long shifts. They put their green dollar bills into
their safes and headed home looking at the moon slowly
starting to beam down on the city. The last flights from the
airport took off in front of the moon, leaving trails of fumes
from their engines. The North Star began to twinkle as the
owl in Central Park hooted, scanning the ground for any

mice. A cool evening breeze started to blow around. A road sign squeaked as it gently blew in the light wind and leaves blew into the lake in the center of the park. The old park warden swept up the rubbish, the sound off his brush scrubbing against the new path echoing. Mice ran off as he hauled the wheel barrow along the short cut grass. He looked up into the clear night sky as the stars continued to gleam down onto the planet and the city. But New York was going to get a surprise, a very big surprise; something which would make a piece of history remembered for eternity.

* * * *

Circo looked out of the front of the huge ship as the rest of the Armazoids scanned the surrounding computers for Gremlon's tracker. He listened to his people speaking to one another as the craft gently glided through the universe, skimming past the other planets as they looked at them. He suddenly jumped at a sudden beep coming from behind. He slowly turned around and looked at the small digital table in the bridge of the astronomic ship. He stared down to see the little white light gently flickering on and off.

"Is that him?" Circo asked.

"Yes," one of the Armazoids, replied. "The signal is very weak I only just got the figures of the location."

Circo looked down at the digital board. "Where is that?" he asked.

"It's about from our current position here," the Armazoid replied. "It's a very weak signal. We haven't got long."

"Turn to that heading," Circo demanded. "Let's get there."

The two pilots of the Armazoid ship slowly turned the craft and headed towards Planet Earth. They zoomed past all the other planets and looked anxiously for the planet. Circo squinted his eyes as the green and blue planet slowly stared to appear.

"Are we landing sir?" one Armazoid pilot asked.

"Yes," Circo said instantly. "Yes, we are. For the sake of Armazon we have to."

The craft slowed as the two Armazoid pilots looked down onto their computer. They stared at the tiny radar as it looked for a suitable landing spot.

"Are we changing size, sir?" one pilot asked.

"Yes," Circo replied. "No one is to know of our being here."

He walked back as Planet Earth slowly got bigger.

"Sir" one pilot went, "we have just intercepted some sort of space station and it is taking pictures of us."

"Destroy," Circo commanded.

Circo looked out of his spacecraft as the medium sized laser launcher rolled out and pointed towards the Hubble Telescope. The power started to surge up behind the machine, getting to maximum for firing through the air. Circo watched as the ray slammed into the telescope. The fireball ripped through the outdated electronic object. Sparks flew everywhere as the huge space station slowly stared tumbling towards the planet, heating up with the excessive heat of the atmosphere.

"Excellent," Circo said, rubbing his hands together. He watched as the rest of his troops prepared to land the ship on the planet without being spotted. He sat down slowly as the front screen of the ship started to warm up. He squinted his eyes as their ship thundered through Earth's atmosphere.

The Armazoids in the front looked down onto the planet as their ship slowly started to glow a light green color. The craft slowly shrank in size as they descended over the dark blue ocean. Now, with it the size of a remote control car, the shrunken Armazoid pilots looked down onto the computer as they zoomed over the densely populated area below them, without being seen by a single person. They looked on as the tall skyscrapers slowly came into view and their lights shone out as the evening cleaners continued getting them ready for the next day's lot of work. Circo rose as the ship steered towards Central Park. The nose pointed down as Central Park got bigger and bigger. The ship flew over the lake and headed for a small cave in the shrubs and landscape. The engines powered back as the Armazoids slowly flew in, still doing a good job in keeping a low profile for the living things on the planet. Circo watched and listened as the huge sets of landing gear came down from the eight mile long and two mile wide ship. The craft banged down onto the ground, knocking the tiny bits of dust from the small crater it created as the atomic engines shut down one after the other. Circo slowly got up insisting that no one leave the ship without his permission.

"Ok, I want a vehicle to take me around to control room one," he ordered.

Within a few minutes one of the Armazoid vehicles pulled up outside the main entrance to the bridge to the ship. Circo slowly walked down the steps escorted by his armed guards. He stepped into the shiny, white vehicle. It pulled away from the entrance to the bridge. Circo watched as the lights passed overhead. He slowly stepped out of the vehicle as they pulled up outside the entrance to the small control room. He looked along the small shiny corridors of the ship. He walked up the tiny set of steps leading towards the control room as the Armazoid vehicle passed behind him. He walked up the stairs approaching the control room door. He slowly pushed the green button and listened to the airlock slowly open. He walked in and looked at the three Armazoids as they sat around the main table, looking down at the map of the planet.

"Any luck in locating Gremlon?" he asked.

"No sir," Boglon said, standing up.

Boglon looked at Circo as Circo slowly sat down, looking at the map of the planet.

"Can we trace that signal?" he asked.

"No sir," Adamlon said to Circo. "The signal was too weak at the time."

"Who is in charge of this dump?" Circo asked.

"We don't know yet, sir. We're trying to locate its leader," Boglon replied.

Circo looked down again at the plan on the table. "Ok, this is what we are going to do," he said. "We're going to explore the current land we are in, but stealthily."

A short while passed. Circo had to think. He couldn't communicate with the home planet as the antenna was currently under repair.

Two Armazoid soldiers stepped off the shiny red vehicle as it pulled up by the large elevator. Knowing they were less than a third of their size they knew they would need to be careful when they returned to their normal size when out of the ship. The aliens switched on the electric filters on their suits.

"Ok, let's go," one of them said.

The two walked up to the large elevator. The shutter slowly started to roll up. They walked onto the huge metal plate and looked up as the main shutter sealed the outside from the inside. The two stood in their suits, listening to the filter on their backs working as they breathed in the pure oxygen from the ship.

"Here we go," one said.

They looked up as the large elevator slowly took them to the surface. They listened to their filters on their back working as they breathed in the polluted air from outside.

The elevator clanked to a stop. Holding onto their weapons, the two aliens slowly walked over the huge bridge and scanned their surroundings. Tiny bits of dirt fell off the side of the deep cliff and slowly disappeared into the black hole of the crater. The two aliens walked across the bridge as the stars from the night sky twinkled down onto the city while it slowly started to quiet down and ready for the next day's work although night clubs and bars started filling up. The two aliens climbed out of the cave. They looked at one another. Their eyes sparkled and their slimy bodies started to glow. The ground slowly got further away from the two aliens as they slowly grew back to their original size. They looked at one another and pulled out their ray guns.

The moon shone down onto the city as the stars gently twinkled. The old road sign gently squeaked as the breeze gently blew it back and forth. The leaves brushed against one another as the aliens slowly turned their heads to the left and continued scanning Central Park. They looked over through the bushes at one of the park benches to see a hobo lying down and covered with newspaper. They slowly walked through the bushes towards him. They listened to the twigs breaking beneath their feet as they placed their ray guns back into their side pouches. The stars gleamed down on the man reeking of whiskey. The two aliens took a deep breath as they approached the man. One slowly placed his hands over his mouth.

"What the hell?" the man yelled at the top of his voice. "Who are you people? Communists?"

Nobody cared. "He is always shouting," the people said to one another as his voice dissipated with the evening breeze. The aliens picked the drunken man up and pushed him towards a cave entrance.

"Help," he shrieked and looked around in shock as the two aliens walked him into the cave. "Who are you people? Help!"

The two aliens laughed as they approached the bridge

leading to the ship. "Put this on him," one said, shoving a huge mask toward him. "This will stop him being over come by carbon monoxide."

"What?" the hobo yelled? "What is this? Help!"

The red rays were switched off by the alien on the other side. They walked across the new shiny bridge towards the large elevator ready to take the hobo down into the ship. The hobo looked around in disbelief as the brakes clunked off one after the other. The lift lowered down into the ship as the two aliens held onto the man.

"Get away, you communists," he yelled "I dealt with you people in 'Nam, I can do it again."

The lights traveled past the two aliens and the man as they approached the floor below them. The brakes came on. The hobo looked around the ship in amazement at the shiny glossy floor as the rest of the aliens looked at him. The two aliens bundled him into the back of one of their awaiting vehicles.

"This is a violation of my rights." the hobo yelled. "Did you hear me? I have rights."

The aliens continued to laugh as they sped through the ship towards the labs at the back. The lights zoomed past the window almost hypnotizing the man who continued yelling as the vehicle pulled up outside the labs. The two aliens stepped out of the vehicle and walked around to the back. They swung the door open pulling the man out as the alien leader slowly slid towards the labs.

"What have we here?" he said.

"This is a violation of my rights," the hobo yelled again in a loud voice.

"God, you stink," the alien leader remarked and looked down at him again. "Ok," he said. "I want a full analysis of-of this- this thing."

The two aliens walked over to their computer as the hobo continued looking at the aliens.

"I have rightttssssss," he shrieked again. "Do you know what they are?"

The two aliens continued giggling at the man as the experiments went on into the night.

4

A small blackbird landed on the tree branch outside Bradley's bedroom window. It looked through his window at him as the new, red alarm clock showed only a minute from seven-o clock. The cool morning breeze blew gently through his feathers as he chirped and looked around the clean, well kept garden. It was most probably looking for something shiny. Bradley slowly opened his eyes to the croak of the crow and shut them. The night had gone by very quickly. The sun beamed in through the blue curtains as Bradley's alarm clock started to beep. The crow shot off the branch, knocking tiny leaves onto the ground as the beep continued. Bradley again opened his eyes slowly looking at the flashing alarm clock as the crow headed off into the distance. It beeped on and off, echoing in his ears and he tried to block it out. He slowly rolled his hand out from under the soft quilt, switching it off as he felt his eyes wanting to close again. His small eyes stung from the long night's sleep and his black hair was ruffled up into a fuzzy ball.

"Shit," he mumbled.

Bradley slowly got out of bed looking at his casual clothes all ready to be worn ready for the big day ahead. He felt his legs go slightly wobbly and the blood rushing down from his head. His curtains gently moved back and forth in the morning breeze blowing through his window. The sound of the birds singing entered his room as he listened to the shower running opposite his room. He waited outside the bathroom as his mum walked out with the towel wrapped around her thin body.

"Oh morning, Bradley," she said to him.

"Morning," he replied, walking into the shower.

Steam gushed out of the bathroom. Bradley walked slowly into the new bathroom. He looked at the clean, green tiles. Tiny drops of hot water ran down them from the last shower. The clean mirror slowly got drier as the steam disappeared out of the small, open window. The sun beamed in, adding to the intensely muggy, heated atmosphere. Bradley showered, and then slowly got ready looking out of the window as he got into his casual clothes. He put his small string bag onto his back as he picked up his dollar filled wallet. He walked slowly down the stairs looking at his dad running out of the room, running late for work. He watched as he lumped his briefcase out of the door, paper documents sticking out. Bradley turned right into the front room and looked at his mum sitting down at the dining table and slowly eating her toast. She was dressed and ready for the day. He sat down, pulling at the tiny bits of toast as he looked up at the new clock on the wall.

"You look tired," she said.

"A bit. Can't wait. I've never been to New York," Bradley replied.

"I have. I used to work there," his mum said.

"Where? What part?" Bradley asked.

"Oh god," she said. "It was an office, right in the city center. I met your dad when I was once on a coffee break. I will never forget that day. I was walking into the coffee shop a few minutes' walk from where I was working, I walked in and there he was - just standing there. Spiked hair and in a suit."

Bradley smiled as he looked up at the clock again. "Ok,

I have got to go now," he said putting the piece of toast into his mouth before his mum could go off on one.

"Hope you have a nice day," she said, watching the crumbs roll off his mouth onto the clean tea table.

"Thank you," Bradley replied. He walked over to the front door, slowly opened it, and felt the morning sun on his face as he walked down the clean swept path and onto the sidewalk leading to his school.

"Excuse me," his dad said.

Bradley watched his dad run out the front door. "What's up?" he asked.

"I'm running late," his dad said.

Bradley watched as his dad got into the car and started the engines up. He stopped by the front door as he heard the radio news come on. The young male reporter took a deep breath as he began to speak about the day's news.

"Good morning. New Haven news at seven thirty," he said "It has been confirmed by the United States government that the Hubble telescope has crashed into the mid Atlantic Ocean last night. Investigators are currently on their way to the location of the crashed vehicle. How it happened has not been confirmed as yet."

Bradley walked along the clean sidewalk. "What on earth brought that down?" he asked himself.

He kept his head high watching the sidewalk as a young female jogger ran down the road, head phones on, listening to the same bass music repeating itself over and over again. He smiled as the young blond jogged past him. He slowly turned his head around and watched the young girl run up the sidewalk in her bright pink, silky trousers. Bradley smiled again as he continued down the clear sidewalk. The roads were quiet. The early morning buses sped past as they headed towards their destinations within New Haven City and surrounding areas. Bradley turned left. He slowly walked down the narrow alleyway and headed down towards his school, looking in on the gardens of the other houses. He looked ahead at the huge, brown gates wide open as the students walked into the school, ready for the lessons and the trip ahead. He walked in slowly, looking at the huge statue of the school's founder as it cast its huge shadow on the clean swept ground and over the newly laid flowerbed. He took a deep breath and slowly walked around to his classroom, He saw the school students slowly walking into the classroom. He followed them into the classroom and looked over to see Kevin, Max and Eric sitting at a table, waiting and ready for the trip with their string bags.

"Morning," he went and sat down on a plastic chair. He placed his small string bag down on the table, reached in and pulled out the small can of energy drink. He placed his small fingers on the tiny ring, slowly pulling it back. He listened to the hissing sound as he lifted the shiny can to his mouth.

"Yoh," Kevin said.

The clock ticked on as Ms. Javies walked in. She was dressed in a purple skirt and blouse and was holding a huge plastic box full of schoolwork and homework from the day before. She slammed it down onto her desk and gasped for air as Bradley watched her.

"Morning, people. Ready for the day?" she asked.

"Not with you," Bradley mumbled.

"Sorry, Bradley," Ms. Javies said. "You got something to say?"

Bradley tried not to smirk. "No, Miss," he answered innocently.

Ms. Javies began to take the register as Colin Coxendale walked up to her.

"Hello Ms.," he quickly said.

"Oh, hi Colin," she replied. "How are you?"

"I heard what Bradley said," he whispered to her.

"What did he say?" she asked.

"When you asked if we were ready he said, "Not with you, Ms.""

"Don't worry, mate," Ms. Javies said.

Colin went and sat down as Ms. Javies continued with the register.

Bradley and the group waited at the back of the classroom waiting to go.

"Is Kung on tonight?" Bradley asked.

"Em," Eric went. "I don't think so."

"Kevin," Bradley went.

"Yeah?" Bradley asked.

"Is it on?' Bradley asked again.

"Yes it is," he replied. "I got a call from him last night."

"Oh," Eric went. "Sorry."

The huge six-wheeled bus pulled into the front car park. The shining silver wheels gleamed in the sun as the driver switched off the engine and looked into the rear mirror at the caretaker emptying the rubbish bins. He stood in his old ratty green overalls as the janitor slowly walked up to him chucking in the blue bags of rubbish after the early morning clean. Bradley pictured their morning chat in his head- football, women, and politics- anything stupid enough to lighten the day. He gently giggled as Ms. Javies looked out of the window, looking at the back of the bus as she locked her old wooden desk.

"Ok, let's go," she said to the group.

They slowly followed her out of the classroom and along the narrow corridors. Bradley held onto his string bag as he felt his arm muscles aching from the previous day's work-out.

The group walked out into the car park and stared at the huge bus as the driver, dressed in his shaggy shirt and un-ironed red tie, stood outside. Bradley climbed into the bus with Kevin, Max and Eric. He sat down and listened to the sound of the generators rumbling as the air conditioner blew the cold air onto his spiked black hair. He looked at the other students strapping their belts on as the windows gently vibrated from the generator's rumbling. He looked down at his watch to see the clock it was nine o'clock. The driver climbed into the bus. He chucked his cigarette onto the floor and stamped it out with his old black shoes, already wanting the day to come to an end. He sat in the driver's seat and started up the huge engines. The birds in the trees nearby flew out as the huge engines roared in the car park. The driver released the brakes and slowly pulled towards the front gate as Ms. Javies put her jacket into the overhead locker. When the caretaker's dog ran in front of the bus, the driver slammed his brakes on and listened to them hiss as the dog continued along the grassy side into the distance. Ms. Javies lost her balance and stumbled onto the floor of the bus.

"Oh, classic," Bradley laughed.

Colin jumped up, out of his seat, helping Ms. Javies up into her seat.

"Do you want a dog?" the driver yelled out of the window at the top of his voice.

"Just drive," the caretaker yelled back to the driver as he looked at his dog.

The driver pulled out of the gates as Ms. Javies staggered into her seat after the horrific fall. Bradley continued to giggle as she strapped herself in beside Colin. The bus pulled onto the main road and headed down towards New York. Bradley looked out of the window at the passing motorists. The driver pushed the accelerator down, picking up speed along the busy highway. Bradley lay back in his seat and relaxed as the sun beamed in through the window. He felt his forehead burning. Ms. Javies sat back in her seat, as the bus passed over the smooth road. The radio sounded in the background over the talking students and teachers. The bus pulled onto the highway as Bradley pulled out his new cell phone and looked down at the screen.

"That new?" Kevin asked.

"Yep, brand new," Bradley replied.

The middle-aged driver looked out through the windscreen onto the busy highway as he still felt the taste of the morning tea at the back of his throat and tongue. He opened his eyes wide as a small red car pulled in front of him from the entrance to the highway.

"Shit!" he gasped, hitting the brake.

Bradley dropped his phone onto the clean carpet in front of him as he felt the bus jerk forward. "Oh shit!" he went hitting his head on the seat in front. Reaching down, he picked up his phone and looked out of the window again as the small, red car pulled away from the bus.

"Jesus Christ!" the driver moaned and started the engine up again.

Ms. Javies looked around, making sure all of her pupils were ok after the sudden skid.

"Typical woman!" Bradley joked.

The bus pulled out again from the middle of the highway, heading away from the school and closing in on one of the highways that would take them down to New York.

*   *   *   *

Central Park was quiet. The early morning commuters rushed along the pathways swept by the cleaners the night before. The sun started to warm the lakes. A young child kneeled down looking at the ducks swimming on it. Leaves from the trees dropped, one after the other, in the breeze.

Circo looked out the front of the vehicle as he was

driven to one of the control rooms on the ship and felt it grind to a halt as it stopped outside. He watched the side door open. He stepped out, feeling his ray gun dangle by his side. The lights beamed down on him as he walked up the steps. He made a left turn, looking at the entrance to the room. He pushed the small button. The two doors slowly slid back. Circo looked up to see Boglon and Adamlon as they stood around the digital table. Circo walked over. "Ok," he said. "Bring me up to speed."

Boglon took a deep breath as he sat down and Circo looked at the map of Manhattan as it was displayed on the table.

"Ok sir," Boglon said. "We have landed at a place called Planet Earth, but the location we are currently in on the planet is called America."

Circo looked up at Boglon.

"I have run some tests on this planet," Boglon said, "and after my research I have learnt that these people are ill prepared for an alien invasion of any kind."

Circo smiled. "Excellent" he said. "Any news of Gremlon's tracker?"

"No sir," Adamlon replied. "We are still looking for that."

Circo looked at Adamlon. "Continue looking for him," Circo said. "The fate of Armazon rests on that ship."

"I agree sir," Boglon replied. He clicked onto the map of Manhattan. Circo watched as it got smaller. It showed a map of Central Park.

"That's our location," Boglon said.

Circo took a deep breath as he continued to dig for information on the planet. "Tell me about the planet's defence system," he asked.

Boglon looked up and smiled. "A joke," he replied "Our tanks could rip theirs to pieces. They do have weapons but the only damage they can do to us is penetrate our suits, so if we do invade we will have to be careful."

"Excellent," Circo said. "This is turning out to be easier than I thought. Do we have enough manpower?"

Boglon laughed. "We have more than enough troops to take out this part of the island," Boglon said. "Would you like me to ask the armory to prepare all the tanks and space fighters?"

"No," Circo said. "Save that for later. I want to get the message across to these people first."

Adamlon stood up. "We are still looking for the planet's leader," he said. "Are you going to invade before or after we communicate?"

"Before," Circo said.

"Why's that, sir?" Boglon asked.

Circo stood up and turned to look around the control room.

"Because I want to get the message across to these people," Circo said. "The Armazoids do not mess around."

He took one last look down on Manhattan, knowing that taking over the planet was going to be a very easy job.

5

The bus pulled past the end of Newark Airport's main runway. Bradley watched as the huge jets shot past and touched down. He looked over at the huge city skyline with the long line of yellow taxis ready for their day shift of taking the people and tourists around the city and to many locations. The bus slowed down in the heavy traffic as they arrived at the bus station. Bradley admired the huge skyscrapers and skylines as they headed north into Manhattan. The bus made a left turn pulling into a small side street. The trams pulled into the station and he reached for his cell phone checking for any texts to be answered. Kevin looked at the new trams parked up in the bays ready to be used on the trip into the city as their driver pulled into the parking bay and shut down the engines. The windows stopped vibrating one after the other. Bradley slowly got up and pulled his trousers up as they had slipped half way down after the long ride down into the city. He reached into his overhead locker, took down his small string bag and checked his wallet to make sure his cash was still strapped up and safe.

"How much did you bring?" Kevin asked.

"Hundred," he replied.

Colin overheard the short conversation. "Ms. Javies," he went.

"Yes, dear?" she replied.

Colin took a deep breath. He looked over his shoulder

45

watching Bradley walked down the bus towards the exit.

"You know you said we could bring only fifty dollars," he said.

"Yes," Ms. Javies said.

"Well," he went. "Well, Bradley has brought a hundred."

"Has he?" Ms. Javies went. "Thank you, Colin."

Colin watched Ms. Javies walk down the narrow aisle of the bus.

The group slowly got out of the bus and waited on the side for the other students, ready to go to the new tram system to take them into the busy city. Ms. Javies stepped out of the bus. After her two falls during the trip into the city, she staggered down, still shocked by them. Bradley giggled as she walked over to him.

"Bradley," she called.

"Yes, Ms. Javies?" he replied innocently.

"Show me your wallet."

"Why?" he asked. "Husband left you again?"

"Just show me your wallet," she demanded.

Bradley reached into his pocket pulling out the brown tatty leather one. He showed it to her. "Happy?" he asked.

"Don't backchat me," she said.

Bradley didn't answer as she counted the set of notes in the pockets of the wallet.

"Ten, twenty, fifty," she counted.

"I didn't know you could count," he went.

Ms. Javies looked up at Bradley over her purple glasses.

"How much did I say you could bring?" she asked him.

"Fifty," he answered.

"Correct," she went.   "And you have bought a hundred."

"My god, you're clever," Bradley said sarcastically.

"I'll keep this till we finish," she said.

Bradley took a shallow breath. "Look," he gasped.

Ms. Javies quickly turned her head. Bradley reached out and pulled the wallet out of her hands. "Joink," he went.

""Hey," she went.

Bradley put the wallet back into his zip pocket. "I think it's safe with me," he said.

Ms. Javies walked away, saving her breath. She slowly walked up to Mr. Knightsbridge. "Ready?" she asked.

"Ready when you are," he replied. "What happened over there?"

"Nothing," she said.

The group met on the lawn as the smell of the bacon sandwiches from the depot wafted out and into the atmosphere around them. Bradley, Max, Kevin and Eric stood by Mr. Knightsbridge waiting for Ms. Javies and the other tutors to take them onto the tram for the trip into the city.

Ms. Javies walked up to Mr. Knightsbridge as she slipped her cell phone back into her old handbag. "Ok, class, here we go," she said. "Now stick together." The group walked up the new path, heading towards the tram station. "Oh, before we go on, have you all got my cell number?" she asked.

"Yep. We're ok," Mr. Knightsbridge said.

The driver of the new tram rang the bell as he pulled into the station, slowly pulling the control lever back to idle. The brakes locked on to full. The doors slowly slid open. Bradley watched as the last few passengers stepped out of the new tram ready to catch their buses to destinations around America.

The group boarded the brand new tram. Bradley sat down on the clean seat looking into the driver's cab. The driver slowly walked into his cab and placed his small blue bag next to him. He pulled out his mobile as he placed his feet up onto the stand, looking up at the digital clock in the station. Bradley watched as he fiddled with the tiny buttons as the crumpled up timetable waited on the clipboard for him to read. The digital clock showed eleven-o clock. The driver positioned himself in his seat. The doors slowly locked into place and shut as the other trams pulled into the station dropping people off. The driver slowly pushed the control stick forward. The new tram slowly picked up speed as it trundled over the new shiny points as the cars sped past them down into the city. Bradley looked up at the new poster on the side of the tram. He looked up at the laminated bold black text.

"City Runlink is New York's brand new finest state of the art tram link system. City Runlink operates the world's newest and upgraded trams. There are many safety aspects of the new trams. If there is a sudden loss of power the tram will not roll. Emergency brakes will move into action quickly, stopping the tram and preventing injury. These trams are more powerful than the normal ones. They are wheelchair friendly and carry up to fives times more people than the original ones. The future is big for City Runlink, as there are plans to increase the system further into the city and maybe into New Jersey via the Brooklyn Bridge. We have planning permission from the New York Borough Council. The future is in our hands."

Bradley looked away from the board and through the driver's cab. He looked at the clean, silver, shiny tracks as they sped along down by the main road zooming past the yellow taxis as they drove their fares to their destinations in the busy city. He closed his eyes, relaxing in the new plastic seat as they stopped at all the stations in the city. Then the tram pulled into the turnaround. Bradley looked out at all the different trams going in different directions throughout the city. The doors slowly slid open as the brakes hissed on locking the wheels into place. The group stepped of the tram. Bradley looked up at the skyscrapers lining the sky as the sun beamed on them on the hot summer's day. The jets from Newark Airport zoomed over head to other destinations throughout the country. As the driver got out of the cab and headed down the new tram to the other end ready to go back to the bus depot, Ms. Javies walked up to the waiting teachers ready to go round the huge city.

"Ok, class. Have a good day. Remember you have my mobile number if you get lost," she said. She looked at Mr. Knightsbridge. "Do you want to go to that coffee shop?" he asked.

"Yeah, why not?" she replied "Doreen is going that way and you look like you need a drink."

"Yeah, a drink," Mr. Knightsbridge said.

"We can save that till tonight as it is Friday," Ms. Javies said to him.

The group began heading in different directions with their assigned teachers. Mr. Knightsbridge followed Ms. Javies up the busy roads scanning the streets for pickpockets. He thought back to the days when he was a student studying here at the New York College University for his teaching degree and all the great times he had when he was younger. Bradley looked up at the skyscrapers as two police officers walked into the café for their late morning breakfast. He smelt the morning coffee as it wafted out of the clean glass door into the street and the young female stood behind the counter, taking orders. He looked at her. 'Most probably a student,' he thought. He looked through the window as they approached a sharp corner. He looked at the tall trees as they blew in the gentle breeze. As the sun slowly got hotter and hotter, Bradley felt the top of head heat up. They approached a small café opposite the park. Bradley pulled out a chair and looked around at the green park and the people playing around happily. A young Brazilian waiter wearing a white pinny walked up to Ms. Javies. Bradley looked down at the clean, shiny tables as the smell of fresh coffee whiffed out of the new coffee shop. The sound of the hissing water out of the machine echoed from the shop as the passers-by looked down into their newspapers staring down at the stock market figures. Aircraft passed overhead. As Bradley sat down the warmth went up his thin body. Ms. Javies placed her brown leather handbag on the pavement as she pulled her chair out. "Blimey, it's warm today," she said.

"Yep, it's lovely. Just what we need," Mr. Knightsbridge replied as he sat back in his chair. "Better than the rain we've had."

"Suppose that's true," Ms. Javies replied. "I spoke to Amber Richards yesterday."

"Oh, yeah? Is she ok?" Mr. Knightsbridge asked, sitting up. "I heard her parents are going downhill a bit."

"No, she is not. She was taken to the doctor's yesterday. She is not well at all. Her parents keep arguing and fighting," Ms. Javies said.

"Depression," Mr. Knightsbridge said.

"Yes I think it is," Ms. Javies replied.

"Can we arrange something for her?" he asked.

"Yes, I'm having a word with Frances about that," Ms. Javies replied.

"Go for it. I'm not letting her go downhill," Mr. Knightsbridge said. "She is a nice girl."

"I see Ivan Peterson did a good assignment for you," Ms. Javies said.

"Yes he did," Mr. Knightsbridge replied. "Top marks to him."

Bradley looked over his shoulder listening to Ms. Javies and Mr. Knightsbridge talking. He looked into Central Park as the group of people slowly walked through the busy walkways kicking up the tiny stones with their shoes and looking around at all the well kept gardens. He took a deep breath as the young Mexican waiter slowly walked to the seating area outside.

"Ah, Ms. Javies. How are you?" he asked politely. "Nice to see you again."

"Oh, hi, Demmio. I'm fine, thank you. Enjoying the sun shine," she replied. "How are you?"

""I'm fine, thank you. We Brazilians are used to this sunshine and heat," he said. "Will it be the usual?"

"Yes, please. Mocha chino," Ms. Javies said.

Demmio walked away from the table back into the coffee shop.

"You going out tonight?" Bradley asked.

"Yep, downtown New Haven. Star bright Club - the best," Kevin went.

"Yep. I'm going to get totally high and wasted," Max laughed.

"How can you?" Bradley asked. "You're only seventeen."

"I have my ways," Max went.

"Do you know Boris, the bouncer?" Bradley said.

"Yep. He knows my mum," Max said.

"How is your dad?" Bradley asked.

"He's ok. Going up to see him soon," Max said. "He's moving to Florida."

"I've been there. It's wicked," Bradley said.

"Oh, is that how you get into the club? He knows your single mum?" Eric went.

Max smiled at Bradley as he shook his head in disbelief.

"Eric, you have got one sick imagination," Bradley said.

"You can talk," Eric went.

"Eh?" Bradley asked.

"Remember that day we were in sports?" Eric asked.

"We have done sports on many occasions," Bradley said.

"Remember Sports Day?" Eric said. "We were getting changed and you found that hole leading into the girls changing rooms."

"Oh yeah," Bradley went. He smiled, looking over his shoulder at the three girls as they looked over at them from their table.

"Thank you, Eric," Bradley said.

"You're welcome," Eric replied, smiling. "Did Colin here…?"

"Probably," Bradley said. "Dick-head."

Demmio returned, holding Ms. Javies' drink.

"Here we are, my sweet," he went.

"Ah, thank you very much," Ms. Javies replied, taking the drink from him.

Bradley watched as the waiter walked back into the coffee shop and some more people turned up.

"Do you think he likes her?" Max asked.

"Who? Ms. Javies?" Bradley asked.

"Yes," Max replied.

What, him and her? I don't think so," Bradley said.

The waiter walked back out of the coffee shop to Ms. Javies as the sun beamed down onto the gleaming tables.

"Are you ok Ms.?" the waiter asked.

"Yes, I'm fine, thank you," Ms. Javies replied.

"So tell me, Ms. Javies, do you have any family?" he asked.

Ms. Javies' face slowly turned a light red as Bradley and the group looked over at him. "Look at her," Bradley went.

Ms. Javies went bright red. "Emm, no I haven't," she quietly answered.

Bradley stared laughing as the waiter walked back towards the coffee shop. Ms. Javies got up and headed towards the ladies toilet as Bradley called the waiter over to clean the table.

"Hello mate. Listen, do you really want her?" Bradley asked.

"Emm, Emm, yes. I really like her," the waiter said. "She's a very nice lady."

"Where are you from?" Bradley asked.

"Me?" he replied, "I'm from Brazil."

"Did you know some of the prettiest and sexiest women come from there?" Bradley asked. "When I have enough money I'll be over there like a shot, and Kevin will, too."

"Oh yes," Kevin intervened.

"Emm, no," the waiter replied as the sun shone on him. "I don't know- sorry." He walked away back into the café. Bradley smiled at Kevin as he placed his hands behind his heads. Tommy looked at Ms. Javies as Bradley lay back in the shiny silver seat. He looked up the road to see a police patrol car drive up.

The hobo staggered slowly out of the park. The two officers turned their heads and looked at the aged man as he held onto his whiskey bottle. "HEEEEELP" he yelled. "HELP."

The word 'help' from the hobo seemed to carry on.

"Oh for god's sake," the officer went. "Now what?"

The two officers stepped out of the vehicle and looked at the man. The group of onlookers tried to figure out what he was saying.

"Is there a problem, sir?" the officer asked.

"It's coming - the invasion," the hobo yelled. "The Apocalypse."

The two officers looked at each other.

"It's coming. Everyone run while you can," the man shrieked at the top of his voice. "IT'S COMING," the hobo continued yelling.

"Ok sir," the officer said. "I think you should just calm down."

"The end is coming. I saw it," the hobo yelled in a freaky voice walking up to the officer. "They tied me to a bed." He walked closer to the officers and looked into their eyes. "They molested me," the hobo said quietly.

The officers stepped back as they smelt the strong smell of whiskey on the man's breath. A group of young Chinese students stood laughing at the man as he walked around in a circle holding the old bottle of whiskey.

"Jesus!" the officer exclaimed, waving the smell away from his face. The officers continued watching the drunken hobo as he walked around in circles. Bradley stared across the street as the drunken man still held onto his bottle of whiskey warning of the invasion that was going to happen. He giggled as he lay back in the chair still watching the two officers dealing with the man.

The two aliens came out of the ship and slowly sneaked through Central Park after returning to their normal size. They were ready to explore some more of the city, but headed out a bit further. They saw and heard the hobo yelling.

"God, what a creature!" one said.

"Yeah," the other one replied.

They crept through the green terrain, slowly approaching a manhole. They scanned the area around them. People walked past them without seeing them as they hid in the bushes. They looked at the dirty manhole. As they leant down to look at it two businessmen walked towards them, down the crooked path.

"Quickly," one urged.

The two of them dragged off the old metal lid of the manhole. They stared down into the long tunnel as hot steam slowly flowed out into the air above. The two of them then slowly climbed down the hot, metal ladder, dragged the lid back over the manhole, and sealed it shut. They pulled out their small flashlights and looked around at the steaming walls as the water ran down them. They slowly crept through the long tunnels looking around.

"What is this place?" one asked.

The other pulled out his tiny computer and looked at it. He looked at the red lines indicating which way was safe to go. "This way," he said.

They moved along the hot sewer in the intense heat. The steam heated up their suits as they trekked along.

They looked up a short while later to see another metal ladder leading up to the surface. They looked at one another as they slowly climbed it. The surface of the city got closer and closer to them as they untwisted the cap in the metal cover. They peeped through the tiny gap and as they looked around the quite run down area, two drunks staggered along, not knowing the time of day. The aliens climbed out of the manhole into a dark and murky alley as the two men rested against the dirty walls. They were high on drugs as well and were obviously wasting their lives away. The green paint from the graffiti marks slowly faded as the two aliens looked around the dirty alley. They stared down at the drunks as they lay on the pavement still trying to take swigs from the empty alcohol bottle.

"God! Look at these things," one alien said. "We should just leave this shit hole and never return."

The two aliens walked out of the alley and looked around the New York docks. A ship's horn hooted in the distance as old yellow cranes lumped the containers onto the ships. The aliens stared, trying to keep out of sight of the human beings as they went about their daily jobs. They then walked into the middle of the road, and looked around but saw nothing. The sound of a horn blasted in their ears. They swung their heads to the right just in time to see a city truck speeding towards them. The horn blared as the driver rammed his brake down and skidded away from the two aliens. The huge tanker started to roll onto its side as the driver kept the brake and clutch down to the full, struggling to stop the runaway vehicle. Sparks flew everywhere. Not

many people heard the skidding as the truck came to a stop.
The two aliens picked themselves up and looked at the
driver as he panted for air in his cab which was on its side.
He kicked the old door open and climbed out onto the road
as the two aliens stood and looked at him. The man looked
around as he walked towards the dirty alleyway. He
watched in fear as the two aliens walked up to him. He
swung his head around looking at the open manhole. He ran
up to the old metal ladder and descended into the hot,
steamy system. The two aliens followed him down.

"Get away," the man yelled at them and ran off into the
sewage system, still being chased by the aliens.

The two officers stood looking at the hobo as he
continued walking around. Their two radios stared going
static as the operator came over on them. "Attention, all
units it's an emergency in the vicinity of Twelfth Street,
crashed truck."

The two officers looked at one another as the hobo
walked of back into the park.

"He'll be alright," the officer said. The two officers
walked back to their patrol car and got in. The onlookers
watched as the car sped off into the distance.

They turned up at the crash scene. They stared at the
onlookers, as the truck stood smashed into the lamppost.
Fuel poured out of the engine. One officer stepped out of
the car and walked over to the cab but saw no one inside it.

"Did anyone see what happened?" he yelled.

"No," a lady said. "We heard a crash and came
running."

"Ok. Can you step back, please?" the officer asked. "If
this thing blows…"

The people started to slowly back away from the truck
as the other officer walked over to the open manhole. He
felt the hot steam blow up into his face.

"GET AWAY," a voice rang out.

"What the hell?" the officer went. "Let's get down there."

"No, we should call in SWAT," the other officer said.

"No time," the other officer said as he climbed down into the hot sewers.

The two officers watched up the road as the rest of the New York emergency services rolled up to the emergency scene followed by two fire trucks. The officers went down the old rusty ladder in the sewer and looked up as the hot steam blew out into the warm New York air. Their flashlights shone brightly as they walked through the tunnels of the sewer system, smelling the dampness from the steam as it still lurked around from the late morning steam out. The screams from the man got louder as they crept along the tunnel, looking down at the burnt rats. The two officers felt their heads burning as the steam swirled around their heads. The ground vibrated from the subway trains as they thundering along the track nearby. The officers continued through the tunnels. The two men turned the corner feeling their hearts pound as they did not know what they were about to deal with. They clung to their handguns as the steam settled down onto the metal work. The torches shone brightly on the walls in front of them. The officers blinked their red eyes as the steam picked up in the sewers. They stared forward to see the truck driver lying on the floor of the damp sewers. They walked up to him as the line to the subway ran next to them. The thundering trains echoed around the thin tunnels as the two officers kneeled down looking at the dead truck driver, the blood dribbling from his neck.

"What the hell?" the officer went. He felt the driver's pulse but it slowly stopped the second he touched it. A small snarl came from his right. The men slowly turned their heads and looked into the corner. They stared with fear at the two aliens standing and snarling at them. The officer swiped his gun from his side pouch. One alien reached into his back pocket as the two officers stared at him in fear. It looked down through the crack in the ceiling of the sewers as the light from the fast moving train came closer and closer, and then threw its small, high powered grenade towards the two officers. Seeing their opportunity, the two of them then ran away into the dark tunnels. The grenade flew through a crack ceiling and landed on the old railway track as the driver, not seeing what had just landed in front of the train, continued heading towards the station. The grenade exploded as the old train passed over it. The driver gasped as he was swung off his old metal seat. The glass along the old carriages shattered into it as the screams echoed over the thundering train. The old carriage turned onto its side as the middle aged driver fell against the old ratty doors and the speed slowly stared to decrease. 28th Street station came into view. The station workers looked up the platform as thick, black smoke poured from the dark, murky tunnel. One of them ran over to the red plunger, slamming it in. The alarms wailed as the train slowly rolled into the station with people struggling to get out as it came to a stop.

"EVERYBODY OUT," a station employee yelled. He stared in fear when he saw the driver lying in the back of his seat, unconscious and with blood dripping from his head where he was hit when he was flung against the old metal door. A fire loomed from under the train as a few people staggered out of the carriages onto the platform. They cried with fear as they looked for the exit. The man slowly walked up to the passengers as the rest of the station staff ran down the old shiny escalators, looking at the people as they staggered out.

"You ok?" he asked a woman. She didn't say a word as she slowly staggered along the platform towards the stairs, looking down at the dirty yellow line, arms folded. The

NYPD officers ran into the station, covering their mouths as the dead driver sat looking up at them. The whiteness of his eyes gleamed.

The red fire trucks pulled up outside the station as onlookers watched the people being helped out of the station towards the waiting ambulances.

Bradley and his group slowly walked along the busy road towards the outdoor shopping center passing the many stores along the sidewalk. Ms. Javies stopped and looked at the New York news channel in the small television store. She squinted her eyes, looking at the camera view of 28th Street station, as Bradley clicked his knuckles. Mr. Knightsbridge looked at the young newsreader as she stood by the New York News van. "I'm standing outside Twenty Eighth Street in Manhattan, where a New York subway train has, erm, well just exploded as it approached the station. Oh my god it's terrible in the station. Some people are dead and trains leading to the station have been stopped and re-routed. Police and fire service officials are on the scene. Fire has engulfed one of the carriages and they are struggling to get people out of the station," the reporter gasped.

Bradley looked on as people slowly walked out of the station gasping for breath. "Dear god," Mr. Knightsbridge said.

"Come on" Ms. Javies said.

The group started walking on again. Ms. Javies looked away from the scene and slowly started walking up the road as Kate and Jane walked in front of Kevin and Bradley.

"Look at that ass," Kevin went

Kate looked at Jane with disgust as they slowly continued walking up the small sidewalk towards the shopping center as the sun beamed down on them.

"Ignore him girls," Colin said.

"Oh I will," Jane went. "You ignore them, too."

"I do," Colin replied.

Bradley laughed quietly as the group turned the corner and walked towards the shopping center. He looked up at the huge shops as some young girls walked out holding their cardboard bags walking into the city.

"More hotties," Max said.

"Will I ever find love?" Eric asked.

"I doubt it, Eric," Max said.

"Why?" Eric asked.

"Don't ask," Bradley joked. He sat down on a bench as the group went off in all directions. Seeing a game shop, he looked over. Then he got up. "I'm going in there," he said. "You coming?"

"Yeah, I am," Kevin replied.

The two of them walked over to the game shop and went in, feeling the air conditioner blow onto their faces as they looked at the young Mexican behind the counter. They stared at the games lined up behind one another.

"Oh, look, Fight Buster Three!" Kevin exclaimed.

Bradley looked out of the shop door as Kate and Jane walked into the shopping center and saw Ms. Javies.

"You girls ok?" she asked.

"Yeah, we're fine," Kate said.

"Is Bradley giving you problems?" she asked.

"A bit," Kate replied.

"Don't worry about him," she said. "You two ok to go off by yourselves? Remember what I said yesterday after class."

"Yeah, we have your cell number," Jane said.

"Can I come?" Colin said. "I'd love to keep you two company."

"No," Ms. Javies said.

Kate looked at Jane. "He can if he wants to," Jane said.

Ms. Javies took a few seconds to think. "Ok, but be back at the bus station by six o clock," she said. "I can't afford to lose you."

"We will," Kate replied. "Promise."

"And don't forget to ring me if you have any problems," Ms. Javies said again.

Bradley watched Kate, Jane and Colin set off towards the other stores, holding onto their bags, not knowing they had been let off by themselves. He walked out of the game store towards the seating area. He sat down looking around as if not knowing that Kate and Jane had gone.

"Right," Ms. Javies said. "Split up time."

"Ok," Mr. Knightsbridge said. "I'll take my group. I'd love to go and look where I use to hang around when I was a student."

"You go for it," Ms. Javies said.

The group split up and headed towards the subway station. Bradley looked over his shoulder as Ms. Javies walked off. He didn't care about Colin as he knew he was never far from her. The group arrived at a subway station.

"Shall we?" Mr. Knightsbridge asked?

"Go for it," Bradley said.

The group walked down into the murky underground station. Bradley looked at a busker on the side of the platform, playing his saxophone and trying to collect money to earn his living. The breeze from the trains blew up the stairs as they rolled in and out, avoiding 28th Street Station. An old train shambled towards the station. The blasts of cold air blew through Bradley's spiked black hair. The group walked onto the platform, Bradley looked at the daily newspapers blowing around on the track as a passenger waited for the train to take him home. He looked up the platform as the lights from the approaching subway train came closer. He felt the wind blowing onto his face as the old piece of metal quickly rolled into the station and slowly came to a stop. The doors slid open. The group stepped onto the train and sat down. Bradley looked at an old newspaper as it gently blew in the breeze as the beeps from the doors echoed around in the interior. They slammed shut as the brakes shuttered off. The train started rolling out of the murky station. Bradley watched as the smartly dressed man's tie swung round his head in the breeze blowing around the station when they entered the tunnel. He looked down at the hobo with his old rucksack and shaggy top. He could smell stale food with the smell of napalm from the Vietnam War as the man lay back in the old chair, chomping away at his sandwich. Bradley grimaced as the tiny breadcrumbs landed in the man's shaggy, old beard. He probably wouldn't shave for another week or two.

The train slowly pulled into the next station. Bradley and the group stepped off the train, one by one, and headed up the stairs of the old underground station. Bradley ran up the stairs and walked out of the station, looking around at the clean streets of the city. He felt the sun burning down on his head as he held onto his string bag. Kevin, Max and Eric walked out of the station followed by the other students. They looked around the mad city as the NYPD police cars passed by them.

"This city is magnificent," Mr. Knightsbridge remarked.

"Were you born here, sir?" Kevin asked.

"I was born in New Jersey, but I went to school here," Mr. Knightsbridge replied. "And college and university."

"Where's New Jersey?" Eric asked.

"About four miles from here," Mr. Knightsbridge replied.

"It's quite an active city, isn't it?" Bradley said.

"Oh, yes. It never stops. It would take a lot to bring this place to a stop," Mr. Knightsbridge replied.

6

Circo stood up after a brief rest. He looked around his quarters at the back of the bridge. The first start of the invasion was to begin. He had made up his mind to invade the part of the land they were in and then try to communicate with the leader of the planet. He slowly walked over to his staff as they worked at a small camera. He took a deep breath and sat down in front of it.

"Ready?" he asked quietly. He watched as the other Armazoid nodded.

"To my fellow Armazoids," he said, "The time has come to begin the takeover of this land. You know what to do, if you encounter any of these creatures- annihilate them. The state of our home planet and people depend upon this invasion."

The Armazoids started to arm themselves, ready to begin the invasion of Manhattan. The first wave of aliens headed towards the elevator, looking around at one another as they prepared to invade New York City. The large elevator, carrying some of the aliens on it, started up and lifted towards the top of the craft. As the large metal plate slowly rolled to the top of the craft, the people in the city walked through Central Park, heading to their destinations.

The aliens walked out of the underground cave and looked around at all the green plants and shrubs. They gleamed green as they returned to their normal size.

A middle aged woman was sitting down on an old

wooden bench reading her small, tatty magazine. Her eyes slowly opened wide with fear as two, green, slimy aliens slowly walked towards her and snarled at her. She dropped her coffee onto her gray old suit as she stared at their gleaming white teeth. One of the aliens pounced on her and sliced her neck with its weapon. She screeched in pain as the blood from her throat ran down the wooden bench onto the mucky walkway. The aliens calmly walked away into the park, looking around as people ran in all different directions. They ran out into the streets from the exit the park. As cars crashed into one another, passengers and drivers staggered out in pain and shock. Water gushed up from a damaged fire hydrant and rained onto the dusty road. Tiny streams of water ran down into the drains as the people continued running away from the pursuing aliens.

A young, black police officer stood dressed in his smart navy blue uniform looking down at his parked car. He slowly lifted his head and watched the people running around the corner onto the busy street. He watched in horror as people fell to the ground, blood gushing from their necks into the storm drains. The young officer swiped his small handgun as his radio went berserk with help calls.

"Come on, run," he yelled. He aimed his new, black, shiny weapon at the aliens as they charged towards him and the innocent people. He watched as the golden shiny bullets fell from the weapon and hit the floor and he thought about his new born daughter only a few days old. The officer looked at his gun as the coupling flung back. He reached into his pocket and pulled out a full magazine of cartridges, ready to start firing again. The young man didn't have any time. He stared ahead, looking at the alien charging towards him. He shut his eyes as he felt the strong sharp weapon slice into his neck. He struggled to push the alien off him as his new black handgun fell onto the clean sidewalk splattered with blood. The officer fell slowly, blood rushing out of his neck into the drain. He listened to the echoing sound of his blood as it trickled down into the dirty storm drain as he looked up into the sky. Small white puffy clouds passed by. The wail of police sirens sounded in the distance and news helicopters flew overhead, looking down onto the city. He slowly closed his eyes, as he lay helpless on the sidewalk, blood continuing to pour down into the drainage area. He listened to the echoing sounds as his eyes slowly closed, the blood running down his neck still echoed as it ran into the drains.

Ms. Javies walked out of the small side shop. She dropped her shopping into her bag and looked around at the people screaming and running down the road one after the other.

"What the hell is going on?" she said to her group. "I mean what's this? A riot?"

The students looked at one another as the screaming people ran up the streets, looking for a place to hide.

"I don't know," one girl said. "One minute it was quiet and then they just started panicking."

The students looked down the road as the sound of explosions started.

Ms. Javies stared as an old rusty lamp post fell onto the street, the yellow bulb inside sparking as the people fell over it. "What on earth...?" she said in a shocked voice. She felt her phone vibrating in her pocket. She pulled it out and saw Doreen on the screen. "Hello," she yelled over the screaming people.

"Oh, hello. It's Doreen. Javies, you ok? What is going on?" She sounded panicked.

"Calm down," Ms. Javies ordered trying not to panic herself. "What is going on?" She listened to the sound of her fast breathing and the screaming people in the background as the signal started to crackle and fuzz. Too many people were trying to get through.

"We were in this shop and these things just came out of nowhere. We are on our way to the police station at… oh I don't know," she said to her.

"Ok, what things?" Ms Javies asked asked.

Ms. Javies slowly turned her head to the right, only to see a group of aliens walking towards them, wielding their weapons. She stared in fear over at them. She slowly put her phone to her ear. "Ok, we will see you at the station," she said.

She looked around the streets of New York as cars crashed left, right and center. She couldn't imagine what the people were thinking as they crashed into lampposts. Water gushed up from the fire hydrants fallen down onto the streets as the aliens attacked the people one after the other. She heard a sudden screech in the street, as her pupils stood next to her, frightened out of their lives like a pack of dingos in the Australian desert. Ms. Javies looked ahead again as one of the NYPD SWAT vans skidded to a halt. Two armed officers stepped out of the van holding onto their loaded MP5 machine guns. They pulled out two yellow barriers from the back as the remaining officers stepped out of the van. The barriers were spread across the narrow side street.

"You," The officer went. Ms. Javies looked over at the armed officer as he walked over to them. "Where you heading to?" he asked. "Come on, tell me."

"I, I, I don't know," Ms. Javies said in a freaked out voice. "The police station."

"Ok. Head straight down this road for about a third of a mile. Our main police headquarters is there. Now, come on, move," the officer ordered.

"What's going on?" she yelled.

"Come on, just go," the officer ordered.

Ms. Javies watched as her group started to run down the road. They stared down at the dead bodies sprawled out in the middle of the street as they passed them, then looked at the water gushing up from the ground. They walked around the huge fountain as it ran off into the storm drains carrying the blood from a young lady as she lay in the middle of the street.

"Come on," Ms. Javies said.

The group quickly made their way along the dead and dying street. Screams rattled their brains as the New York News helicopters circled above, looking down onto the city through their cameras, trying to figure out what the hell was going on. The group made it to the police station. They looked around at the armed officers as they helped sick and injured people into the station. Ms. Javies ran up the concrete steps as people turned up from all directions.

"Come oooooooon," she yelled.

The group ran through the glass swing doors, looking at the officers running around in all directions. Ms. Javies slowly walked through the busy corridors as the staff ran in all directions.

"In here," an officer directed.

Ms. Javies followed the officer to a large back office. She sat down on a plastic bench and looked at all the frightened people. She looked at two, seemingly calm, old age pensioners as they sat down, trying to hide their nerves from the other people.

"You ok?" the old man went.

"Yes, I, I, I'm fine," she replied. "What the hell is going on?"

"We don't know, darling. We were happily walking through Times Square doing our weekly shopping when suddenly these things just came out of nowhere and started attacking people. We haven't got a clue about what is going on," the man said.

"How did you get here?" Ms. Javies asked.

"We were helped by two officers," the lady said.

"I've lost two of my group," Ms. Javies said. "And I've got to find them." She pulled out her cell phone and stared at the no signal sign on it.

"Oh god," the lady mumbled. "I hope you do."

Ms. Javies sat back in her seat trying to calm her nerves as they got the better of her. She quickly got up and walked over to the window of the huge, open office looking out into the street. Police officers were running in all directions. People were running out of the subway station, looking around at the other frightened people by the main station waiting to be evacuated.

Two young students stood on this warm summer's day holding their music players and taking in the aroma of the cooking noodles coming from the stand in front of them. They most probably were students from Japan or China, over here in the US, learning a bit about their culture. They looked at the very old man in his old white apron smeared with brown noodle stains, and took the wipes from him. One young student heard screams in the distance, from the lower part of the town. He turned his head to the left and looked at busy Chinatown and people sprinting and running through the wide shopping districts.

"What's with these people?" he said in a quiet voice.

His friend slowly turned as the screams from the frightened people echoed around and seemed to be getting louder buy the second. The two boys looked in fear as a horde of aliens slowly walked down the shopping district of the town, attacking people on the way. The two students started running away from the pursuing aliens as they attacked people left right and center. Cars skidded to a stop as the people ran across the busy streets. The three officers looked out of their patrol cars and then suddenly jerked to a stop as the yellow taxis smashed into one another.

"Quickly," one officer went. "That way."

The officers looked up the road as other patrol cars

screamed down the road and skidded to a stop at the entrance to Chinatown. The two officers opened their doors and got out from their car, drawing their weapons. They stared down into the district as the aliens ran after people killing them one after the other.

"Get out of the way," one officer yelled. "Get out of the way." He held on to his pump action shotgun, looking through the scope as the aliens ran towards them. He pulled the trigger. An alien fell onto the ground and his green blood spattered everywhere. The officers continued firing at the oncoming aliens. People continued running in all directions which slowed the officers down. The first officer watched the top of his handgun ping back. "Fuck it," he gasped.

He reached into his side pouch to pull out his last magazine but something caught his eye. He turned his head and looked over his shoulder. There stood three of the aliens behind him, their weapons still in their holsters all charged and ready to be used. The officer trembled with fear as a sharp razor came out of an alien's suit. It gleamed in the sun as the two other officers turned around looking at the three aliens. "Oh dear god," one went.

The three aliens snarled at the three officers as they approached. The blue and red lights on the patrol cars were still on as people still continued running in all directions, struggling to get to somewhere safe. The aliens approached the three officers when the sound of heavy gunfire was heard. They twitched as AK47 rifle bullets ripped through their suits, killing them. Then they slowly fell to the ground. The officer turned his head and looked at two young Chinese men as they stood holding their AK47 assault rifles. The officers slowly got up. The two men turned around and headed into the alleyway behind them.

"Wait," one officer yelled. "WHERE DID YOU GET THOSE?"

But the two men disappeared into the darkness of the alleyway, not to be seen again.

"Come on," one officer said.

The three officers helped people through the city as they stood running around in fear. They clung to their weapons as they walked slowly along the walkway looking at the aliens attacking people everywhere.

Bradley looked around as they walked down a quiet street more towards the north of Manhattan. He looked down at his watch. "Twelve fifteen," he said quietly.

"What's up mate?" Mr. Knightsbridge asked. "Bored?"

"No," Bradley replied. "Just thinking about college."

"Have you applied yet?" Mr. Knightsbridge asked.

"No," Bradley said. "Not yet."

"You should," Mr. Knightsbridge advised. "Places can get really hard to get."

Bradley slowly walked along the sidewalk trying not to bump into any of the passers by.

"You ever thought of studying here?" Mr. Knightsbridge asked.

"I haven't, no," Bradley replied. "Never thought about it."

"Well, what do you want to study?" Mr. Knightsbridge asked.

"I wouldn't mind joining the army," Bradley said "Then maybe the police."

"Hear, hear," Kevin said.

"So why don't you two study law here, then?" Mr. Knightsbridge said. "The University is not far from here. We could pop in."

Bradley slowly walked along the sidewalk when a sudden rumble was heard in the distance. It seemed to go on and on.

"What was that?" Bradley said, looking around.

Mr. Knightsbridge froze for a few seconds. "There are a

lot of construction sites up here," he answered. "Perhaps it's something there."

"I suppose," Bradley replied.

The group continued walking along the sidewalk, Bradley stopped to look into the window of a TV store. He saw a young news reporter standing outside Grand Central Station, looking around and holding her head as people ran into the station.

"What's the matter with her?" Bradley asked.

Mr. Knightsbridge looked in through the window. The reporter pulled the microphone to her mouth as the TV screen started to flicker. They could only just about hear the TV set. "I'm standing outside Grand Central Station where people are trying to flee the city due to this, well, invasion which I don't know I can even explain," she said and paused.

"What the…" Eric went.

The middle aged officer stood in Central Station as the people shoved and pushed, tying to get onto the old double decker trains. He clenched his shotgun as the driver started up the engines. The smoke from the exhaust puffed out as the doors slowly closed and locked into place. The officer watched and held on to his shotgun as the people were pushed against the doors. A train slowly pulled out of the station away from the city. A second train slowly pulled into the station as an oncoming fuel tanker sped towards the station. The officer watched as the people pushed and fought and struggled to get onto the huge train. The glass doors at the train station burst open as more people ran for the train. The driver looked out of his cab window as hordes of people, pursued by the aliens, made for the train. The two officers fell to the floor, trampled by the panicked people.

"Oh shit!" one officer went. He pumped his shotgun. He knelt down on the clean platform looking at the hordes of people as they charged towards them and the train. He struggled to get a clear view of one of the aliens. He was very concerned about hitting an innocent person. "Get out of the way, get out of the way," he yelled.

He pulled the old metal trigger. The cartridge flew out and smashed into one of the pursuing aliens. The alien fell onto the floor. His green blood spilled out onto the platform as the pursing aliens continued chasing people along the platform. The officer stared as the single alien dove for him, his gleaming teeth coming closer to him. The alien landed on the officer as the sound of the tanker train sped through the station. The alien pulled his sword out slamming it into the officer's neck. As he fell back he pulled the trigger on his shotgun. The bullet exited from the weapon, whistling through the sky and hitting the oil tanker on the train. The rusted metal sparked and oil fumes rushed out from inside the tank. The people at the station dropped to the ground as a huge fireball ripped through the tanker. The explosion then ripped through the station, wiping the rest of the tankers out. The huge fireball ripped through the station incinerating some aliens as they tried running from it. The TV screen went static.

Bradley jumped as he looked at the grey and white picture on the TV screen.

"What a good film," Eric went. "Wonder what it's called."

Mr. Knightsbridge slowly walked away from the TV screen feeling his heart pound. He walked slowly along the quiet sidewalk. "It's just a film," he mumbled to himself.

Bradley looked over his shoulder, listening to the sound of police sirens slowly getting louder and louder. He watched as three New York patrol cars and van zoomed past them, skidding around the corner.

"What's going on?" Eric asked.

Mr. Knightsbridge felt his heart start to pound as the

sound of shooting came from around the corner. "I think we should head back," he said, "back to the subway."

"Nah, let's have a look," Bradley said.

The group slowly walked around the corner. Bradley opened his eyes in shock. He just couldn't believe them. The three police patrol cars swung next to one another, the officers slowly got out when a group of aliens pounced on them as they reached for their handguns. Mr. Knightsbridge looked at the car crashed up on the sidewalk with smoke poured from the running engine, door wide open and blood splattered on the leather seats. Max turned his head to the left and look into a casino.

"This way," he yelled.

Bradley followed the group up the concrete stairs into the casino. He walked in, listening to the manager as he slammed the glass doors shut, turned the key and locked the door. He stared at him as he trembled with fear and the people looked at him for advice.

"What's going on?" Kevin asked.

Everyone was quiet. They were shaking with fear. Bradley turned around and stared down into the new casino as people stood around wondering what the hell was going on. An armed security guard ran up to the entrance, sidearm ready to be used if the need arose. Bradley kept a calm head, as he knew the rest of the day was going to be as smooth and as quiet as he predicted. He scanned the group as Mr. Knightsbridge's phone started ringing. Knightsbridge pulled his old phone out of his pocket. "Hello," he went in a shaken voice.

Ms. Javies was on the other end of the line. He listened in spite of the sheer panic and confusion in the police station, and voices clashing with one another.

"Oh god, Alan, thank god you're there," Ms. Javies said "I've been trying to get through to you for ages. Are you ok?"

"We're fine. Where are you?" Mr. Knightsbridge said to her.

Ms. Javies struggled to hear and think over the panic and confusion in the police station. "We're at the police station. It's the main one in the middle of the city about a mile and a half from Grand Central," Ms. Javies replied. "I think we should be able to make our way there and try get a train out of here."

"No point," Mr. Knightsbridge said. "We have just seen it on TV. It has been completely destroyed."

"Oh," Ms. Javies said.

"Don't worry," Mr. Knightsbridge said. "We'll be there soon."

"Be quick," she urged. "These things are everywhere."

"Tell me about it," he replied.

Mr. Knightsbridge turned around as more people, scared and confused, dived into the casino and looked around,. The young security guard held onto his sidearm ready to pull the trigger as the light music in the background continued playing. Bradley sat down on a chair, as he knew he was going to need all the energy he could save.

Mr. Knightsbridge walked up to Bradley, Kevin, Max and Eric. "Ok, we have got to get out of here," he said. "Ms. Javies is at the main police station about a mile and a half from Grand Central."

"Where's Grand Central?" Eric asked.

"It's about..." Mr. Knightsbridge started when he was distracted.

Bradley looked at the front door of the casino. He watched as the three aliens walked up to the door and staring in at the people. Bradley clenched his fist desperate to use it. Just you try it, you shit bags," he mumbled.

The aliens walked back away from the glass door. The security guard breathed a sigh of relief as they walked away. "See? Stand up to them and they walk away," Eric said. He opened his eyes again to see the aliens charging towards the door. He closed his eyes as the sound of smashing glass came into the casino. Bradley jumped up out of his seat as Mr. Knightsbridge swung around and looked at the door as the three aliens dived onto the security guards. Screams filled the casino as they ran down into the huge building trying to get away. Bradley looked again at the security guard as his blood gushed out onto the carpet, destroying the patterns on the floor. The alien jumped on the guard, ripping his sword out of the guards neck. He slowly closed his eyes feeling his heart coming to a stop. Bradley looked to see his handgun lying on the floor next to his nightstick baton. He dived over the chair and leaped onto the floor. He picked up the blood stained handgun and nightstick. He continued looking around the casino as people sprinted in all different directions. Mr. Knightsbridge looked at Bradley as he held onto the handgun and slipped the stick into his trousers, ready to react if provoked. "Come on," he urged, hanging on to the handgun.

The group followed him around the side of the casino trying to keep out of sight of the attacking aliens. They came to a small set of stairs. Bradley looked down, checking to see if the coast was clear. "Go," he whispered.

The group walked down the steps as the casino slowly started to go quiet. The screams slowly faded away into nothing as Bradley clung to the firearm. The multi- colored lights continued shining down on their heads as they slowly crept along through the quite casino. It felt different, seeing empty blackjack and poker stands, Bradley said to himself as he continued escorting the group through the casino towards the back exit. He looked forward as he held his head up. He looked at the two shadows on the floor in front of him. He grasped his sidearm as he slowly crept along the wall. "Two," he whispered.

Kevin and Max nodded. Bradley clung to the handgun as he swung out from the wall. He looked at the two aliens as they stood inside the casino looking around for people to attack. Bradley pulled the trigger, launching the bullets into the aliens. "Oh, that felt good," he said.

The two aliens fell to the floor as the group sprinted through the casino and up the carpeted stairs towards the rear fire exit. Bradley looked round at the bar and the glasses on the counter half filled with drink. "Come on," he went.

Mr. Knightsbridge ran over to pick up a glass of gin. He swallowed it to the last drop in an effort to ease his nerves, but it didn't seem to work.

"Come on," Bradley said. "We'll save that till later when we are out of here."

"If we do get out of here," Mr. Knightsbridge said.

Bradley looked at the back exit to the casino. He pushed the silver bar down and ran out into the street. He looked on with consternation as people were running in different directions. Two yellow taxis had crashed into each other. Bodies were lying everywhere and fires raged through the buildings. "Jesus Christ!" Bradley went, holding on to the sidearm. He didn't have a clue about who or what to shoot at first.

"Right, follow me," Mr. Knightsbridge ordered.

"Bet this will be a joke," Bradley mumbled.

The group walked cautiously down the concrete steps onto the sidewalk as people still ran helter-skelter. Bradley followed Mr. Knightsbridge down the small flight of steps onto the sidewalk. He crept along slowly, listening to the sounds of the screaming people as vehicles continued slamming into one another. Water gushed up from the destroyed fire hydrants. Mr. Knightsbridge felt his heart pounding as the fear of death overtook him, but Bradley calmly followed on behind. The breeze picked up as the NYPD helicopters circled above and the police sirens started to fade away into the distance. Bradley looked ahead, at the parked police car. It stood smashed into the lamp post, the door, through which the officers had made their escape, wide open.

"This way," Bradley went. He ran in front of Mr. Knightsbridge, and then ducked down, looking over the bonnet of a vehicle as aliens pounced on innocent people. He looked at one of the overturned cars and saw a middle aged lady in it, most probably dead. She wore a red skirt and her business bag was flung on the roof of her car. She had most probably been on her way to a business meeting.

"Come on," Max said. "She's dead."

The woman slowly opened her eyes a few seconds later, coughing up small drops of blood from her mouth. She had heard the small group talk about her being dead. She felt the blood rushing around in her head. Her heart pounded as she slowly turned her head to the left and looked out of the rear window at the people as they ran in all directions through the city. Police sirens wailed through her ears into her brain. She took a deep breath and felt her chest push out against the strong material of the seat belt. "HELP," she yelled.

Bradley and Mr. Knightsbridge stopped. The small stones on the sidewalk kicked up into the air. They both turned their heads back and looked at the green sedan as the lady driver tried to break open the door. Her screams echoed in their ears.

"Shit!" Bradley went. "Come on."

"Bradley, no," Mr. Knightsbridge yelled. "Come on."

"We can't just leave her," Kevin said. "What would you want in her situation?"

Mr. Knightsbridge shook his head as Bradley led Kevin, Max and Eric over to the car. Then he followed close behind. Bradley dove to the ground and looked into the green estate car as the engine hissed. "You ok, Miss?" he asked.

Bradley struggled to hear the woman as she slowly turned her head and looked at him, blood running down her face. "I, I, I'm ok," the woman said. "Get me out, please."

"Ok, ok don't panic," Bradley said to her. He slowly crawled into the car through the broken window. He smelt the fuel leaking from the engine as the tiny shards of glass started to dig into his stomach. "Jesus Christ!" he went. He looked at the woman again and continued to push the red clip in. "Kevin," Bradley yelled.

Kevin leant down and looked into the car. "What's up?" he asked.

Bradley took a deep breath. "See that smashed up fire truck? Go and get me something like clippers or any bloody thing," Bradley said.

"Got it," Kevin said and left.

He ran across the road towards the fire truck when Bradley called him again. "Bring an extinguisher, too," he yelled.

Kevin nodded and walked up to the truck as the screaming from the frightened people continued. He looked over his shoulder constantly for any of the aliens as people ran in all directions.

"Got it," he said as he found what he was looking for. He
hauled the cutters and extinguisher over to Bradley and as he was passing the cutters to him, two of the aliens came towards him.

"Shit!" Kevin gasped. He pulled out the tiny plastic pin and activated the extinguisher. He pulled the knob and blasted the aliens away from him. As they were blinded Kevin swung his foot round kicking them in the head.

Bradley turned his head around and looked at Kevin.

"Not what I had in mind," he said, "but there we go."

The flames in the engine started grow. "Shit!" Bradley gasped. "Kevin, spray now."

Kevin sprayed the car engine from the hydrant. He struggled to control the fire. Bradley opened the cutters and slowly started cutting through the material. "Come on," he started to groan. "Come on, you fucking things."

The thick black smoke started to fill the car. The lady in the car struggled to breathe as the tiny fires inside the engine started to intensify. Finally, the last of the metal was cut. The lady stretched her hands out, stopping herself from falling. Bradley chucked the cutter away from the car and looked at Kevin as he guarded them from any attacking aliens. Kevin grasped his fist as an alien charged towards him. He swung his back foot around, kicking one away. "Ha," he yelled. "You ok down there?"

He watched Bradley help the lady down as the burning hot fire slowly got closer and closer to the leaking fuel. The fumes still lurked where the woman was. "Come on," he went. "That fucker's gonna blow."

Together they helped pull the lady out of the car as Mr. Knightsbridge looked on. "You lot move," he went. "Get well away."

The lady stood up, trembling with fear and terror. "Thank you," she said haltingly.

"Come on," Kevin said to her. "That's gonna blow."

Kevin, Bradley and the lady quickly ran up the sidewalk away from the burning car. The fire slowly crept into the engine, igniting the fuel and fumes. The green sedan was thrown up into the air from the explosion. Bradley looked up as the car cast a shadow down on him. "Fuck!" he mumbled. "Come on, move."

The glass from the window shattered outwards, landing on the ground. Bradley fell forward as the explosion rocketed through the street blasting other car windows out.

He looked up at Kevin. They both turned their heads around and looked at the burning car as they lay in the middle of the sidewalk.

"Jesus Christ!" the woman said. "Thank you so much."

"No problem," Bradley said. "You ok getting up?" He lay back down on the ground.

"Come on," Mr. Knightsbridge yelled.

"Name's Amelia," she said.

"Hi Amelia," Bradley said.

"Hello," Amelia said.

Bradley looked around and saw a group of aliens charging towards them. He reached into his pocket and pulled out the security guard's handgun. He took aim and pulled the trigger repeatedly. The aliens dropped to the floor one after the other as their suits were penetrated. He turned around and caught up with the group. He shook his head as the blood from the people poured onto the ground. He continued scanning the streets. He looked into the patrol car to see a pump action shot gun loaded and ready to be used. He reached in through the open window and pulled the weapon out. Mr. Knightsbridge looked up at him as he fell against the car trying to catch his breath. Bradley pumped the shotgun lever looking over the car bonnet as he stood looking down at the group. He felt the nerves in his hand twitch as the long metal and wood weapon pushed into the palm of his hand. He slowly turned his head to the right and looked at three aliens as they stood looking at the group. Their teeth gleamed white. As Bradley held on tighter to the shotgun, he swung his body around and pulled the trigger, launching the shell. It whistled, as it flew through the air and slammed into one of the aliens who fell back onto the ground, blood spilling out everywhere. Bradley watched as the other two aliens looked at one another. They reached for their ray guns from the pockets.

"Shit" Bradley went. He ducked down behind the patrol

car. The blue rays from the ray guns zoomed overhead and smashed into a lamppost. Bradley quickly jumped back up. He felt the cold rushing air hit his face as he looked through the shotgun scope. He blasted the two aliens away as they stood looking at the car. "Move," Bradley ordered. He held onto the shotgun and peered over his shoulder watching Mr. Knightsbridge slowly creep along the sidewalk. "Oh, for God's sake," he moaned. Mr. Knightsbridge started coughing as he fell against the wall of a shop. "You ok?" Bradley asked.

"Yeah," he replied.

Kevin looked at him as he looked at Bradley. Bradley scanned the area around him when he heard a sudden crash. He blinked his eyes. He saw one of the aliens jump onto Mr. Knightsbridge.

"No," Kevin yelled and pulled the alien off him. "Oh, no, you don't," he said. He fell back onto the road as Bradley walked forward holding the shotgun. The shell flew through the air. The alien's blood drained into the sewers as Bradley looked down at Mr. Knightsbridge. He slowly got up as he looked over into the streets. The aliens came back with a greater force.

"There's too many of them," Bradley yelled.

"Too fucking right," Eric replied.

Bradley looked around at Mr. Knightsbridge. "Go, go, go," he yelled.

"What?" Mr. Knightsbridge asked.

"Don't argue," Bradley yelled. "Just go."

"Amelia, you go as well," Max ordered.

Bradley pushed Mr. Knightsbridge up the small alley as he pumped the shotgun. He took aim and pulled the trigger blasting the aliens away.

Kevin looked over at Bradley as Mr. Knightsbridge and Amelia disappeared. "He's well gone," he went.

Bradley laughed as the rest of the aliens charged for

them. He kept his cool as he started to run low on shells. "Come on," he said. He crossed the road, looking both ways at the smashed up vehicles. As he reached the other sidewalk he looked at Eric fall to the ground with the aliens chasing him. Bradley swung his head. "Come on," he said. He picked Eric up off the ground. He looked down the long sidewalk, as the aliens seemed to be charging towards him at a great speed. "Shit!" he gasped. "Come on."

Bradley pushed Eric along the sidewalk. Kevin ran ahead as Bradley spun around holding onto the shotgun he had pulled out from the patrol car. He pulled the shiny metal trigger, launching the last remaining cartridge through the air. The aliens fell back as he turned around running along the sidewalk trying not to run into the fleeing people as they ran in all directions.

"In here," Kevin yelled as he pushed a set of wooden doors open. Bradley followed Eric in. He slammed the two doors shut pulling two huge dining tables across to hold the door shut.

"What the hell?" Eric said.

"Yeah, what is going on?" Max asked.

There was a small pause. Bradley turned around as the aliens from the outside started banging at the door.

"Shit," Kevin went.

"What do we do?" Max went.

"I've got it," Eric said as he walked up to the door. Bradley watched Eric walk up to the restaurant doors as the two aliens continued trying to break in.

"Stay back. I've got a chainsaw," he yelled. "Ram nam, nam, nan, nam, nam, ram, nam."

Bradley, Kevin and Max looked at Eric as the two aliens stopped banging and started looking through the door at them. Eric looked at the two aliens through a hole in the door.

"Who is this joker?" one alien said to the other in their

own language. They both looked at Eric as they started banging again.

"Did it work, Eric?" Bradley asked.

"No," he replied. "Sorry."

Bradley took deep breaths as bits of muck rained down each time the aliens banged on the door. He handed Kevin the handgun he had picked up off the dead security guard before he ran into the kitchen.

"What?" Kevin went.

Bradley didn't answer. He walked into the kitchen to look for the fire exit. "Come on," he yelled when he found it. "Go."

"Wait. What about you?" Kevin asked.

"Don't worry," Bradley said. "I'll catch up. Now go."

Kevin pushed the fire exit open just as three aliens burst into the restaurant. They slowly pushed the old metal tables out of the way. Bradley walked back into the lounge and looked at the aliens as they stood looking at Bradley. He clenched his knuckles. "Bring it on," he yelled.

The three aliens charged towards him. Bradley felt his heart pound as all the martial arts and fighting he had learnt over the years were called into action. He took a deep breath and swung his leg round, slamming it into a running alien. Bradley watched as it flew back through the air and slammed into the other two. He knew he had to get out of there. He sprinted for the exit, diving over the broken tables and chairs trying not to slip on the broken plates and glass. He ran out of the restaurant and sprinted along the sidewalk as the alien continued to chase him. Not many people were around as he continued along the sidewalk, his heart pounding in his chest. He spun around running back as he held onto the night stick, ready to use it as he approached a small side alley. He skidded to a stop, and then ran up it, away from the chasing aliens, hoping to give them the slip. He looked to the right. Running up the next side alley, he skidded to a stop as he came face to face with a brick wall.

"Shit!" he gasped. "Now where the fuck do I go?" He knew he did not have enough time to climb over it.

The two aliens ran around the comer looking at the wall. "Shit!" one went. "Where is he?"

"He's gone," the other alien said.

"Never mind. There's plenty more out there."

The two aliens looked around for a few seconds as the screams of the frightened people started to slowly fade away into the air of the city and they heard other frightened people running along the sidewalk. Bradley gave it a few minutes. Then he slowly lifted the cardboard box up off the floor and got out of it. He felt his heart starting to slow down. He wiped the tiny drops of sweat away from his face as he looked around the dark alley, looking for a way out, trying to avoid the main roads. He looked up at the wall. He reached up, grabbed the edge and pulled his thin body up. He looked down at the ground as he landed on his two feet. The screams had faded away. Not many people were now left in this part of the city, and he wondered where his group could be. He felt his pulse slowing as he continued to wipe his forehead. "Fuck me," he mumbled.

Kevin ran down the set of steps behind the shop. He watched as Eric and Max followed. "In here," he commanded. He opened a small door leading into a quiet, dark café. He closed the door slowly trying not to make a noise and draw attention to them. He stopped and looked around the small building. The coffee machine was still running, gently dripping onto the silver plate. The chairs were overturned from when people had tried to run from the attacking aliens.

"What are we doing here?" Eric asked.

"Staying out of sight while we figure out what to do," Kevin replied as he closed the door and slid the bolt across.

"Guys stay down," he ordered.

Eric hit the ground and looked up at the window.

"Ok, now what?" Max asked.

"We wait here for a while," Kevin said.

"How long?" Eric asked.

"For as long as it takes," Kevin snapped. "Until we can find out what to do."

Eric remained silent as he stayed down on the floor. He looked up at the window as the smell of the coffee from the machines that still hissed lingered around the small building. The shadows of two aliens fell across the coffee shop. Kevin trembled as the shadows passed over his head. The two aliens slowly walked past the windows. Kevin looked at their shadow through the blinds again, watching them slowly walk past. "What are they?" he asked quietly.

"They're aliens," Eric replied.

"I know that," Kevin replied, "but where are they from?"

"The thing is where they came from," Max said. "No ship, nothing. They just appeared out of nowhere."

"Beats me," Kevin said "But before we start with the science fiction, let's try and get out of here..........alive."

"I agree," Max replied.

Kevin, Max and Eric stayed down on the ground as the two aliens stood outside the small café. Kevin looked over his shoulder, looking for the back exit so he would know where to run in case things got worse.

"Where the hell is Bradley?" Eric asked.

"He's ok," Kevin replied. "I know he is."

"But where is he?" Eric asked again.

Kevin let his breath out. "Eric, listen to me" he said. "He is ok. Keep quiet."

Eric looked up as the two aliens stood outside the café looking at one another not knowing whether the group was inside the small café or not. One of the aliens turned the shiny golden handle. The lock slowly pulled back. Kevin clenched his fist ready to fight them. The door moved back and forth as the bolt held it closed. Kevin held his fist tightly closed. He felt relieved as the two aliens started to walk away. Eric looked around to see his leg poised against a few plates dropped on the floor by the frightened people. Kevin looked over as they fell against his legs. "Do not move," he whispered.

"What?" Eric went.

"Don't move," Kevin said again.

Eric didn't move as the pile of plates slowly started to slip over the top of his leg. Kevin closed his eyes tight as the plates fell to the ground and smashed with a loud noise. He swung his head forward, looking up at the two aliens as they looked through the blinds of the small café down onto the group. "Shit!" he gasped. "Come on." He jumped up, grasping the handgun. He opened fire through the windows. "MOVE, MOVE," he bellowed.

Eric and Max ran out of the back exit into a quiet side street, looking for a place to escape to. Kevin looked around at the huge warehouses in front of him. He looked up at the seagulls flying above. They were not aware of what the hell was going on below. Kevin skidded to the right. He looked to see a medium sized warehouse entrance. "This way," he yelled. He ran down the small side alley towards the back entrance of the huge building. He looked at the wide open door ready to be run into. He skidded to a stop. "In here," he yelled. "Come on, come on"

Kevin watched as the chasing aliens followed Eric towards the back door. He reached out and pulled it closed. The aliens slammed into the door as Kevin got his breath back.

"Shit!" he went.

Eric looked at Kevin. "What do we do?" Eric asked as he started to panic.

"Eric, calm down," Kevin said. "We should be safe in

here for a while. They are tough doors."

The banging continued on the back door. The group ran up the narrow corridor into the warehouse. They looked at all the empty offices and rooms.

"What is this place?" Eric asked.

"A warehouse," Max replied.

"I know that," Eric replied. "I mean what do they produce?"

The group turned the corner looking out over a long balcony. They looked to see orange gas canisters piled up.

"Bloody hell," Kevin said.

"What are they?" Eric asked.

Kevin slowly walked down the metal steps to the concrete floor. He walked up to the orange canisters and looked at the labels. "Gas," he said.

"Gas," Eric repeated.

Kevin heard a sudden bang. He looked over at the shiny silver shutters to the warehouse as they rocked back ad forth when the aliens outside slammed into it.

"Shit!" Kevin went.

"Is there another way out?" Eric asked.

"We must be surrounded," Kevin replied. He didn't know what to do. He was also worried about Bradley.

Bradley peeked his head around the corner as he walked out of the alleyway. He looked both ways down the quiet street and then at the two motor bikes that stood smashed in the middle of the road, fumes seeping out of the engines. The old black crash helmets in the middle of the road were still rolling about in the gentle breeze. Bradley didn't feel right. He continued to look over his shoulder as he advanced out of the alleyway onto the sidewalk, looking into all the empty shops wondering which one to enter. He raised his head only to see a patrol car smashed into one of the street lamps. He walked over to it, looking over his shoulder, as the door stood wide open. He reached in, then

jumping back, took one last look over his shoulder into the
streets. Nothing came into sight. He slowly crawled into the
police patrol car looking down onto the black leather seats
He looked over the steering wheel and placed his finger in
the tepid coffee which had partly spilled on the seats. He
pulled the red boot lever releasing the back of the seat. He
slowly crawled out the vehicle and walked alongside it after
looking around at the empty streets and side roads. He
opened the boot. His eyes widened in surprise and he felt
the adrenaline surging through his body as he saw an AK47
assault rifle lying there. "What the..." he gasped. "An AK!"

Bradley reached in and pulled the weapon out. He took
the magazine out and looked at all the rounds stacked up,
ready to be used and fired. He pulled the weapon out of the
vehicle, placed the leather strap over his head, and grasping
the weapon, looked back around the city. He took a deep
breath and nearly choked on the fumes from the burning
vehicles. He turned around and walked down the sidewalk
happily holding the AK47 rifle and wondering why on earth
it was in the back of a police car. He slowly walked along
the sidewalks looking out for any of the aliens. He heard a
sudden crash from the road ahead. He looked to his left to
see an overturned car. He dived down behind it and looked
at the glass as it fell to the ground. Bradley took a shallow
breath as the strong taste of petrol went down the back of
his throat. He looked up to see a long stream of the alien
invaders running down the road in one direction. "What
the...?" he asked himself.

Bradley looked out onto the main road. He moved along
the sidewalk to the quiet street leading to the industrial
estate north of the city. He kept his head down and watched
as the aliens ran towards a warehouse. "What are they
doing?" he wondered.

He came out of the alleyway onto the main road. He
grasped his AK47 assault rifle ready to use it if he had to.

He stared at the aliens as they attacked the main entrance to the warehouse. They slammed into the metal door struggling to get in. The door was slowly starting to give way. "I wonder..." Bradley said.

He ran up to the entrance of the huge building and looked into the security shack. Blood covered the swivel chair. Bradley turned his attention to the roof of the building. He looked up to see a metal ladder leading to the top, probably for maintenance of the air conditioners. He sprinted over to it, all the while keeping an eye on the aliens as they continued trying to break into the huge building. Bradley quickly climbed the ladder, staying out of the aliens' view. He blinked his eyes as the huge fireballs ripped up from the ground and the sound of explosions echoed through his ears. "Shit!" he gasped.

Bradley shook his head and walked onto the roof of the building. He came across a small, glass skylight. He kept back trying not to cast a shadow down into the huge building. He blinked. He looked down through the skylight to see Kevin leaning against a small wooden crate looking at the door as the aliens continued ramming into it. He shook his head as he caught sight of a roll of wire, most probably left by the builders when they finished building the huge warehouse. He continued staring down as the aliens finally got the huge door open.

"Shit, they're getting in," Eric yelled. "What are we gonna do?"

Kevin held onto the sidearm. He was too scared to shoot as they were surrounded by gas canisters.

"Shoot, Kevin," Max yelled.

The aliens walked in as Bradley's shadow fell on the floor of the warehouse. Kevin looked up as the huge skylight glass shattered. The tiny shards of glass started raining down on them as the unraveling wire tumbled down towards the floor.

Bradley took a deep breath as he looked down into the old warehouse. The aliens didn't have a clue what the hell was going on. Bradley grabbed the copper wire. He looked down as he started sliding down, still holding the AK47 assault rifle in one hand. Eric stood looking up at Bradley as he opened fire on the aliens. The tiny golden bullets shot through them.

"Jesus Christ, Bradley," Eric yelled. "There's fucking gas around."

Bradley released his hands from the copper wire, looking at the group. He gently smiled as he spun around. "GET OUT," he yelled.

Kevin, Eric and Max ran to the back exit of the warehouse. Kevin kicked the gray bar and ran down the dark alley, away from the warehouse as Bradley stood looking at the aliens. "Come on, then," he mumbled. He curled his finger round the trigger and fired. The bullets spewed out, penetrating the large group of canisters. Bradley turned round and ran to the exit as the last bullet hit the ground. He spun around looking at the building filling up with gas. He released the AK47, chucking it through the air as the aliens tried to escape. The weapon landed on the floor and skimmed along the top of the metal pipes. A tiny spark lit up from under the old weapon. The gases throughout the building erupted traveling along through the warehouse. Bradley sprinted out of the building as the huge fireball seemed to be following him. "Fuck, fuck, fuck," he mumbled.

The force slammed him to the ground. He tasted the ground as the tiny particles blew up into his mouth. "Ouch," he moaned.

Kevin ran over and looked down at him. "Brad, where the hell you been?" he asked.

"Just around," Bradley replied as he got up off the floor and brushed off the bits of muck from his clothes. "You guys ok?" he asked.

Bradley slowly got up and, leaning against the wall, looked at the group.

"We're ok," Eric said.

"Good," Bradley went. What have I missed?"

"Not much," Max replied.

Bradley looked down the alleyway. He stared at all the garbage bins as the old newspapers blew around them in the breeze. His ears were still ringing after the explosion. He shook his head as he took another look down the alleyway. "Come on," he said. "Let's get out of here."

The group started walking up the alleyway, keeping an eye out for any of the aliens who could be hiding, waiting to pounce on them.

7

Lieutenant Kipling clambered into the Ft-17 tank holding on to his rifle as he stared across the empty Queensboro Bridge. He slowly turned his head to the left as the sun beamed down on his head. He looked over as a few puffs of smoke came out from under the bridge. The huge shockwave from the explosions rippled through the air as he jumped to the explosion. The Williamsburg Bridge went up into flames. He watched the burning twisted metal work slammed into the Hudson River. The splashes were huge as the current took it away. "May god have mercy on our souls," he said.

The atomic motors on the tank roared to life. He felt the burning fumes go down his throat as the tracks slowly started to roll forward. The tan rolled onto the bridge. Kipling looked behind as he looked out the top of the tank He grasped his rifle as the end of the old bridge was near. The roads were clear ahead. "Standby," Kipling said.

He ripped the machine gun lever back looking at the golden bullets dangling beside him. He grasped the trigger, ready to squeeze it as the tank rolled out from the bridge. The roads were covered with smashed up vehicles. There was an eerie silence as Kipling raised his hands for the brigade to stop. Kipling looked around the dead quite streets. The manic sounds from Queens now behind them disappeared as he continued to observe the streets around him. Not a soul in sight. Only the hissing of a taxi engine which has been slammed into a lamp post. "My god!" he mumbled.

The tanks slowly started turning to the left, heading up the street towards the police station which was just over two miles away. Kipling's eyes twitched as they slammed through smashed up buses and trucks. But something caught his eye ahead of him. He raised his fist, stopping the tanks again. He stepped down from the tank holding onto his rifle. The surroundings were horrible. There was not a sound or gust of wind, only small pieces of newspaper blowing away with the very gentle breeze. Kipling stared ahead at the dead corpse of a middle aged woman lying in the middle of the road. She was smartly dressed. Red skirt down to her knees, long blonde hair; must have been going to a family get together or a date. Kipling kneeled down next her. He placed his hands on the corpse, slowly turning her onto her back as two more of his troops ran over, scanning the area around them. Kipling stared down at her face. The blood had dried on her neck where one of the aliens has stabbed or shot her. "Jesus," Kipling said.

One of the young troops looked down at her. "Fwooor," he went. "Very nice."

Kipling continued looking down at her. Her eyes were still wide open with shock.

"Where was she off to, then?" The soldier said.

Kipling looked down at her as he felt his inner emotions start to turn.

"Let's see what she is made of, then," the soldier said, using his boot to start lifting her skirt.

"Hey," Kipling snapped. "Show some goddamn respect."

The soldier lowered her skirt.

"Don't let me see you do that again," Kipling ordered.

"Sorry sir," the soldier replied.

Kipling looked over at the sidewalk. "Move her over

there," he ordered.

Kipling closed her small eyes. Two soldiers started to move the woman's body. Kipling looked around as he walked over to the tank and pulled out a small map. He looked down at it to see the police station was about a mile away. The two soldiers placed the young lady down on the sidewalk. The soldier looked over at Kipling as he looked down at the map.

"Go on. One look," Kipling said.

The young black soldier placed his rifle by his side as the tanks started up again. He was just lifting the young lady's skirt when he heard a sudden scuffle coming from the shop next to him.

"What was that?" his companion asked.

The two men peered into the dark shop as the lights had gone out.

"What is it?" the soldier asked again.

The two men slowly walked into the shop crunching on the glass below their feet. The sound echoed around the empty shop. The two soldiers stared into the shop, when suddenly a burst of light came towards them.

"Yaaah," one soldier yelled. The purple ray slammed into the soldier.

Kipling looked up as one of his troops fell to the ground. "Man down," he yelled.

Kipling looked up as the other soldier fell to the floor.

"Shit!" he gasped.

He jumped into the tank, grabbed hold of the heavy machine gun and swung it over to the shop as the two aliens sprinted out. Kipling squeezed the trigger as he stared at them. The two aliens fell to the ground. He stared down at their slimy bodies as the green blood ran out of their wounds onto the sidewalk, and covered the young lady.

"Come on," Kipling yelled "Let's go."

The tanks started to pick up speed as Kipling brushed the loose golden shells onto the floor of the tank. His eyes were peeled as they moved along the road. He grasped the machine gun as he looked down at the map. They were approaching the police station.

"I want all side roads blocked," he ordered over the radio. "Let's get a clear route back to the bridge." He stood up and watched as the tanks slowly pulled into the wide side roads, pointing their turrets down the road, waiting for one of the alien invaders to appear. Kipling looked ahead at the police barricade as it blocked the way to the station. He watched the new white cars slowly roll back to make way for the brigade of troops. Kipling looked down at the officers. He saw the look of terror in their eyes as they watched the huge tank roll past to the police station.

Ms. Javies quickly got up from her seat in the police station office at the sound of military jets flying overhead. The drinks in the cups on the table rippled as the engines roared off into the distance. She felt relieved as more people turned up at the police station and walked out of the office, trying not to walk on anybody as the floor started vibrating. It was very warm and she felt very hot. She walked down the concrete steps looking down the street at the people standing about, all looking very scared. The sound of crashing vehicles was heard. She slipped her old glasses on and squinted her eyes. It was not the sort of thing one saw everyday. Ms. Javies watched the United States Military tanks rolling down the street, smashing into the crashed taxis as the armed officers moved the yellow barriers out of the way for them. Ms. Javies stepped onto the sidewalk as the tanks pulled up in front of the police station.

The noise from the engines was horrendous. The soldiers climbed out of their vehicles, arming up and looked around at the panicked and frightened people. The lieutenant walked up the concrete steps into the police station past Ms. Javies. She turned around and watched him walk briskly through the station with his comrades. They turned to the left and headed up the stairs towards the Chief of Police's office. They banged on the glass door and the three soldiers walked in, looking at him as he listened to his radio. The sound of shooting and cars crashing from the radio filled his room as the cries for help got worse and worse. The chief turned his head and looked at the soldiers as he stood in his dark uniform, the badge on his hat shining gold in the light from the outside.

"Chief Irons?" Lieutenant Kipling said.

"Yes," he replied. "Yes, that's me."

There was a short pause from both the men.

"Lieutenant John Kipling, sir, New York city and the surrounding areas and districts have been put under martial law as you may be aware. Now we are going to need as many men as possible here, so can you get your officers back here?"

Irons got onto the radio. He called his officers back to the station knowing that not many of them would be returning.

"We also have put a call out for all emergency service personnel to report here," the lieutenant continued. "Everything - fire, ambulance, all military as well."

Chief Irons walked out of his office over to a window. He took off his hat and looked out at all the injured people as they staggered about, trying to find their loved ones. He turned round and shook his head. "How are you evacuating?" he asked.

"I've not had my orders yet, sir, but from what I know there is going to be one way out only," Kipling replied.

Irons was shocked to hear that. "What?" he gasped. "There are many bridges and tunnels you can use."

"I'm sorry sir but I cannot disclose that information as

of yet, sir," Kipling replied. ""I will be keeping you informed of the situation as my men and I progress."

The chief looked out of the window again as people staggered out of the underground stations, looking for help, blood gushing from their wounds and cuts.

"What's the status on the subway?" Irons asked. "All lines seem to be totally blocked. The people are obviously making their way through the city to here," he said to Kipling.

The lieutenant took a deep breath. "Grand Central Station has been destroyed and is on fire I have been told," he said to Irons.

"What?" Irons said in a shocked voice. "Grand Central?"

"Yes, sir. It's in a blaze. People tried to evacuate it but things just got out of control," the lieutenant said.

Irons looked out of the window and at the people again. "Once our people have cleared a route out of the city we will begin evacuating them, but it is too dangerous right now," Kipling said.

He tuned around and walked back downstairs, through the station and out into the street, looking at all the military vehicles as they rolled into the city in search of survivors who could still be alive. He and the onlookers watched as two tanks rolled into place to guard the entrance to the station. The officers watched in relief as they now had help for the rest of the day. The young officer looked over at an aged man as he sat on the concrete steps hiding his old walking stick. He looked at the fear in his eyes. He was most probably a veteran of World War Two or Vietnam. He pictured his fear of a bomb which could be dropped on New York at any time. The officer shook his head as more people came out of the subway station toward the police station. He knew it was going to be filled up very quickly. It had turned out to be the busiest day of the week.

8

Bradley slowly walked up the alley. He kept looking over his shoulder at the group as they followed him like a pack of dogs. He didn't know what to think as he was leading a group of people through an alien filled city. Kevin looked up as Bradley walked forward. Max caught up with Bradley. "Hey, Bradley" Max said.

"Yes?" Bradley replied.

"That AK," Max said. "Where did you get it?"

"Just found it," Bradley said.

"Just found it?" Max said.

"Yep," Bradley replied. "In the back of a patrol car."

"Lucky sod," Max went.

Max took a shallow breath. "What's the plan then?"

"To stay alive," Bradley replied. "That's about it."

Bradley looked at Kevin as he stuck his fist up into the air ordering the group to stop. Kevin slowly pointed at the shadows on the ground as they moved. Bradley silently nodded as he knelt down on the ground. The two shadows slowly moved away. Bradley took a deep breath as he crept forward along the alley. He tried not to step on the cracked cement as the light from the main street beamed in. The screams from the frightened people could no longer be heard. Bradley peeked around the corner of the alleyway. He looked out into the streets to see the aliens walking around together, wielding their weapons, ready to use them. The smoke poured out of the crashed vehicles. Glass lay scattered about on the ground. Bradley slowly moved back into the alleyway, back to the group. He kneeled down on the ground and looked at Kevin. "Ok," he whispered. "I'm going across first. I'll call you soon"

"Got it," Kevin said.

Bradley looked down the entrance to the side alley. He looked at the two aliens as they looked out on the city. He crouched down and sneaked along. He spun around and knelt down on the ground as he swiped the night stick. He put his hand up, calling Eric across. Eric crept along as he stared at Bradley holding onto his night stick. Suddenly he stumbled to the ground.

"Oh shit," Bradley went. He crawled out and grabbed hold of Eric. He pulled him in as Kevin and the rest of the group dove behind a few of the large wheelie bins left outside. He dragged Eric behind an overturned set of boxes. "Get down," he whispered.

Two aliens walked into the alleyway. Bradley looked up into the whiteness of their eyes as he gripped the night stick. He heard his heart pounding in his chest as the aliens looked both ways after they heard the noise. Bradley watched as the aliens then walked away.

"Phew!" Kevin said.

Bradley turned and looked at Eric. "Why is it always you?" he asked.

"I don't know," Eric replied.

Bradley shook his head as he looked over at Kevin. He carefully peeked his head around the corner to see if the coast was clear of aliens. "Come on," he then whispered.

The group started creeping along. It passed behind Bradley as he slowly walked backwards holding on to the night stick. He felt the muscles twitching in his hand as he clung to the wooden weapon. He walked back into the alleyway feeling free of the aliens for a short while. He ran ahead of Kevin, scanning ahead, trying to find away out of the alley ways and back into the main streets. "Ok, guys, take two," he said.

Bradley kneeled down and looked around as he scanned the alleyways. It was quiet. Not a living soul was around.

"Hey," a voice suddenly went. Bradley looked up toward the back window of a shop. The group looked up to see a middle aged man looking down at them. "You ok?" he said. "Come inside. I'll let you in."

Bradley stood up and looked at Kevin. He shrugged his shoulders as the back door slowly started to open. The creak of the hinges seemed to go on and on. Bradley held onto the nightstick as the shop keeper helped him in. He looked around the dead dark corridor as the light from the main store shone out into the hallway.

"Name's Rodger," he went.

"Hi Rodger," Eric went.

"Name's Bradley," Bradley said. "What the hell is going on?"

"I ain't got a clue. I was happily behind the counter in my uncle's shop looking after it while he is on vacation in Las Vegas when I suddenly saw people running in all directions. I walked up to the entrance of the store to see these things attacking people left right and center," Rodger said. "It was horrible to watch."

Bradley walked into the store. His eyes widened with amazement. There, in front of him, stood stack after stack after stack of weapons. Bradley, Kevin, Max and Eric had walked right into a weapon store.

"How come you weren't raided for weapons?" Kevin asked, folding his hands as he leant against the wall.

"I put the shutters down straight away and got the door locked, but I don't think people had the time" Rodger said looking at the group. "What I saw was horrible."

Bradley walked up to the huge silver shutter admiring all the weapons as they stood stacked on the shelves. He peeked through the tiny holes in the shutter looking out into the city as the aliens walked past. He slowly looked to the right seeing the shutter control box. "How did you shut it from inside?" he asked.

"We have an emergency switch behind the counter," Rodger said. "What you boys in New York for? Vacation? Field trip?"

"Just a field trip," Kevin said. "At least it was a field trip."

"Where's your school teacher?" Roger asked.

"He was getting in the way," Kevin said.

"Oh," Roger said.

"So we sent him packing," Eric said.

Bradley turned around. "Have you got a TV?" he asked.

"Yes. Why?" he replied.

"Is the news still broadcasting?" Bradley asked.

Roger turned around and walked up behind the counter. He turned on the small television standing on the metal stand looking out over the deserted shop. Bradley stared at the static screen as he flicked through channels.

"No," Roger went. "This is a dodgy machine, anyway."

"Ok. Do you have any plans for survival?" Bradley asked.

"No," Roger said. "I'm just staying here as long as I can. What are you doing?"

"We should head off and get back to our people at the police station," Bradley said. "Where is that?"

"The main one?" Roger asked.

"Yes, so we were told," Bradley said.

Roger pulled out a small pocket map from under the counter. He unfolded it and looked down onto the Manhattan area. "Ok," he said.

Bradley leaned over the counter and studied the map.

"Ok, we are here. The main police headquarters is here," Roger said. He circled the station as Bradley looked down.

"That's not far," Eric said.

"It's about three and a half miles from here, south, but I suggest you take the alleys and back routes all the way down to here," Roger said.

"Where's the bus station?" Bradley asked.

"The bus station is here," Roger said, circling the station with a red pen. "Why do you want that?"

"Our bus and our driver may be there. He could help with the evacuation," he replied.

"Cool," Roger went. "Ok, boys. I wish you luck in getting to your friends. Take what you want."

Bradley shook his head. "Anything?" he asked.

"Yep, anything. This place will be gone soon if they start bombing the island anyway," Roger said.

"That won't happen for a while," Kevin said.

"Don't bet on it," Roger said.

Bradley didn't want to get a long conversation going. "Right. We had better get armed and get out of here," he said.

He turned around and walked into the shop. He looked at all the weapon utility belts. He pulled one down off the stand and strapped it to his body. He felt the tight straps cling to his leg as he placed the handguns in the pockets, all fully loaded and ready to be used. He continued round the shop putting two sub machine guns on the sides. They were followed by the SPAS shot gun on his back, ready to be used in the event of them being in a crowded place.

Kevin turned the corner. He looked at the shelf to see some flick out batons all lined up, ready for purchase. "Wicked," he went and pulled a selection of the truncheons off the shelf. "Brad," he said. He chucked one into the air and Bradley reached up and caught it. He flicked it out, admiring the small weapon. "Cool," he went.

Bradley closed the weapon and put it into a pocket on

his leg strap as he continued scanning the shop. He looked to his right to see a large, leather jacket. He pulled it down off the coat hook and placed it over all his weapons. Kevin watched as he swung around walking towards the group as they stood by the entrance, ready to leave. "Ready when you are," he said.

Roger handed Bradley the map. "Oh Bradley," he went a second later. Bradley turned around. "Here, take this," Roger said. He handed Bradley a small silver weapon.

"What's that?" Bradley asked.

"That's a flare gun," Roger said.

"A flare gun?" Bradley asked.

"Yes," Roger said. "When you fire it into the air it sends out a burning bright light, blinding anything for a short while. This can be seen from a distance away."

Bradley tied the tiny weapon holder to the lower half of his leg. He locked it into place. "Thank you, Roger," he said.

They shook hands and Bradley slowly turned around and headed for the exit. He pushed the exit door open. Instantly sounds of glass smashing came through the door. Bradley turned around and ran back into the store. He looked over the counter at the group of aliens that had broken into the shop via the skylight.

"GO," Roger yelled.

Bradley turned around. He slammed the back exit door shut.

Roger stood looking at the two aliens as they looked at him.

"BRING IT ON," Rodger yelled. He pulled the trigger of his weapon. Bradley listened in from the outside as the semi automatic machine gun opened fire.

"Come on," Bradley ordered.

The group ran down into the alleyway as the sound of the shooting from the shop faded into silence.

9

Mr. Knightsbridge felt his stomach turning as the thick saliva started to build up in the back of his throat and mouth from all the running and sprinting he had done. He turned his head to the left and looked at the old basketball court in the side alley as Amelia followed on behind. He thought back to the days when he used to play there, not ever dreaming that ten years later he would be running past it with Amelia, running from attacking aliens.

"You ok?" Amelia asked.

"Yeah," Mr. Knightsbridge said. "Just fine." He felt his heart thumping in his chest as he placed his hands on his hips and leant his large body against the bent lamppost, trying not to spit out the saliva in his mouth. His heart missed a beat as he looked around at the destroyed city. It felt different with only smashed up cars to be seem and no business men and women on their phones heading to their destinations throughout the once magnificent city. There were no happy tourists photographing the landmarks around. The sound of the police sirens slowly started to fade away in the distance. His blood ran cold each time an occasional scream was heard.

"You ok?" he asked Amelia.

"Yes, I am, thanks," she replied. "Still a bit shaken up, though."

"We shouldn't be far now," Mr. Knightsbridge reassured her.

Death lurked around Mr. Knightsbridge and Amelia as they slowly started walking along the rubbish filled path, looking at all of the trash bins rolling around in the street. Blood was splattered on the streets and there was the occasional dead body.

"Oh my god," Amelia gagged.

"Come on," Mr. Knightsbridge said.

The splats of blood on the pavement dripped down into the gutters. Mr. Knightsbridge looked at the trashed bus stop. He sat down on a red plastic seat, feeling the weight come off his burning legs as he continued looking around at all the smashed up taxis and police patrol cars with their police lights slowly fading away from lack of power. The smell of burning lurked from the vehicles as the small fires slowly extinguished themselves. Mr. Knightsbridge lay back and waited for his heart to stop thumping and the energy to rebuild in his system.

"So what were you doing here in New York?" Amelia asked.

"Well," Mr. Knightsbridge said. "It was meant to be a field trip."

"Were those boys with you?" Amelia asked.

"Yes," he mumbled. "They were. You?"

"I'm on business from New Haven," Amelia replied.

"I'm from there," Mr. Knightsbridge said. "How come I haven't seen you around?"

"It's quite a big city," Amelia replied.

Mr. Knightsbridge looked around. "Come on," he said. "Let's get out of here."

"I agree," Amelia replied.

Mr. Knightsbridge helped Amelia of her seat as he looked over his shoulder. He opened his eyes with fear as a single alien looked out of the alleyway at him. He looked at the gleaming white teeth as it snarled through the plastic window of the bus stop. "Oh shit!" he exclaimed.

The alien snarled again, running for the plastic window. Mr. Knightsbridge closed his eyes. He heard a sudden slam and opened his eyes again, looking at the alien as he stood splat against the glass panel of the bus stop. He laughed as the small sized alien slowly started to slide down the paneled plastic, and though his heart was pounding he laughed again. "Ha."

The alien fell back onto the mucky path. Mr. Knightsbridge looked down at him and it shook his head violently. "Oh shit!" Mr. Knightsbridge went again. He sprinted along the center of the destroyed road weaving in and out of the cars as aliens leaped over the smashed up vehicles to get at him. "Come on, Amelia," he yelled.

He didn't have a clue where the police station was. He looked over his shoulder again at the chasing aliens that were catching up with him. Mr. Knightsbridge felt the side of his large body start to weep as he came to a stop and the stitch in his side got worse. He placed his hand on his side as he felt the pain power through his side. He fell against the lamp posts and the chasing aliens surrounded him.

"This is it," Amelia cried.

Mr. Knightsbridge held onto Amelia's hand as his heart banged in his chest. The sun beamed down on the aliens as they slowly swiped their ray guns from their side pouches. Mr. Knightsbridge closed his eyes, peeking through the two bits of skin, as death looked at his head. He watched in fear as a single alien leaped through the sky towards him. He closed his eyes tight again, looking death in the face as he thought about his short life. Then he jumped as the sound of banging came from behind him. He swung his head around and looked at the three US soldiers as they stood in the middle of the road wielding their rifles, their gas masks covering their faces. Mr. Knightsbridge watched as the golden bullets landed on the ground. The tingling still rang through his ears.

"This way," the soldier commanded.

Mr. Knightsbridge released his breath from his exhausted lungs. "Come on," he said to Amelia.

The two soldiers helped him along the deserted road towards a barricade. He squeezed through the yellow, rusty barriers looking over his shoulder as the two young soldiers slowly stepped back and scanned the roads ahead, guns drawn and ready to be used again. Mr. Knightsbridge had walked into a military zone. He stared at all the parked tanks guarding the main police headquarters as people ran about in different directions. "Jesus Christ," he said quietly.

"God! What a mess!" Amelia said.

Mr. Knightsbridge watched as the two Humvees pulled up outside the entrance to the station and coaches started turning up. The frightened, confused people struggled to get their seats. Knightsbridge walked along, heading towards the police station entrance. He struggled to get up the concrete steps into the station as he was still low on energy. He listened to the phones constantly ringing as the police staff headed in all directions. As he looked into one office he saw Ms. Javies.

She was standing, looking out of the side window onto the busy streets as the military vehicles continued rolling in. She slowly turned around holding her small half puffed cigarette in her mouth as her students looked at Mr. Knightsbridge, his shiny pink tie half undone and his jacket half hanging from his huge body. "Alan," she yelled.

Mr. Knightsbridge watched as Ms. Javies crashed into his body. She wrapped her long, thin arms around him as he struggled to keep his balance. "Thank god," she said. "You ok? You injured?"

"No, I'm fine," Mr. Knightsbridge replied. "You?"

"I'm ok," Ms. Javies said.

"Where were you," Mr. Knightsbridge asked, "when

this happened?"

"We were about five minutes from here," Ms. Javies said. "You?"

"We were right at the other end of the city," Mr. Knightsbridge said. "You sure you're ok?"

"I'm fine. Where are Bradley, Kevin, Max and Eric?" she asked "I want to see them and make sure they are ok."

Mr. Knightsbridge looked around the room as his students looked over at him. He could see the questions about Bradley and the group in their eyes.

"Bradley, eemmmmm, well we had this little situation," Mr. Knightsbridge stuttered.   "They left me and went ahead."

"Ok," Ms. Javies said in a dull voice. Then she suddenly started, opening her eyes wide. "What?" she asked furiously.

"I lost them," Mr. Knightsbridge went. "I was attacked by one of those things and Bradley insisted that I go."

"You mean to say you have left four of my students out there in this invasion all by themselves? They are probably dead, she wept, "and you left them."

"No, they're not," Mr. Knightsbridge went. "He's a tough lad."

"What do you know about him?" Ms. Javies yelled.

"A lot more than you," Mr. Knightsbridge replied in an abrupt voice. "All you ever do is throw your negative attitude towards him.

"What?" Ms. Javies yelled.

Mr. Knightsbridge and Ms. Javies continued arguing as Amelia walked up to them. "And who is this?" Ms. Javies asked.

Mr. Knightsbridge turned to look at Amelia. "Oh, this is Amelia," Mr. Knightsbridge said.

"Hi," Amelia said.

"And where did you find her then?" Ms. Javies

groaned.

"Alleyway."

"Excuse me," Amelia went, "I'm not some street hooker. I was here on minding my own business."

"I didn't say you were," Ms. Javies said. She turned back and looked at Mr. Knightsbridge. Amelia walked closer to Ms. Javies, arms folded, ready to ram her words back ˙down her mouth.

"Bradley and Mr. Knightsbridge actually saved me from my vehicle which overturned," Amelia said, "so I owe him and Bradley my life."

"Oh good for you," Ms. Javies replied. Amelia clenched her fist.

"Ok, don't worry," Mr. Knightsbridge said.

Ms. Javies looked to see two girls run into the station office. "Ms. Javies we can't raise Kate or Jane on their phones" one went.

"Oh my god," Ms. Javies cried, falling against the wall of the office.

"Where's Kate and Jane then? Who were they with?" Mr. Knightsbridge asked, folding his arms.

"They, they, they... I let them go off by themselves," Ms. Javies said, looking up at Mr. Knightsbridge. "And Colin went as well."

"So you let two young school girls and Colin go around New York city by themselves. That explains it all," Mr. Knightsbridge replied in a static voice. "That explains it all."

Ms. Javies ran out of the office. She turned around the corner and headed up the stairs towards the control room, listening to Mr. Knightsbridge as he moaned to her. She kicked the glass door open, walked in and looked out of the window at the coaches and buses evacuating people as they turned up one after the other. Ms. Javies felt her heart pound as she reached into her coat pocket. She pulled out her old cell phone. She slowly scrolled down the names list looking for Kate. The phone beeped as the signal failed. "Oh shit!" she yelled. "Now come on. You can do it."

Ms. Javies slowly turned her head, looking out of the window again at the city as the smoke from burning vehicles slowly climbed out all over it. Military personnel slowly walked around the area as people ran out of the subway station. The evacuation area was soon filled to capacity. "Where are they?" she quietly said. "They must be alive."

10

Bradley held onto his shiny sidearm as he felt the huge leather jacket he picked up from the weapon shop rubbing against his thin body. The smells of the burning vehicles and of death pervaded the air around him and the group. He felt his heart pounding as he scanned the area and saw nothing but trashed vehicles and burning buildings.

"Bradley," Eric called.

Bradley looked over at Eric as he stood on the sidewalk pointing towards a new police patrol jeep smashed into one of the bus stops. Bradley walked over to the jeep, keeping his sidearm at bay, ready to be used.

Eric stood looking at the jeep. "Could we drive it?" Eric asked. "Or anything else around here?"

"No, look at the roads. They're too blocked," Bradley said. "Let's see what's in here." He opened the jeep door and slowly brushed aside the tiny shards of glass. He looked down at the vehicle radio and slowly reached in to switch it on.

"Nothing," Eric went.

Bradley looked behind the box to see the wires pulled out and destroyed. "Ok, let's keep moving," he said. "Don't want any attention." He pulled his string bag off his back, and pulled out the tiny chocolate bar he had picked up from the shop the day before. He slowly unwrapped the silver shiny paper and placed the small bar in his mouth. He kept his eyes open as he slipped his weapon back into his side pouch continuing to look around the deserted street.

"Where is that station now?" Eric asked.

"About four miles this way," Bradley said to him.

Bradley dropped the shiny blue packet of chocolate onto the floor, past caring as he scanned the crossroads ahead.

"Bradley," Kevin whispered.

Bradley looked over at Kevin, as there was a sudden gust of breeze. Kevin pointed at the two aliens standing at the cross roads.

Bradley felt a sudden rush of adrenaline in his system. "Ok" he said. "This way." He held onto his sidearm as he ducked down by the broken shop window watching the two aliens. Eric slowly walked up behind. "Keep quiet," Bradley whispered. "They might move in a second."

Eric stumbled forward over an empty coke can lying on the sidewalk. "Oh shit!" he gasped. "Sorry."

Bradley rolled his eyes and looked up at the two aliens as they looked over their shoulders and snarled at them. Bradley swiped his handgun out of his pocket, aimed at them and pulled the trigger. Bullets were launched through the air. Bradley spun and turned around, looking down the packed roads as hordes of aliens charged towards them from out of nowhere. "This way," he yelled. He knelt down on the floor as Kevin, Max and Eric ran up towards the crossroads. Bradley looked through the scope and pulled the trigger, taking down the aliens one by one.

"Bradley," Kevin went. "Come on."

Bradley ran forward, looking for an entrance to one of the New York Subway stations. He looked at the yellow sparks raining down on the mucky steps as an electric sign dangled on its wires.

"Come on," Max yelled.

Bradley approached the subway stairs. He looked down them as he grabbed onto the metal bars. He sprinted down them. He felt the coke cans rolling under his feet and into the dark tunnel. He quickly turned the corner. He skidded to a stop and looked into the eyes of Kate. Bradley stood and looked at Kate in shock. "Kate!" he exclaimed.

Kevin, Max and Eric ran down the stairs. They too, stopped and looked at Kate as she stood looking at Bradley.

"Where's Jane?" Kevin asked before Bradley could say anything. "Is she ok? Where is she, Kate? Tell me."

"I'm fine," Jane said walking out of the toilet.

"Calm down, Kev," Bradley said. "She's here."

"That's good news," Kevin replied, slowly walking up to her. He heard a crash in the men's toilet. He pushed her to the side as a small shadow started to appear. He held onto his sidearm looking through the scope as Bradley looked over as well. Slowly appearing from the darkness of the murky, stinky toilet was Colin.

"What?" Kevin went. "You?"

"Yes, me," Colin said. "What's going on?"

Kevin turned to look at Jane. "You ok?" he asked again.

"Yeah, I'm fine" Colin replied.

"I'm not asking you," Kevin said in an abrupt voice.

Bradley slowly walked up to Colin. "So, dossing with these, are we?" he asked

"Yes," Colin replied. "Good fun."

Kevin placed his arms around Jane's soft shoulders as she shivered from fear. "Yeah, I'm fine," Jane said again.

Kevin quickly turned around and watched a group of aliens running down the stairs into the station.

"Come on," Kevin went. "Jane, stick with me"

"Colin, stick with Eric," Bradley commanded. Colin jumped over the ticket barrier holding onto his sidearm as he did.

"Go," Bradley went. "Ill catch up."

"You better," Kevin said. "The last time you said that you disappeared."

"Don't worry, I'm right behind," Bradley replied. He

ducked down behind the plastic barrier. Kevin stood back by the tunnel leading to the station. Bradley opened fire on the running aliens as they dived down the stairs and Kate and Jane jumped over them. He watched as two aliens dived into the station, looking around the murky place and at the people and personal belongings everywhere.

"Come on," Eric yelled.

The group ran down the stairs to the platform. Bradley looked around at the blood stained platform as old newspapers blew onto the tracks. He felt his heart pound as he looked towards the sets of stairs and saw the shadows of the two aliens as they ran down them. "This way," he said.

The group jumped onto the railway track. They slowly ran along and headed into the dark tunnel. Bradley stopped and knelt down on the floor as he held on to his side arm. The small group of aliens looked down the platform and around for the group. Bradley kept quiet as the two aliens slowly turned around and walked back into the station.

"Phew!" Bradley went. He turned around and walked into the tunnel once more, taking one last look over his shoulder. "You two ok?" he asked the girls.

Kate didn't reply for a few seconds. "I guess. What the hell is going on?" she then asked.

Bradley didn't know what to say. "I have no idea," he said "One minute we were walking down a road and the next it all just hit us."

"Where's Mr. Knightsbridge?" Kate asked.

"He got in the way," Kevin went.

"So he left you?" Jane asked.

"No, we left him," Bradley said.

"Oh, I see," Kate said.

"Come on, let's get out of here," Bradley insisted.

The group continued trekking up the tunnel. The sound of the breeze flying in from the platform echoed around the dark tunnel. Bradley kept looking over his shoulder to see if any trains were approaching. He couldn't tell the difference between the sounds from the trains and those from the wind and breezes.

11

Washington, D.C.

Washington, D.C. was under Martial Law. US Troops were to be seen everywhere. People were desperate for answers on the invasion. The young black man, dressed in his black new suit, stood as the sun beamed down onto the well kept gardens of the White House. He turned his head to the left looking out onto the clean gates of the huge building as the people yelled, demanding answers from the other side of the fence. He squinted his eyes, looking into the distance as the large blue Sea King helicopter sped over the city towards the huge building. He looked up into the air as the small white puffy clouds passed overhead. He watched as fast moving military jets flew over in pairs, and as the helicopter slowed down and landed on the clean, well kept heliport in front of him. The huge blades began slowing down. The man watched as the long blades of grass stopped blowing around. The military pilot stepped out of the helicopter and ran to swing the back door open. President Green stepped out. The young black man watched as his tie flew over his back from the force of the blades. "Shall I bring you up to date with the situation, Mr. President, sir?" he yelled over the engine.

"Yes. What the hell is going on in New York?" the president asked. "Some alien invasion?"

"Well, sir, intelligence from our troops on the ground

say New York City's Manhattan has been invaded by an alien life form," the man yelled over the engines. "We have had no contact from any leader of the force and all we know is they have killed many, many people."

"So they haven't come in peace," President Green said.

"No," the man replied.

"Dear God!" the president exclaimed.

"It's our worst nightmare," the man commented. "So our generals have mobilized the troops in the city as you requested, and have set up a unit around the main police headquarters. But apparently the roads are jammed with trashed vehicles so they are clearing a one way route to the Queensboro Bridge where a command post has been set up."

The two of them walked into the White House. The president felt the air conditioner blow onto his face as he walked up towards the spiral stairs towards his office. He admired the well-kept carpets as he approached the first floor and walked up to the small, white door. The young black man swiped his ID card through the reader and pulled the door open. The president walked into the command center. He looked at the digital computers as the TVs on the screen showed the Queens command center at Manhattan burned down. President Green looked on in horror as the small buildings and burning offices in the background coughed out smoke as helicopters circled above. He sat down in his char and looked at the smartly dressed military personnel assembled there.

"Ok, bring me up to speed," President Green said.

A general in a smart green uniform stood up. "Ok, Mr. President, sir," he said, walking over to a digital board.

The President looked at the digital board as it showed Manhattan Island.

"Sir, my men have set up a unit around the main police headquarters here, and at the hospital just down the road.

People are turning up left, right and center. The only way out is across the Queensboro Bridge," the general said. "Any questions on this part of the situation, sir?"

President Green rubbed his face. "Is that the only way out of the city?" he asked. "What about the New Jersey tunnel?"

"No, sir, sorry. We have had to seal that off in case the alien invaders tried to get through to New Jersey," he replied. "But we have set up a ton of semtex on the Queensboro Bridge ready to blow it up if the invaders try and break through the barricade we have on it."

"What about any of the other bridges?" President Green asked.

"No, sir. We have only one way out for evacuation and that is the Queensboro Bridge. We have up to White Plains co-cordoned off," he went. "All the other bridges have been destroyed to prevent invasions of any other fellow town"

"What about J F K airport?" President Green asked.

"The airport has been closed," the general said. "So also La Guardia and Newark. Apparently all US Airspace is being closed by the aviation authorities."

"Have any other countries been invaded?" Green asked.

"No," the general replied. "No. just Manhattan."

"Ok, that's good. Have we heard from any leader of their kind?" President Green asked next.

"Not yet, sir," the general replied. "Nothing at all."

"Well, we have to plan for the worst. We don't know how many more of these things there are, so I want your people ready for immediate action," the president said.

Just then the general slowly stood up and looked down at President Green. "May I speak, sir?" he asked.

"Yes," President Green replied.

The general took a deep breath. "I have currently on standby at Edwards Air Force Base, six B 52 Bombers ready to roll and go to New York, plus a few F- 16s ready to bomb the island," the general said. "Then our B 52 Bombers can take out the island to finish these things off once and for all."

"Ok. Get your jets to New York but I want them flying over the Arctic. I don't want to cause unnecessary panic," President Green said.

"Yes, sir," the general replied.

President Green sat rubbing his face. "So we are the only country that has been invaded by these things?" he asked again.

"Yes, sir," a naval commander answered.

"What am I going to say? The whole world is waiting for me," the president said, rubbing his face again for s moment. "Ok. I'm going up to my office. Let me know if any of their leaders make contact with us," he instructed.

He walked out of the Oval Office and headed up to his room. He looked out of his window at the panicked people, as they stood by the fences yelling and demanding answers.

12

Bradley looked forward as they walked through the mucky train tunnel still keeping an eye over his shoulder for any of the aliens or even worse, trains. There was an eerie sound going through the tunnel. The stones beneath their feet crunched as they saw the lights from the next station slowly start to come into view. Bradley looked ahead to see a parked up subway train in the station, blocking the way. "Oh dear," he went.

"Going under?" Eric asked.

"No," Bradley said. "Through." He walked up to the back of the train, slowly climbed the metal stairs and looked into the cab. There was not a soul in sight as he looked down the long metal vehicle. The door swung open. He pulled his thin body up into the front of the train. He looked around at the newspapers and shopping bags left behind. He peeked over his shoulder as Kevin helped Kate into the front of the train. Kate stepped into the carriage and folded her arms as Bradley walked down the carriage, looking out onto the platform through the dirty windows. "Ok." he said and walked up to the closed and sealed carriage doors. He placed his two hands on the door and tried to pull them open. He listened to the creaking of the doors as they remained tightly closed. "They're stuck," he said.

"Ok, give us a hand, Bradley," Kevin said.

Bradley and Kevin tried to pull the doors open as Eric

climbed onto the train. He looked down at the motor as the power was still running through the train. He stared at the open door button. He looked as Kevin and Bradley still trying to open the doors. Eric slowly pushed the button down. The two doors shot open at a faster speed.

"Woooh," Kevin and Bradley yelled.

The adrenaline surged through their bodies as they looked at Eric walking onto the train.

"Cheers," Bradley went.

He turned around and looked at the group as he stepped off the train onto the platform. He kept his firearm ready to use as he scanned the empty station. The breeze blew around the platform gently pushing the newspapers around. Kate watched as Bradley kicked the small bits of paper away from his trainers as he continued around the corner holding onto his sidearm. He turned the corner of the station and looked at the static escalator as the tiny coke cans rolled around. "Up we go," he said.

Bradley slowly walked onto the metal stairs, trying not to make a noise as the ringing from the metal pinged around the quiet surroundings. He looked through the scope as Kevin slowly got closer behind him.

"You ok?" he asked.

"Fine," Bradley replied. "Never felt better."

"Where are we going when we get out?" Kevin asked.

Bradley slowly continued to climb the frozen escalator. "I have no idea," he said.

Colin kept by Eric's side. "You ok, Eric?" he asked.

"No," he said. "I've got you."

Bradley laughed. They made it to the top and he stepped off the escalator. Looking down the short empty tunnel, he noticed the small puddles of blood on the mucky floor. He slowly walked towards them looking through the sight of his handgun waiting for aliens to jump out of nowhere and attack them.

Colin came to the top of the stairs. He followed Kate and Jane along the tunnel looking at the adverts, most of them covered in blood. He looked over as his shoulder as Max turned around and guarded the stairs while the group progressed down the tunnel and headed towards the exit. Bradley continued walking down the tunnel. He looked around as they moved to the exit. The breeze from outside blew around the spooky corners and the sound of it scraping crisp packets along the ground made Bradley's blood run cold. Bradley looked forward as he headed out beyond ticket vending machines. He looked at the beeping machines and at an orange paper ticket hanging out of a slot. Kevin slowly walked over to the small orange ticket. He looked around at all of the muddy foot prints as they covered the tickets on the floor. He leaned forward and pulled out the small ticket. He looked down at the small print as he listed to the breeze blowing around the dark, mucky station.

"Times Square," Kevin went. "What a waste!"

Bradley nodded his head as he walked to the stairs. He looked down at the tiny puddles that ran down the steps into the station. He walked out of the station into the quiet streets. He stared around at all the broken shop windows and burning vehicles. Kevin walked out of the station too. He held onto his firearm and, like Bradley, looked around. The breeze continued to blow around the city. It blew into the fires as they crackled one after the other. Bradley let his breath out as he leant against the wall of the subway station entrance.

"Where now?" Max asked.

Bradley looked around the quite area. "I remember this place," he said. "We drove through here when we were on our way to the bus station. Let's go there."

Bradley walked along the sidewalk. He looked to his right to see the shiny track on which the tram ran along through the city. He walked down the empty road towards the bus depot. He continued scanning the roads ahead for any of the aliens as the station came into view. "There we are," he finally declared. "One bus station."

The group looked over at the huge, new building. Shadows were cast on the ground. The area around them was quiet. The group slowly crossed the road as Bradley approached the concrete steps. He climbed them and looked around the bus station as he walked through the entrance. Tickets were strewn everywhere in the office and the cash registers lay open. Blood splattered the glass windows. The breeze blew around the quiet station as they walked out into the depot. Two silver buses stood smashed into one another as the blood from the driver splattered over the advertisement banner on the side.

"Jesus!" Kate went.

"Don't look," Bradley said to her.

Kate looked away as Bradley held onto his pistol. He walked into the dead bus station. The wind slowly picked up as the gentle drops of water ran down onto the pavement from the rain the night before. He felt his heart pound as he looked for their bus. He turned his head to see the long, new bus parked in the same spot as earlier. He gently jogged over to it and looked through the front door which was wide open. Could the driver be hiding? Bradley slowly crept along the side of the bus. He felt his back rub against the side of the bus. He took a deep breath as he approached the door. He swung his body around and looked into the bus. He jumped back as he looked at the driver's seat. He stared at the large, stumpy body of the late driver as he lay back in the seat, slash marks from alien swords over his face, and blood running down it, as the ignition barrel sparked.

"Shit!" Bradley whispered. He climbed onto the bus. He looked down the long aisle at all the empty seats as the air conditioning generator continued running gently. He slowly turned around taking one last look down at the ignition switch and at the small sparks. He shook his head and slowly walked out of the bus to the depot and back through the empty car park to the group as they stood by the terminal building, waiting for him. His weapons dangled from the side of his tall, thin body.

"Anything?" Kevin asked.

"Sorry," Bradley went. "The bus is there but it's undrivable."

"What's up with it?" Kate asked.

"Don't ask," he replied.

Kate looked down at the ground.

"Are there any others?" Kevin asked.

Bradley looked over his shoulder. "No," he replied "It's just our one."

"Great!" Kate said. "Now what?"

Bradley took a second to think. "Let's just get to that police station," he replied "There must be a safe way out of the city that way."

Kate let her breath out. Bradley heard a sudden crash coming from behind him. He swung around. His long, leather coat blew around him as he reached into his pocket and pulled out the silenced sidearm. He looked at the groups of aliens as they jumped into the bus station. Bradley took aim and slowly pulled the trigger. He hit the aliens one after the other.

"There are too many," Kate yelled.

"Oh, no, there aren't," Bradley replied. He stopped shooting and turning around, looked over at the group to see a parked up tram in the station, doors wide open and ready to roll. Bradley spun around and his heart started pounding as the hordes of aliens jumping from corner to corner, charged towards them.

"This way," Bradley yelled. The group ran with Bradley

through the empty bus park towards the tram station. He turned around and pushed Colin towards the vehicle. "Come on, got to go, got to go," he yelled. He ran in through the open doors of the new tram and looked down the long vehicle as he walked up to the cab.

"In, in, in," he yelled. "Come on."

Bradley pulled the door open and stepped into the cab as the aliens continued charging towards the tram. Bradley looked down at the new tram's digital gauge. He flicked on the tiny switches which started up the engines. Power surged through the vehicle.

Bradley pushed the door button. The doors slowly slid closed and locked into place as he looked out of the window. He pushed the small control lever forward and pulled out of the station. The group watched as the aliens pursued them along the clean shiny tracks. Kevin and Max watched as they pulled onto the main road, picking up speed slowly, and the aliens gradually disappeared from sight.

Eric looked at Colin panting for breath. "You tired?" he asked.

"Yeah," Colin replied.

"Get used to it," Eric said. "The day isn't over yet."

The tram moved along the shiny track. He looked at the dead bodies hanging over the sides of the crashed cars as the light smoke poured from their engines into the outer air. He shook his head as he continued along the track when he caught a glimpse of something moving in the rear view mirror. He opened his eyes in horror to see another one of the city trams catching up with them.

"Oh fuck!" he whispered.

Bradley looked over his shoulder as Max pulled the cab door open. "Bradley," he said.

"I know," Bradley said before Max could finish.

"What do we do?" Max asked, looking back.

Bradley looked into the mirror again. "Hold on," he yelled.

Bradley slammed the control lever to full throttle. He felt his hand jerk as the tram quickly picked up speed, zooming along the long, straight, shiny track. The chasing tram slowly caught up.

"How're they catching up?" Bradley asked. He held the control lever at maximum as the chasing tram rammed into them.

"Shit!" Colin yelled. "They're ramming us!"

Eric turned and looked at Colin. "You don't say," he replied sarcastically.

The tram sped along the track at full speed. Bradley looked in the mirror as the other tram stayed close behind them. Kevin slowly ran down to the end of the tram and looked out of the back cab window. He watched the aliens as they loaded their ray guns.

"Holy shit!" he gasped, running down the aisle of the tram.

"Bradley, they're gonna fire," Kevin went. "Come on."

"Alright," Bradley said. "Don't panic. I'm going as fast I can."

The aliens stood at the side of the tram aiming their ray guns at the pantograph cable over the top. They pulled their triggers, firing at it.

"Shit!" Bradley gasped. He looked ahead as they passed empty stations. The Armazoids continued firing onto the pantograph, trying to stop the tram.

"These wankers don't give up, do they?" Bradley yelled.

"No, they don't," Kevin replied.

Bradley felt his heart pounding as the tram struggled to keep its speed up to maximum. Then he saw something on the dashboard next to him. He looked at the two orange point switches. With these he could change to a different line on the tracks. "Kevin," he yelled.

Kevin didn't hear him as he was too occupied looking out the back at the chasing tram. "Oh, for fuck's sake!" Kevin mumbled.

"KEVIN!"

Kevin ran towards the door of the cab after hearing Bradley yell his name. He pulled the door open and looked at Bradley as he held onto the power lever, keeping it on full.

"What's up?" he asked.

Bradley took a deep breath. "Right. When I say 'Now,' shoot at that chasing tram," he went.

"Got it," Kevin replied.

Bradley looked down at the speed indicator as he sped along at fifty miles an hour. The aliens continued shooting at the pantograph. Kate watched as the sparks ran down the side of the tram. The electronics in the cab flickered on and off. Bradley felt the tram suddenly pick up more speed. "Hmm, sixty and rising" he laughed. He stared ahead to see the green sign zooming towards them, and the tiny white line leading to the left. "Ok, Kev," he yelled. "Now!"

Kevin shot out the back window of the cab. He aimed his handgun, taking shots at the driver of the tram, and the green rays zoomed into the tram as Kevin ducked down. He peeked over the broken window taking out the alien. The tram slowly started to fall behind. Bradley looked into his mirror as the chasing tram continued to slowly fall behind.

"We've lost 'em," Max yelled.

"Good," Bradley said.

He placed his hand on the orange button as they approached the left-hand turn. He pushed the tiny button down switching the points to the left. "Hold on," he yelled.

The tram swung around the corner to the left. Bradley grabbed a pole as he felt his thin body flung to the right. The tram straightened up on the long line, He looked into the mirror hoping the tram behind would go straight on. He rolled his eyes as the tram with the aliens swung around the corner. "Oh, what?" he went.

He looked forward as the tram slowly started descending down a hill. It picked up more speed. "Ninety," Bradley went. "Wicked!"

The tram picked up more speed going over a hundred. Kevin walked into the cab. His weapons dangled in his pocket as he held onto the green pipe. "They're still after us" he went. "Now what?"

"We keep going," Bradley replied.

Kevin's eyes opened wide with fear. "What?" he asked.

Bradley slowly turned his head, looked down the narrow hill and saw the red sign showing the end of line. "Ohhhhhhh shit" he went. "Not to worry. We just pull this back a bit and …."

Bradley pulled the red lever back slowly as the tram started to head down towards the bottom of the hill. He laughed at Kevin as he pulled it back to the maximum. He felt an adrenaline surge through his body. He rammed it back and forth as they sped through the last remaining stations. "Not to worry," he said again, trying to reassure Kevin.

Bradley clenched his fist and looked at the red emergency stop plunge. He rammed it down. The tram continued to pick up speed. "Cock!" he went.

He jumped out of the cab seat and looked at the notice board behind the driver's seat. Then he looked up at the skylight in the roof. "Kevin, bunk," he ordered.

Kevin bunked Bradley up to the skylight. He grabbed the metal poles kicking it open and dragged himself onto the roof of the long vehicle. He staggered along to the pantograph as the freezing cold air blew into his face. He reached into his inside pocket and pulled out the flick out baton. He clenched the rubber handle as he flicked the long truncheon out. He slowly approached the long pantograph. As he turned around, he saw the double red buffers slowly coming towards them. He took a deep breath and swung the bat around hitting the pantograph. The plastic graph swung away from the overhead wires. Bradley slowly walked away from the pantograph as Kevin stood looking out the top of the tram. The clanking sound went through the cab of the tram. Kevin looked up at Bradley as he jumped over the rubber joiners holding the carriages together. The front left brake fired into action but the rest failed. Bradley fell forward on the tram, and he struggled to keep his balance, He skidded along the shiny paintwork towards the open skylight. He slipped forward falling through the small hole. "Hello," he exclaimed.

"You could have just switched the power off," Kevin said.

"Never thought of that," Bradley said.

Still gripping his baton, Bradley leant down and flicked it as the sparks came out of the front left wheels.

"Ok, get to the back," Bradley yelled, "NOW."

The group ran to the back of the tram. The speed slowly reduced as they approached the end of the track. Bradley dove into the wheelchair bay at the back of the tram. The front tram slammed into the metal buffer, the glass shattered into pieces as the carriages slammed into one another. Bradley held his head down as the engines crumpled up to the insides of the tram and the carriages burst into flames. He listened to the windows smashing on the tram as it slowly came to a stop. He slowly opened his eyes and looked up as he listened to the hissing sound of the tram's engine. Sparks flew out the front of the tram. Fire burned from the front left brake. Bradley slowly staggered up, looking down the narrow aisles of the car. The long overhead lights dangled from their hinges as well. Shattered glass lay everywhere. Bradley slowly walked up

to the set of doors. He pulled the red lever down. The two
doors slowly popped open and he held on to his sidearm as
the warm summer air blew onto his face. "Come on," he
said to Kate. "And you, too, Colin."

Kate slowly walked away from the tram. She looked up
the track to see a set of headlights coming towards them.
"Oh shit," she went.

"Yes," Bradley said. "Oh fucking shit!"

Kevin watched the chasing tram heading on the same
track towards them.

"Right over here," Bradley ordered.

The group went down a small set of steps leading down
towards a small walkway. Bradley knelt down on the steps
as he watched the chasing tram running towards the other
tram. He swiped his sub machine gun and got it in his
sights. The tram with the aliens inside smashed into the
back of their tram. The front crippled up into the back of
the tram as it quickly came to a stop. The carriages
continued folding up into one another as the two at the back
stood up in the air from the force of the crash. The two
trams stopped crippling one another. Bradley looked at
them as they pointed into the air. The hinges holding them
together broke away.

"OHHHHH SHIT!" he yelled. "Stay down."

The carriages slammed back into the ground, ripping
the overhead wires down as well. Bradley slowly got up as
he held onto his sub machine gun. The dust and muck
slowly started to clear. He started walking slowly out to the
tram. He looked around as he approached the cab entrance
trying to see through the smoke. Kevin walked up to the
smashed set of doors. He slowly walked in and looked
down the aisles looking at the dead aliens as they lay on the
floor of the tram.

"Clear," he went.

Bradley looked into the cab at the dead alien lying on

the power lever as Kevin stepped back onto the road. "You ok?" he asked.

"So what now?" Kate asked, walking up to them.

"Can we rest?" Colin asked.

"We can't here," Bradley said. "That noise might have alerted anything near by."

"We'll rest in a while," Kevin said.

"So we'll go to the cop shop quickly," Bradley replied. "I'll look at my map when we find a secure place."

"Why? Are they there?" Kate asked.

Bradley looked at Kate. "I can only assume that they were sent there as it is the most secure place in the city right now," Bradley said. "Anyway, let's move before any of those things come here."

"He's right," Kevin said. "There has got to be a place we can rest at, a short way from here."

The group slowly got up from the benches and looked around the deserted place as the smell of electrical fires from the two smashed up trams lingered.

Bradley looked down at the dirty floor of the side alley as he held onto his small handgun. He looked down at the used needles and the old sleeping bag left by the hobo as they slowly moved over the tiny cobbles. The smell of stale urine filled the alley and sunlight peeked in from between the sky scrapers. The old rusty tin cans slowly rolled over into the drains.

Kate looked around as she kept pace with Bradley, slowly followed by Jane, followed by Eric, followed by Kevin. The path in the alley was up a gentle slope. Bradley felt the pull on his leg muscles as he held onto his handgun and scanned the area ahead for any of the aliens. Bradley looked forward to see a small crossroad ahead. The alley led off in four directions. He looked to the left hand and saw two shadowy figures slowly coming their way. Bradley clenched his fist up in the air. Kate gasped and jumped at the same time. Bradley stood dead still as the two dark shadows slowly got bigger. Bradley raised his hand signaling the group to get down onto the ground. Kate looked over Bradley's shoulder and watched the two aliens walk down the alley past the group. Bradley's finger slowly crept along the soft metal towards the trigger of the handgun. He prepared to pull the trigger at their heads. The two aliens walked off into the depth of the alley.

"Keep quiet," Bradley said. Slowly he got up and signaled Kevin forward. Kevin crept past Eric towards Bradley.

"You, that wall," Bradley said. "Me, that one."

Kevin nodded. Bradley and Kevin went to the opposite walls looking down each alley.

"Clear," Kevin said.

Bradley looked down his alley to see if the two aliens had gone. As he turned his head he saw Kate. He looked at her as she slowly got up and leaned against the wall. She placed her hand on her head. Bradley slowly walked up to her sliding the handgun back into his side pouch. "You ok?" he asked.

Kate nodded her head. "Tired," she said "And a stitch, plus a head ache on the way as well."

"Ok," Bradley said. "We'll find a place to sit down. We can't do it here."

"Why not?" Colin asked.

"Too compacted," Bradley said. "They might arrive and surround us. He walked up the alley.

The group slowly turned around the corner and walked out into one of the main roads. Bradley held on to his sidearm, ready to pull the trigger at the first sign of any aliens. He had got used to his heart pounding with fear and the police station did not seem to be getting any closer to them. The group walked out of the alleyway, looking across the deadly quiet street at the six police cars smashed into one another. Bradley looked around and over the street. He noticed a small red cross on the top of a large building.

"That's a hospital," Eric went.

"Yes, that is," Bradley replied.

"And where there's a hospital," Kevin said, "there's people."

"Do you think there will be anyone in there?" Kate asked.

"Only one way to find out," Bradley replied. He walked out of the alleyway still looking up the road for any of the aliens. He crossed the road, walking between the smashed up police patrol cars.

"Any weapons?" Max asked.

Bradley looked into a car, seeing nothing. "Nothing," he said. "We have enough to last us, anyway."

The group continued across the deserted road over towards the hospital entrance. The breeze in the air felt spooky and the entrance to the hospital seemed to get further away as they approached the ambulance bay. Bradley looked at the new white vehicle, as it stood smashed up into the concrete bollards in the middle of the bay. The red emergency lights were slowly starting to die away as the battery was being drained of all its energy. Kevin slowly walked up to the front of it staring in through to the back of the vehicle. The old stretcher hung out the back of the vehicle from where the paramedics had obviously tried to save a patient. Kevin looked away as Bradley walked up to the set of automatic doors. He reloaded the old handgun and walked into the hospital. The doors slowly slid open. The screams from the frightened people still hung about in the hospital. The rubber doors still gently moved back and forth with the breeze from the outside. The building was modern; quite new with new equipment, smells of disinfectant and all the rest.

"Keep together," Bradley went. "Come on, Colin."

"I'm right behind," Colin replied.

Bradley slowly walked up the corridors smelling the detergent where the cleaners had tried to clean up the blood and vomit of frightened people.

"Come on," Bradley went.

"Where are we going?" Jane asked.

"To look for survivors," Bradley said.

"Shall we split up?" Colin asked.

Bradley stopped. "Ok, Colin" Bradley said. "You go that way and we will go that way."

"I aint going by myself," Colin protested.

"Well then, shut up and follow," Bradley demanded.

Colin stood quietly. Bradley walked on as Max walked past Colin, shrugging his shoulders at him. He looked up to see a set of stairs. He slowly walked up to them and stepped onto them. He walked up them, scanning the way ahead. No one in sight; not a single doctor or nurse.

"Do you think they've evacuated?" Kevin asked.

"I wouldn't have thought so, Kev. No time. Look how fast things moved over at the city," Bradley said.

They came to the first floor of the huge hospital. Bradley walked in. There was still no one in sight. It was a totally dead place. Bradley feared what could be around the corner. He looked down into the ward. There were no nurses and doctors running back and forth, no beeping of the heart machines and no kids running around as the mourning parents sat at family bedsides. Bradley shook his head as he walked over to the ward reception. He looked at all the patient files scattered all around the reception. "Anyone here?" he asked in a low pitched voice.

No one answered. The light blue curtains gently blew in the breeze as he turned around and headed back towards the exit. "The hospital appears to be empty," Bradley said.

He walked out of the ward and headed towards a walkway leading to the hospital refectory. He looked forward to see a pair of old shiny elevator doors. "Up or down?" he asked.

"Up," Eric said. "People might be hiding upstairs."

"Good thinking," Bradley said. "Not like you."

"I have my moments," Eric smiled and said.

The group slowly walked towards the huge silver doors. The beep from them dinged through their ears. "Not up or down," Eric went, grabbing Kate's arm.

Bradley looked around frantically. "This way," he whispered. He pulled Kate by the arm over to the walkway. He turned around watching the two shiny doors slowly slide back. Two aliens walked out of the lift and headed into the hospital. Blood dribbled off their swords from where they had attacked their innocent victims in the city. Bradley turned around, pointing towards the refectory. "Go," he whispered.

He held onto his sidearm, ready to pull the trigger and flicked his head around looking at the group as they disappeared to the top of the walkway. Then he slowly turned around and walked back. The two aliens turned around as the shadow of Bradley headed up towards the refectory. They looked at one another, swiping their side arms. Then they quietly followed the group.

Bradley came to the top of the passage. He quietly stepped through the wooden and glass fire doors and closed them, trying not to squeak them or bang them. He stared around at the quiet room and at the food still simmering on the stoves. The workers must have fled the scene but most probably didn't get very far. Eric slowly walked over to the counter looking at the food lined up on the counter, ready to be served, as Bradley looked over at him. Bradley walked over to the counter, too, and stared down at all the practically dried up food. He turned his head again, looking at the small fridge beside the counter. He walked up to it, looked at all the drinks neatly stacked up inside, and then took a bottle of water out. "Over here," he said.

The group walked into the far corner of the refectory and sat down at the clean table. Not many people had been around at the time of the attack. Bradley felt a sense of relief as he sat down on a chair and looked out of the window onto the city. He looked at the small puffs of smoke blowing out of the burning cars and subway stations. A few people were still trying to take shelter in what was left of the city.

"Shouldn't we be moving?" Kate asked.

"No, let's let the ones downstairs clear out," Bradley said.

"How far is the police station?" Eric asked.

Bradley pulled out the tiny pocket map he was given by Roger at the gun shop. "We came down here, so …" he said looking at the hospital logo on the map. He scanned it planning a route. "Ok. We are here. The main HQ is about three and a half miles away but we will have to keep to the side streets, so we are looking about a two hour walk" Bradley said. "So drink up. This will be the last stop for a while."

"Can't we run it?" Max asked.

"No," Bradley said. "We take it easy and only run if we have to."

Bradley sat back in his seat looking down at the map. He turned his head and looked at Kevin. "Do you think Mr. Knightsbridge got to the police station?" he asked.

"I don't want to answer that," Kevin said.

"Yeah, I suppose," Bradley said. "Do you think that assignment will have to be in on Monday?"

"I don't think so," Eric said.

Bradley looked out the window again as he folded the small map and placed it in his pocket keeping it safe in case he would have to use it again. Kate slurped her water down, oblivious to what was going on around her. Bradley pulled out his cell phone. He looked at the shiny plastic piece and stared at the small screen.

"Still no network?" Eric asked.

"Nothing," Bradley said. "It must come and go."

"Well, people must be struggling to get through to people,"

Kevin said. "My mum, for example."

"Mine too," Bradley said as he slipped the phone back into his pocket and looked at Kate as she slipped her sunglasses off feeling the light from the sun burning them. Bradley looked into the shiny metal work as the reflection of the refectory shone in them. He stared into them looking over towards the entrance of the refectory; he felt his heart pounding as he slowly looked into them. "Oh no," he mumbled.

"What?" Kate said. "What no?"

Bradley held his breath as he looked at the entrance and saw the two aliens staring at them as they sat down at the table.

"Oh, what?" Eric went.

"There's aliens- look," Colin said frantically.

"No, you don't say," Eric went.

The two aliens swiped their ray guns. "Down," Bradley yelled.

Kate and Jane fell back off their seats and to the floor. Bradley overturned the table, diving over it as the rays from the alien weapons fired overhead.

"Jesus Christ!" Eric yelled.

Bradley looked into the eyes of Kevin as the wooden table started to burn. He nodded as he pulled out two of his handguns. Kevin got up at the same time as Bradley. They opened fire at the two aliens as they continued firing at the group. Bradley pulled the trigger again, taking an alien down. "Move," he yelled.

He led the way with Kevin and the rest of the group following. He looked down at the two dead aliens as they walked past them towards the walkway. Bradley kept his eyes peeled as they came to the bottom of the new walkway. Bradley looked down the corridor towards the way he had come a short while ago. He still tasted the clean clear water in his mouth. He watched as a group of aliens ran towards them. He looked in all directions. "This way," he said.

The aliens charged up the narrow corridor towards them. Bradley watched as the group ran ahead. Kate slowed down as she panted for breath. Bradley ran up behind her. "Just go," he yelled. "I'll catch up."

He opened fire at the long line of aliens running towards him. Kevin led the group away, towards the exit. "Come on," he yelled.

Bradley looked over his shoulder as the group disappeared into a room. He swung around, sprinting up the long corridor, trying not to slip on the floor. He skidded around the corner looking for the group. He looked up the t-junction corridor as the aliens came from all directions. He slowly turned his head and looked at the stretcher and the two oxygen canisters behind it. Bradley smiled and snapped his fingers. He dropped to the floor and lifted the canisters up. "Jesus Christ!" he gasped.

He slammed the canisters onto the bed. He turned round and fired at the aliens as they came closer towards him. Bradley watched the canister on the top of the handgun fire back. He knew he hadn't enough time to reload. He swung around jumping onto the bed. He flicked out the baton and smacked the canister valves. The blue oxygen vapor fired out of the broken valves as Bradley held onto the metal bed which quickly started rolling along the corridor of the ward.

"OH MY GOD! I GOT TO DO THIS AGAIN," Bradley laughed in a sarcastic voice. He held on to the side rails as the adrenaline powered through his body, keeping his heart going. He watched as the group of oncoming aliens turned around and the trolley bed sped through the hospital corridor. The bed slammed into the aliens as he stared ahead at the exit of the hospital. He looked at the glass doors as they came closer and closer. He pulled out his spare handgun taking a shot at the glass. The glass shattered as Bradley squinted his eyes closed, covering them from any glass which could tear his face open. The trolley continued picking up speed. Bradley peeked out from the corner of his eyes as the speeding bed shot through the broken door. He opened his eyes and looked ahead as the steep steps came into view. He watched and felt it as the trolley lifted off the ground. Then he jumped up and dived out of the bed. He looked down at the well-kept flowerbed in front of him. He closed his eyes as he slammed down into a prickly bush, quickly rolling to a stop.

"Ouch! Shit!" Bradley went. "Ouch! Bastard things!" He looked up as the bed continued on into the destroyed street slamming into a smashed up military tank. Bradley turned his head and looked up at the hospital as he reached for his handgun. He watched as two aliens looked out of the broken window out onto the tanks as the oxygen continued to hiss from them. They turned back into the hospital and put their weapons away as Bradley shook his head trying to refocus on the current situation. He staggered out of the bush, slowly put his hand onto his back and rubbed the tiny graze under his t-shirt as he walked over to the tank. He looked at the huge, green machine as it stood smashed into the side of the street. The lamppost stood bent over the green metal as blood ran down the side of the green paintwork.

Bradley slowly climbed onto the green vehicle. He looked inside through the hatch. No one was to be seen. He looked at all the damaged wires where the vehicle had been destroyed by the aliens.

Kevin, Eric, Max, Kate and Jane slowly walked up behind Bradley as he stood on top of the tank looking out onto the city.

"Is it drivable?" Kevin asked.

Bradley jumped, swiping his handgun as he span around and looked at the group.

"Bradley, it's us," Kevin yelled.

Bradley looked into the eyes of the group but they had their eyes more focused on the tank behind him.

"You ok?" Kevin said.

Bradley didn't want to answer the question. "Yeah, yeah, I'm ok," Bradley said. "You ok, Colin?"

Bradley looked around. "Where's Colin?" he asked.

Colin slowly emerged. "Right here," he said.

"Don't do that again," Kevin said.

"Sorry," Colin said.

Kevin turned again to look at Bradley. "Sorry. Didn't mean to make you jump. We saw that trolley fly out over here," Kevin said. "Kate here thought you were a goner."

Bradley smiled as he wiped some small leaves off his jacket, still looking at the tank. "Even these couldn't hold here," Bradley said, "Shitting hell!"

"It was totally deserted, that place, wasn't it?" Eric said.

"Yes," Bradley said. "I don't think anyone else is left alive there."

Eric turned around and looked up the dead street and at the three ambulances smashed into one another.

"Come on. Let's move," Bradley said as the group stood rooted to the spot. He led the group to the quite alley way, still scanning the road ahead for any of the aliens, and even checking the roofs of the buildings they passed.

13

Mrs. Harrison slowly pulled her new car onto the driveway of her house. She felt the cold air blow onto her face. She sat back in the cream leather seats. The people in the streets didn't seem to be acting normally. She looked at her next door neighbors as they bundled huge bags of supplies into their house. The elderly man looked over at her as she sat in the driver's seat looking at him. She wound down her window feeling the hot air rushing in from the outside. "You ok, Oscar?" she yelled. "Haven't seen you and Mary for a while."

Barry jogged over to her car. "You going out shopping? It's madness down there. That gun club Bradley goes to has been completely sold out of weapons," Barry said. "You ok? You got everything? Need a weapon? I've got a few spare. Look." He pulled out two handguns from his pockets.

"Why? What's happened?" Mrs. Harrison asked.

Oscar's eyes opened with fear. "Don't you know?" he questioned her. "Haven't you heard? It's been all over the news."

"What's going on?" she asked, confused.

"I think you had better go and look at the television," Oscar said. "I hope to see you again soon. We are staying inside in case it gets any worse."

He turned around and ran over to his open garage. Mrs. Harrison watched as he pulled out long planks of wood followed by a tool box. She watched as he started banging the old rusty nails into the pieces of wood over the windows of his well kept house. Mrs. Harrison shook her head wondering if she was lying in bed still and this was a dream. She got out of the car and locked it slowly and quietly. Then she walked over to her front door and unlocked it, all the while watching Barry as he put the planks over the doors and windows. She pulled out her small new cell phone only to see the networks jammed. She walked into her house and shut the door. "Kettle," she said quietly.

She walked in, feeling a shiver go down her back as the floor in her house started to rumble. It slowly got worse as she placed her small cream handbag down on the new wooden table. She looked out of a window into the street. She watched in disbelief as a long line of military vehicles and tanks rolled down the New Haven Street heading towards the highway which led to New York State and Manhattan. The soldiers were armed to the teeth, ready for a fight. She felt her heart pound as she looked into the eyes of one of the soldiers. She could see the fear in him, wondering if he was going home later on that night. The long snake line of vehicles disappeared into the distance. "What is going on?" she said.

The new floorboards stopped vibrating as the military jeeps were just a small blur in the distance. The tenants in the next house slowly walked out and looked down the street, trembling with fear and wondering if it was ever going to end.

Mrs. Harrison turned around. She walked over to the wide screen TV in the corner of the dining room. She pushed in the small button and sat down on the couch crossing her arms and legs. Her heart banged as she watched the New Haven news channel on all stations broadcasting to the people. Mrs. Harrison looked at the sub titles screen. "ALIEN INVASION: NEW YORK'S MANHATTAN"

"Oh my god!" she gasped.

A middle aged man popped up on the screen. "If you are just joining us, we are here to bring you bring you up to speed on the situation in New York City. There has been an alien invasion on New York's Manhattan Island. We don't know the exact figures yet but we know that thousands are dead and hundreds of thousands are missing. We are now going live to an evacuation point in Queens which has been setup by the US Army," the reporter said as calmly as possible.

Mrs. Harrison lay back on the couch feeling her heart pound as her nerves hit her stomach. She turned her head to look out of the front room window onto the driveway as her husband's car pulled up and skidded to a stop. He jumped out of the car, slamming the door shut and not bothering to lock it. Mrs. Harrison got up quickly and opened the door.

"Thank god you're ok. I was so worried. I've just heard the news," she said.

"I know, I know. Are you ok? Have you heard from Bradley?" her husband asked,

"No. I've tried getting to him but the phone lines are jammed," she said in a frantic voice.

"Ok, ok try mine," he said. "It's got a stronger signal."

Mrs. Harrison looked at her husband's phone and saw the signal was operational. She flicked through the phone book and selected Bradley's name. She placed the phone to her ear and listened to the gentle vibration as she waited.

Bradley walked along the back of the apartment blocks looking all around at the broken and fallen bins. Feeling his phone vibrate, he stopped and unzipping his trouser pocket, reached down and pulled out the vibrating phone. "Ok Kevin, keep an eye that way; Max, that way" Bradley said. "Brace yourselves for a long wait."

"Why? Who is it?" Max asked. "Ms. Javies?"

"Not that bad," Bradley replied. "My mum."

"Oh," Max said.

Bradley kneeled down and, slowly placing the phone to his ear, answered the call. "Hello," he said quietly. "I'm still alive."

"Oh god, Bradley! Thank god you are ok. We have just seen the news. Tell me you are out of the city," his mum went. "Please tell me."

Bradley looked around again. "Actually we are right in the city center, stuck up an alleyway," Bradley said.

"Oh my god, oh my god," she panted. "How have you survived so long? Tell me all that's happened."

Bradley released his breath. "Well," he said, "we were merrily walking down a road, when, bam- these things came out of nowhere. We ran into a casino still being chased by them. We pulled a woman out of a car. That bloody thing went bang, but we made it out. We lost Mr. Knightsbridge. Kevin found a restaurant. He dived in there, sealing the door shut. The things found us inside. Eric tried to fend them off with a pretend chainsaw, but did that work? No. They burst in. I sent them packing and they ran. So did I, but in the opposite direction, trying to lead them away. The gang found a cafe behind some of the shops. Eric again led them in. From there they ran to a warehouse and waited there for a while, until I came to the rescue as usual. We got to a weapon shop. Eric again nearly gave us away. We armed up - and I mean armed up, and made it to a subway station where we found Kate, Jane and tit brain Colin. We had to try and hide in the station. We ran up the track out the other side heading towards the bus station and got to the bus station but our driver was dead. We jumped on board a tram, still being chased by another tram full of them things, ran through a hospital and stopped for a drink. I took a ride on an oxygen propelled bed and now we are here."

Mrs. Harrison struggled to take it all in. "Uh," she went.

"Yeah, long day," Bradley said. "Still, we have far more shit to come."

"Bradley, this is dad," Mr. Harrison said. "Can you hear me ok?"

"Oh, hi dad," he went. "Yes, I can just about."

"Hi, Mr. Harrison," Eric yelled.

"Keep your voice down," Kevin ordered.

"Hello," Eric whispered.

Bradley closed his eyes trying not to make a comment to Eric. He felt the small stones digging into his knee.

"Bradley, listen to me. Have you got any sort of weapon to defend yourself with?" Mr. Harrison asked.

Bradley looked down at all his weapons lined up on his tall thin body. "Yes, a few," he replied.

Kevin looked at Bradley as the weapons dangled on him.

"Ok. Have you heard from Ms. Javies?" he asked.

"Yeah, she is at the police station," Bradley said.

"Ok. Now get there ASAP," his dad ordered. "And for god's sake, be careful."

Bradley heard a beep. He looked down at his phone, seeing the signal dying again.

"Bradley," his dad could be heard faintly. "Bradley?"

Mrs. Harrison looked up at him as she started crying. The couple looked at the television as the President of the United States walked up to the dais. Mrs. Harrison felt her heart pounding as the couple sat down on the couch.

"My fellow Americans and other people of other nations that have tuned to this broadcast," the president began. "As you now know, New York city's Manhattan Island was invaded at approximately eleven forty five local time by an unidentified species not from this planet or any planet that we are aware of with a form of life. We have had no luck in contacting the Martian leaders. Our people are still trying to do so. I am asking for all people throughout the country to be brave and remain calm. Listen to your law enforcement personnel and continue to monitor your news stations. All flights across the country have been temporarily suspended, and all international air travel towards the USA has been diverted or sent back to its country of departure. Once again, I ask you to remain calm and I will keep you updated on the situation in New York as I get more information. Thank you."

Press cameras flashed one after the other.

"Mr. President," a journalist yelled, seeking more answers.

But President Green had walked away. The president walked into the White House. He heard the door seal shut. Armed guards were protecting him everywhere.

Mr. Harrison switched off the television and walked back over to the couch. "He's gonna be ok," he said. "He's gonna be ok."

Mrs. Harrison looked out of the window as the sun shone in through the window, warming her face.

14

President Green watched as his two armed guards sealed the door shut. He sat down at his desk slowly, closing the bay window curtains so he couldn't see anybody from the outside as they screamed for answers. He lay back in his chair taking off his red tie and chucking it onto the desk.

"Can I get you anything, sir?" his assistant asked.

"No, thank you," he replied.

He looked up as two of his generals walked into the office. He sat up and looked at them dressed in their smart uniforms.

"Sir, I think we have made contact," one general said.

President Green didn't say a word. He stood up instantly, knocking his paper work to the floor. He walked quickly towards the back exit of his office and headed towards the emergency briefing room. He walked in and looked at all the generals and armed services people as they sat looking at the giant screen on the wall. President Green sat down in his chair and looked at it as well. Circo appeared on the screen. Circo looked into his display unit to see President Green.

"Is this thing on?" Circo asked.

"Yes," another alien said.

"Greetings," President Green said. He tried not to tremble as spoke to the extra terrestrial life form years ahead of him and his family.

"My name is Green. I am President of the United States

of America," he slowly and said quietly. "What are your demands from us?"

Circo didn't reply immediately. He took a deep breath and looked at President Green. "Well, thank you for your time," he then said in a sarcastic voice. "Now let me get this straight. If you are President of this place you should know what happened to one of our ships which crash landed on Earth a few months ago."

President Green was silent for a moment. Then he spoke. "I do not know of any alien spacecraft landing here," he said "Otherwise we would have returned it to you. I give you my word."

Circo looked at Green. "Well, you have got three Earth hours to find out, otherwise we will be forced to intensify our attack," Circo said. "Cheerio." He switched off the screen.

"Shit!" President Green said. "Anyone know of any ships landing here by any chance?"

The group of people slowly shook their heads.

"Right. This is serious. I want every single world president, prime minister and leader asked about this and I want some answers," he demanded.

President Green walked out of his Emergency Briefing Room and headed back to his Office. He walked in and looked at the clean blue carpet and the US flag on its stand. He turned around and looked at the widescreen TV in front of his desk. He picked up the small black remote and turned it on. The static atoms built up on the screen as the power surged through it, ready to show the picture. He watched as the news channel popped up. He stared at the young, female news reporter as she stood beside her helicopter. The pilot was in the seat, ready to take off as she raised the microphone to her mouth to speak.

"I am currently standing on top of the New York Police Department's main headquarters in Manhattan Island," she gasped. "The situation below is horrific. We came up here trying to get away from the sheer panic of the frightened people. If you'll follow me to the edge here…"

President Green watched the shaken camera images as they walked to the side of the police station roof. The cameraman pointed the camera down over the side of the station onto the ground. President Green listened to the sound of the wind as it blew onto the microphone. He also took note of all the US Army tanks and vehicles parked outside guarding the people from the aliens who could strike at any minute or even any second. The cameraman pulled the camera away slowly and walked towards the helicopter, ready to ride over the city to take more pictures. The engine soared to life. The young reporter struggled to keep her hair down as it blew in the force from the engines. She got in and sat down as the camera was focused out of the window onto the top of the station. The engine picked up speed. "As you can see we are flying back into the thick of it," she said into the microphone.

The helicopter flew off to Manhattan. The camera pointed down onto the buildings as fires raged in some of them.

"Jesus, look at them," the reporter said, looking down.

The pilot lowered the helicopter so the cameraman could get a closer look at the aliens walking down the road, looking for people to kill. Cars in the middle of the streets burned where they had crashed. "Get a snap of them," she said.

The camera pointed down, out of the window, onto the aliens. The group of aliens quickly looked up at the helicopter as it hovered above. They reached into their pockets, pulling out their ray guns. The pilot stared down as they looked up at the helicopter, and took aim. "Shit!" he gasped.

The helicopter quickly pulled up as the rays slammed

into it. The pilot looked around. The avionics in the front of the new helicopter sparked as the back rotor ignited into flames. The cameraman cut the transmission as the helicopter started to spin around in circles. He cut the power, taking the helicopter down towards Manhattan. He looked around, trying to find a suitable place to ditch it. He looked out as the ground grew closer and closer. "BRACE," he yelled.

President Green closed his eyes as his TV screen went blank. A few seconds later the news channel came back on. He looked at the misery in the people's eyes as they knew one of their helicopters was down. He switched off the TV, got up slowly and looked out of the window waiting for some news to come in. "Was there a ship which crash landed here? Or maybe in another country which is refusing to speak?" he asked.

15

Bradley slipped his phone back into his pocket after a five minute breather.

"They ok?" Kevin asked.

"They're ok. Just my mum panicking," Bradley said.

"Are you surprised?" Kate went. "I mean…"

"Yeah. Anyway, let's move before things catch up," Bradley ordered. "Come on. Stay close."

Bradley walked forward holding his sidearm and continuing to look into the air for a helicopter to air lift them to safety. He felt his heart starting to slow down as they started to emerge from the back alley. He flicked his head both ways looking around looking around at all the broken and smashed vehicles sprawled across the new tram track, as he held onto his handgun.

"How many lines were there installed?" Kevin asked.

"God knows," Bradley said. He walked up to a tram and looked in through the broken windows as the tiny bits of glass continued falling onto the road. A yellow New York cab stood smashed into the middle carriage. The yellow paintwork was ripped from the bonnet as the glass from the door lay smashed on the floor. He slowly walked up to the tram door to his right. He looked down onto the blood stained floor. Then he reached into his inside pocket, and pulled out the flick out baton as small sparks flicked from the pantograph.

"Is it drivable?" Kate asked.

Bradley looked into the cab. He watched as the digital gauges flicked on and off and the sparks got worse. "No. If we start that up we could blow the whole thing," he said.

Kevin flicked out his baton. Bradley swung his head to the right as Kevin slammed the steel baton through the glass window ripping it from the hinges as Max helped him. The glass sheet flew off the bat and he flung it onto the road.

"What is he doing?" Bradley asked. He watched as Kevin reached in and pulled the red lever. The set of doors half opened and Kevin pulled them apart as Bradley jogged down the side of the tram to them. He watched as Kevin slowly leant down, forcing the baton back into itself. Kevin slowly stood up. Walking into the carriage, he looked around at the belongings left behind and sprawled all over the carriage. Bradley walked into the carriage as Kate sat down on the step keeping her eyes open and scanning the surrounding areas as the sun beamed down onto her head. Kevin looked at a seat on which a leather document bag lay open with documents half falling out. He slowly leant down and picked up the bag. He looked at the pieces of paper. He chucked the bag down onto the seat and looked to the left. Kevin looked forward down the tram and saw a small, black box. He slowly got up and walked down the aisle towards it. He knelt down and, picking it up, he wiped away the dried blood of the tiny screen as Bradley looked over his shoulder.

"That's a television," he said.

Kevin switched on the small portable television and stared at the static picture as he felt for the small switch. He tuned in to the local television station. Kate got up and listened to the crackling sound. She walked down the tram and looked at the group as they surrounded the small television. She looked down onto the small screen at the young female reporter as she stood by the exit to

Queensboro Bridge on which traffic, escorted by the military vehicles, slowly passed.

"I'm standing by the exit to the Queensboro Bridge where thousands, maybe hundreds of thousands are trying to evacuate the city. The NYPD have had to clear one route to the bridge and from what I have experienced back at the main headquarters of the main station, people are turning up injured, shocked and confused. The New Jersey tunnel has had to be sealed. The only way out of the city now is by this bridge. I repeat,- the Queensboro Bridge. If you are watching this now, get to the Queensboro Bridge or the main police station. I've just heard from my command centre that we have an aerial view of the New York police headquarters. We're going there now," the woman said.

Bradley looked at Kevin as Max and Eric continued watching the news broadcast. The picture switched to an aerial view of the police station. Coaches were pulling up outside the station, quickly loading people onto them as the United States Army, armed to the teeth, surrounded the station. Tanks stood parked at either end of the building, turrets pointing directly in front. NYPD officers helped people onto the buses as they were pushed and pulled about. Bradley looked closer as the citizens ran out of the subway stations, struggling to get onto the buses to evacuate the island. Kate watched as the screen flickered. The battery sign flicked on and off.

"Oh shit, no," Kevin said. The small screen went blank. Kevin shook the set. He watched the small green light go red and then off. "Battery's gone," he said, chucking it away. Kate watched as the TV landed on a seat.

"Ok. Let's follow what we just saw. I don't think we should go to the police station. We haven't got a hope in hell of getting off the island quickly so we should just get to the bridge now," Bradley said. "The bridge should be about five miles north."

Bradley bent over and took off his shoe as he leaned against the side of the tram. He slowly emptied the small stones out as he continued scouring the empty streets. He looked over onto the sidewalk to see a small white information board. He slipped his shoe back on and slowly headed over to it as he held onto his sidearm.

Eric looked over his shoulder at the smashed up NYPD patrol car. He slowly walked over to it and looked through the open window. He reached in and slowly pulled out a SPAS 12 shotgun and a belt of shells. "Hee, hee," he giggled, loading the shotgun as he walked over to Bradley.

"What's this?" he asked.

"It's a map of Manhattan Island. See, we are here and Queensboro is right up here. I say that's about five miles, maybe a wee bit less, so I suggest we head up the coast of the island staying out of sight and we should be out of here within a few hours, maybe earlier," Bradley went.

"Got it. I like it," Eric said, pumping the shotgun.

Bradley looked down onto the shiny black weapon. "Where the...?" he went.

"That patrol car... mine," Eric said to him "You're not having it."

"Alright, you can have it," Bradley said. "But only if you behave yourself."

"Like when?" Max laughed, trying to keep their spirits high.

Bradley smiled as he walked over to the tram. "Right. We've got to get to that bridge quickly because I don't think the US army is going to handle this situation too well," Bradley went.

"But they've got guns and stuff," Kate said in a dull, quiet voice.

"Guns, but these things are smarter," Bradley replied.

"Ok, let's go," Kate went. "We get that from Mr. Knightsbridge."

Kate slowly got up, holding on to her arm as Bradley swiped his sidearm from the pocket keeping his eyes open and scanning the busy street as they weaved in and out of the burning vehicles. He looked over his shoulder as Kate held onto her arm. He stopped short on seeing a small trail of blood run out from under her shirt.

"You ok?" he asked.

"Yeah," she said. "I'm fine."

Bradley walked up to her. He slowly pulled her hand from her shoulder. He looked at the cut on her arm as the blood slowly wept out of the tiny slit. "Oh," he went. "Sore."

"I did it as I got off the tram," she went. "And, yes, it is sore."

Bradley let his breath out. "Ok, don't worry. I'll soon have that fixed up," he said. "Eric here has got a first aid badge from the girl guides."

"Hey" Eric went. "Well, seeing that I have a first aid badge…"

"I'm glad you've got a sense of humor," Kate replied to his comments.

"Alright, I'm sorry," Bradley went. He looked around the busy street and stopped as he caught sight of a smashed up ambulance. He looked at the back doors wide open and one of the stretchers half out in the street. "Look," he went. "There." He helped Kate over to the smashed up ambulance, and climbed up the metal steps into the back of the vehicle. "Ok," he went, looking around the vehicle and thinking back to the first aid badge he had earned many years ago. He looked up into the plastic containers as the bandages and bottles of medicine stood strewn about on the floor. He took down a shiny silver bottle and a bandage.

"Show us," he demanded.

"Ok," Kate said. She lifted her shirtsleeve. Bradley broke open the shiny plastic bottle and poured the sweet smelling liquid into the cut.

"Ouch," Kate went.

"That will stop any infection," Bradley said.

"Ouch," she moaned again.

"Shall I kiss it better for you?" Bradley laughed.

Kate gave him a sarcastic, cheeky smile as he wrapped the white bandage around her arm. "Hold it," he said. He pulled down some medical tape and wrapped it around her thin arm. He'd never had so much pleasure in his life. "This is fun," he said.

"What?" Kate asked.

"Nothing," he laughed.

Kate looked out the back window of the ambulance as Bradley finished tying the tape around the bandage.

"There we go. That should tide you over," he went, "until we get out of here."

"If we ever do," Kate said.

"We will," Bradley said. "I promise."

He got up slowly, watching as Kate stepped out of the ambulance. She turned around and looked at Bradley as he put the bottle of sterile fluid back into the plastic box. From the corner of his eye, he spotted a red blanket in the corner slowly start to move. Kate had noticed it, too and looked on in fear as the red blanket continued moving in an odd way. Bradley froze for a few seconds. "Kev," he whispered.

Kevin didn't hear him as he stood guarding the area around them. Bradley reached down. Picking up a small bandage, he chucked it over to Kevin.

"What?" Kevin asked. He swung his head around and looked into the back of the ambulance as Bradley waved him over. He walked up to the back of the smashed up ambulance and looked in at the broken medicine bottles and stain patches. He looked at Bradley as the red blanket continued moving around. Kevin opened his eyes wide as he pulled out his sidearm, looking through the scope at the moving blanket. Bradley pulled his handgun out as well, holding it in his right hand. He slowly reached down towards the blanket and placed his hand on it. He felt the soft material between his fingers. He nodded at Kate and Kevin, and aimed his handgun at the blanket as he pulled it off, jumping back. Kate looked in amazement at the small cat as it hissed at the group and ran out of the ambulance, back into the alleyway.

"Ha," Kevin laughed. "Thought it was one of them, didn't you?"

Bradley looked to the right as he stood in the back of the ambulance. He immediately jumped back in fear as an alien looked through the small ambulance window. He looked at the white, gleaming teeth as it grinned at him. "Oh, crap," he mumbled.

He swung his gun round firing the shiny golden bullet through the window. Max looked up as the alien fell back, away from the ambulance. He swiped his sub machine gun, and pulled out the long magazine, reloading it into the bottom of the modern weapon as he also pulled out the extender making it easier to hold onto. He stared through the scope, shooting at a few running aliens.

Bradley jumped out of the ambulance and looked around the streets as he grabbed Kate's hand. Kevin swung around as hordes of aliens jumped in from around the corners.

"Oh, god, here we go" Bradley moaned, "again."

"Go," Eric yelled. "I'll cover you." He pulled the trigger but missed the alien.

Bradley looked at him. "Ok, I'll come with you," he said.

Bradley sent Kate and Jane off as he held onto his sidearm. He kept it raised as he started taking pot shots at the chasing aliens. He pivoted around on his foot catching up with the group. He looked over at the burnt cars. Eric stopped swinging around. He aimed his gun at the attacking aliens as they charged towards him. He pulled the trigger of the new gun. The large golden shell launched off the cartridge and flew through the air. It slammed into an alien, blasting him into two pieces. Bradley stopped as Kate, Jane, Max and Kevin continued going on. He watched as the aliens flew back one after the other.

"Yeah," Eric yelled. "I want this."

"Come on, Eric," Bradley yelled.

Eric stopped. "Oh, sorry," he went.

Eric caught up with Bradley running ahead.

"I'll take that of you if you don't behave yourself," Bradley said.

Eric looked into his shotgun. He looked through the belt as he started reloading the weapon. Bradley looked forward towards Kate and Jane as they started to slow down. "Come on," he yelled "Don't slow down."

Kate had started slowing down as Kevin stopped at the crossroads, slowly followed by Colin. He looked in all directions as the aliens charged towards them. Bradley looked to the right, up the quiet street at the entrance to an indoor shopping center. "This way," he yelled.

Bradley ran up the quiet road as the aliens charged at them from both sides. Kevin ran up the steps towards the entrance to a medium sized building. Kevin pulled at the glass door-thanking God it wasn't locked. But it wouldn't give. "Oh, come on," he yelled. "Shit ass, fucking thing."

"Move," Bradley ordered.

The aliens charged up the steps as Bradley aimed his handgun at the door. He pulled the trigger, blowing away the lock. He grabbed onto the metal handle and pulled it open. He smiled at Kevin as he walked into the center. Kate and Jane shot into the building followed by Max, Eric and Kevin.

"Where's Colin?" Bradley asked.

Bradley looked around to see Colin running close behind.

"Come on, dick," he yelled.

He held onto the handle as the aliens grabbed it struggling to pull the door open. Kate looked to her left at the shutter control box. The shiny silver key was still left in the box from when the security guard had most probably tried to seal the place in. She ran over to the box as the group struggled to keep the door closed.

"These wankers don't give up," Eric said.

"You don't say," Bradley replied, panting for breath. He looked up as the rusty shutter slowly started rolling down. The glass door slowly opened as the group of aliens struggled to get in. "Push, push," Bradley yelled.

The glass door closed as the rusty old shutter slid down over it locking it down into place. Bradley looked at the old shutters, seeing the aliens slam into it.

"Ha, ha," he yelled. "Look at you."

Bradley turned to look at Kate. "Good thinking, Kate," he said.

Colin slowly walked up to her, and then looked at the shutter as it stopped moving back and forth. Bradley turned round and slid to the ground. He felt his heart racing. He felt his legs start to go dead as the cold floor made him shiver. He took deep breaths shaking his head as he slowly got up. He looked around the empty shopping center as a light musical tune continued to play.

"Look at the size of this place!" Kevin said.

Bradley looked up onto the many floors piled on top of one another.

The group of aliens outside quickly walked around the side of the center, holding their ray guns. They slowly went up the side of the building, approaching the set of steps leading up to the car park of the building.

Bradley continued scanning the empty shops, keeping

his eyes wide open, as he walked forward. Kevin turned his head and looked into a computer game shop to the right as Eric slowly walked forward in the center. He looked up at the multistoried shops all empty of people. Bradley entered the small deserted games shop and looked around it. Only the air conditioner was still running. He walked over to the counter and looked at the open cash register. The dollar notes spiraled out of the shiny tray. They appealed to him.

"Hmm," Bradley went. "No one around. Oh well, let's hope they have a good insurance company." He leant over the counter, pulling out the dollar bills, as Kevin walked into the store.

"You ok?" he asked, looking at Bradley as he loaded the dollar bills into his small string bag. "Good one," he went and leant over, grabbing the dollar notes as well before he looked over at the line of new games. He picked up a small game box and put it in his bag.

"What's that?" Bradley asked.

"Fight Buster Three," Kevin went. "It's new."

"Oh good. I'll have one too," Bradley replied. "Will give me something to do tonight." He reached over and picked out the game from under the counter. He slipped it into his bag and zipped up the small pouch, looking at Kevin. "I don't care. I'm going shopping when we get home," he said.

"If," Kevin went.

"We will," Bradley replied. "We will." He looked around the shop. "Any more? Take your pick," he joked.

Kevin smiled as Bradley looked at the two girls sitting down on the benches in the middle of the floor and looking at the small water fountain as it trickled water into a crater. Kate looked at the small blue tiles as the dirty water ran off, back into the pump.

"I have no idea what must be going through their minds" Bradley said to Kevin.

"I know," Kevin replied. "Shit scared and wondering if this shit is going to stop."

"Possible," Bradley said.

"How far is this police station from here, now?" Kevin asked.

"If I remember correctly it should be about three miles from here," Bradley said. "But we stick with the bridge first. If we can't get to the bridge - cop shop."

Bradley and Kevin slowly walked out of the shop. Bradley turned his head looking at the front entrance, the shutter still sealed down. Not an alien in sight. He looked forward again when he heard a sudden tap. He stopped and looked at Kevin. "What's that?" he asked.

Kevin looked up onto the roof. "Agh, Bradley…" he mumbled.

"What?" Bradley said and looked at Kevin as he looked up at the glass dome roof. Bradley and Kevin stared as the aliens outside started banging onto the glass, trying to break in.

"They won't get in," Eric went. "No way. That's double glazed."

The glass shattered.

Bradley and the group watched as the large chunks of glass rained down onto them. "Really?" Bradley said.

"Oh," Eric went. "Arm up, boys."

"Best thing I've heard you say all day," Bradley replied. He looked up as the glass finished raining down on them, and the wooden roll of wire slowly rolled down to the center.

"Shit!" Kevin yelled.

He swiped his two-sub machine gun from his inside pockets. He felt the small shards of glass landing in his hair as Kate looked around for a place to hide and Bradley slowly aimed the weapons into the air. An alien slid down the green phone wire. Bradley watched as the alien landed next to the girls and Jane fell into the water.

"JANE!" Kevin yelled.

Kevin listened to the shooting as he ran over to her. He reached into the fountain and pulled her out of the water. "You ok?" he asked.

"No, I am not," she said in a fierce voice. "I am not taking shit from these any more." She swung around, slamming her fist into one of the aliens that had just landed next to her. Kevin was shocked to see her slam her fist into it.

"Go for it," he joked.

Bradley ran over. "This way," he urged, looking in all directions for a place to leave Kate, Jane and Colin. He looked to the left and saw one of the see through elevators.

"This way," he said again. He dragged Kate along the slippery floor as the aliens continued dropping down into the shopping centre. Bradley pushed the call button in. "Come on, come on," he insisted. The two glass doors opened. "Come on," he yelled. "IN." He pushed Kate in. "Hold that button in," he demanded.

The doors slowly closed and stayed at the lower level. Bradley looked at the fear in Kate's eyes as she looked at him. "Don't worry," he yelled. He turned around and looked at the aliens as they invaded the shopping centre. "Here we go," he whispered.

He reached into his pocket, swiping out the two sub machine guns. He stared into the eyes of the invaders as they slid down the green copper wire. He yanked the triggers inwards. The golden bullets were launched. The green blood from the aliens dripped down onto the shopping center floor as they fell to the ground.

"Jesus Christ!" Eric yelled.

Bradley looked around. The whole centre was filled with the alien invaders.

"There's two many," Eric yelled.

"No, there's not," Bradley went. "Never too many." He reached into his pocket and took out the baton. He flicked it out as the aliens charged towards him. "Come on, you fuckers," he yelled. "Give it all you got."

He grasped the rubber bit at the end. The aliens charged at him. Bradley flung the baton, slamming it in. He watched as the alien creature flew to the ground.

Eric was standing by the sports shop. He looked in at the huge green bowling ball as it stood on the wooden stand waiting to be sold which was not going to happen. He slowly turned his head to the left as he held onto the shotgun. He stared as the group of aliens ran down towards him. He stepped into the shop and reached for the heavy ball. The aliens skidded to a stop as they looked at Eric and he stood looking at them. Eric took a deep breath. He ran, holding the ball in his hand. He let it go as the aliens turned around and ran away from it. The huge, green ball rolled into the aliens, knocking some down. "Strike!" Eric yelled.

Bradley held on to his two submachine guns as the aliens tumbled to the floor.

Kevin looked around. He saw a small shop and ran over to it. The shop was empty. The shelves had been looted except for one thing. Kevin looked at it to see boxes of fireworks stacked one on top of the other. He rubbed his hands together and picked a box up. The cardboard packing ripped off easily. He stared down at the rockets. The fuses dangled out of the back waiting to be lit. Kevin turned around and looked at the bench by the small coffee shop in the center with coffee and cold drinks splattered everywhere. He ran over to it, carrying the boxes with him. He started loading the rockets into the launchers aiming them out into the center. He squinted his eyes looking over at Bradley as he spun his foot around slamming it into an alien. Bradley gripped his baton. He slammed it into the electric filter at the back of the alien's suit. He jumped as it sparked. The alien coughed, placing its hand over its face. It slowly fell back onto the ground, choking.

"BRADLEY," Kevin yelled.

Bradley looked over at Kevin. Kevin stood up from behind a set of stacked up fireworks.

"Holy shit!" he gasped. "Max, Eric, get your asses here."

Max and Eric started sprinting along the slippery floor towards Kevin and Bradley. Bradley stared through the scope of his handgun, taking pot shots at the aliens as they charged toward them. Kevin looked up as Max and Eric dived over the table. Kevin lit the fuses.

"BRADLEY," Kevin yelled "GET YOUR ASS HERE."

Bradley swung around as the small puff of smoke came up from behind the bench. "Shit!" he gasped and dove behind the bench, placing his hands over his ears. The wick on the fireworks sparked up slowly and headed towards the boxes of gunpowder.

"Fire in the hole," Kevin quietly said, covering his ears.

The wicks slowly burnt down towards the fireworks pointing out toward the shopping center. The two aliens skidded to a stop and looked at the rocket as the wick was almost burnt out. "Oh fuck!" one alien said. "MOVE."

The rocket from the stand fired off the launcher. The smoke poured over them as the whistling got louder and the fireworks all lit up in their cardboard boxes. The smoke slowly started to fill the huge shopping center. The rockets continued screaming as the aliens tried to dodge the fireworks. The huge bangs got louder and the aliens fell to the floor, rolling in pain as the fire engulfed their suits. The blast of rockets left a horrible smoky mist.

Bradley slowly opened his eyes after the explosions had finished. He looked up at the light white smoke as he slowly got up. "You lot ok?" he asked.

He looked over at the wooden bench through the heavy smoke as he slowly started coughing. "Jesus Christ!" he gagged.

He looked over at the elevator as Kate and Jane looked through the clean glass at the group. Colin, next to them, was as quiet as a mouse.

Kevin quickly got up, jumped over the burning firework boxes, and ran over to the lift. Closely followed by Bradley they ran over to the glass doors. Kate let go of the door close button. She watched as the two doors slowly slid open, smoke pouring into the small compact box. She ran out of the lift holding her small hand over her mouth and coughing out the smoke from her lungs.

"Come on," Bradley said. "Let's get out of here." He put his arm around Kate, helping her over to the escalator as she continued to cough. He looked over his shoulder as Colin followed the rest of the group. They stepped into it, putting their side arms back into their pouches as the smoke continued to disperse very slowly.

Bradley looked over to his right as they came to the top floor. He looked at a set of doors that had shutters three quarters of the way down. "Oh dear," he said.

Bradley pulled the silver door handle and the door opened. Not a squeak was heard. Kate struggled to breathe as the smoke filled her lungs. The group coughed the smoke out of their lungs as they looked out onto the river. A cool air blew over them. Not a single ship was in sight.

Bradley looked out onto Queens as the military helicopters circled overhead looking down onto the city. He looked to his right and saw a clean, new, yellow telescope. He felt into his pocket and pulled out a nickel. He looked at the shiny metal as it gleamed in the afternoon sun. He looked out into Queens again as the helicopters continued circling above. He took a deep breath and placed the coin in the shiny slot. He leant down and looked through the clean glass at a military camp. Helicopters and military vehicles scanned the area around as the horrible smell of the burning rubber continued up his nose. The sound of the engines hummed through the cool air as the afternoon started to set in. The sun beamed down onto the camp as soldiers stood guarding the green camouflaged tents which were most probably full of computers and equipment. He felt his heart still pounding in his chest and the taste of firework smoke still lingered in his mouth.

"Yuck," he went, spitting on the ground. He zoomed in and looked at a military command center. He looked at all the soldiers as they walked around in pairs, armed to the teeth, ready to attack any aliens. The tanks rolled in one after the other, ready in case any of them tried to make a break across the river.

"Isn't there a boat," Kevin said, "that we can jack?"

Bradley leaned over the side and looked at the river. "No," he replied.

"Swim?" Eric went.

"Don't be stupid," Bradley replied.

"It may be the only thing we can do," Kate went "Come on."

"No, it's too far. We stand a better chance of making our way through the city towards that bridge," Bradley replied. "Now, come on, let's move."

The group followed Bradley along the side of the river, continuing to look out onto the command center. Bradley wished a nuclear submarine would emerge from the deep river to pick them up and take them away. He looked out again onto the river as the seagulls skimmed over the dirty water. The waves rocked them around. The sun sparkles rippled around as the waves continued dashing against the side of the brick pier.

"Dear, dear, dear," Eric went.

"What's the matter with you?" Bradley asked.

"Tired," Eric replied.

"Aren't we all?" Kevin countered. "Aren't we all?"

Bradley still kept his hands by his side, ready to swipe his weapon. The leather jacket continued rubbing up and down his back as the small string bag hung over. He looked up again to see a set of small steps leading to the top of a small building. He stopped and looked at the open gate as the old golden rusty padlock lay broken in two.

"Look," Bradley said.

"And?" Kate asked, folding her arms.

"Why has the padlock been cut off?" Bradley asked.

"Beats me," Colin said.

Bradley walked over to the open gate, walked up the rusty metal stairs and pulled out his sidearm. He crept up the stairs towards the top of the building. He looked over the side, down onto the city and at the burning vehicles. He wondered if they were ever going to get out of the city. He listened to the air conditioning system as it continued gently running, cooling the building. He took one last look down into the street and walked onto the roof of the building. He looked around to see a sniper rifle aiming down onto the street. He slowly turned his head to the left and jumped back in fright. The group stopped and looked at the body of a dead US soldier. The blood from his body had dried on the building rooftop. He had probably been out looking for survivors. Kate felt her stomach turn as she placed her hand over her mouth. "I'm gonna be sick," she said.

Bradley looked at Kate as she threw up over the side of the building. "You ok?" he asked.

Kate finished being sick. "I wanna get out of here," she wept.

Bradley looked at her as she started to cry softly. "Hey, hey," he went, grabbing hold of her. "I promise you I will get you back home even if it kills me," he went. "Promise."

Kate wiped her tears away. The breeze started to get

cooler as the day gradually came to an end. Bradley took one last look down at the two sniper rifles. "Let's take 'em," he went. "Still could come in handy Max, you're top shot at the club."

"Oh, yes," Max joked.

Bradley and Max started walking over towards the two rifles. Max walked over to the two dead soldiers. He knelt down and pulled off their shiny dog tags. "Rest in peace," he murmured.

Bradley rolled two blankets over their dead bodies in respect to the fallen men. Max let his breath out as he rubbed his face and prayed for the day to come to an end. There was a sudden hint of breeze. Bradley slowly got up and stretched his back as he walked over to the sniper rifles. A rumbling sound came from the distance.

"What's that?" Kevin asked.

Kevin and Bradley both looked out over the city. They continued moving along as the rumbling and vibrations grew louder. Bradley looked at Kevin again as he leant down and picked up the sniper rifle. He stared through it at the bust road. He breathed out in relief as he gently smiled. "Eye up, people, we're skipping this dump," Bradley went "Look what the cat dragged in!"

He handed the scope to Kevin. He put it up to his eye and looked through it down the empty and destroyed street. The green tank slammed through the smashed up vehicles igniting their engines into flames. The huge turret pushed the burnt vehicles out the way as the military jeeps followed behind.

"Ok, guys, we're out of here," Bradley said.

Kevin looked around as Max held onto his sniper rifle. "Come on," he said.

Bradley leant down to pick up his sniper rifle when there was a whooshing sound. He quickly looked up as a rush of adrenaline passed through his body. He felt the goose pimples on his arm as he watched a blue streak pass through the air. He felt his heart start to thump in his chest as the blue streak closed in on the military tank. He heard the screams from the frightened people.

"Oh, for god's sake!" Bradley moaned. "No, no, no." He dove to the floor and was followed by Kevin.

"What's going on?" Eric asked.

"Just get down." Max demanded.

He pulled Eric and Kate and Jane to the ground. He watched as the blue streak slammed into the tank blowing it onto its side. Huge fireballs rushed out from under the vehicle as the military jeeps spun out in all directions, slamming into lamp posts. Water gushed into the air.

"Jesus Christ!" Bradley said, looking down on the burning tanks. "Kev, Max, arm up. We've got a battle." He focused the rifle scope. He watched through it as the soldiers jumped out of their vehicles and the aliens jumped out from all corners.

"FIRE!" Bradley yelled. He pulled the trigger of his weapon and watched as the attacking aliens fell to the floor and the soldiers dived behind the smashed up vehicles firing onto the attacking aliens.

"Come on," Bradley continued, shooting down into the street as he listened to the bullets reloading into the weapon. The cartridges fell onto the ground next to Bradley as he continued reloading the new weapon. The fires raged as the sound of the zapping rays got slower and slower.

"They are dying out," Kate yelled.

"Yeah," Bradley replied, shouting, "But not quick enough."

He pulled the trigger and launched a bullet.

"I'm out," Max yelled.

"Think fast," Bradley said and threw the magazine over to Max. Max re-loaded the rifle as he stared back through the lens again. He slowly started pulling the trigger again, attacking the attacking aliens. The cool breeze blew through his hair as he smelt the string stench of gun powder. Bradley felt the sweat run off his head as he wiped it away. He took one last look around as an Apache helicopter approached the military convoy. It hovered above, getting its weapons ready to finish the aliens off. The turbulence from the blades blew Kate and Jane's hair around.

"Come on. Can we go?" Jane yelled over the engine's loud noise.

"Not yet," Bradley yelled, "I have a bad feeling about this."

"Come on, it's clear," Kate yelled.

There was a sudden rush again. Bradley looked out at the apache helicopter as it cast its shadow down on the military personnel. The young helicopter pilot looked out as one of the alien's rockets slammed into the helicopter. The soldiers looked up as the small fireballs rained down onto the city, further igniting the vehicles. The old helicopter started dropping from the sky as the back rotor slowly failed. The blades slowly stopped spinning as it slammed into the ground. A huge fireball ripped around, incinerating the fleeing soldiers.

Bradley stepped up. He looked down at the burning golden capsules as the smell of burning gunpowder wafted up to his nose. He looked down the tall building and onto the burning vehicles as the soldiers crawled out of the burning vehicles. The screams ripped through the empty streets as the small fuel tanks erupted. "Jesus!" he went.

"I'm gonna be sick," Kate said.

"Me, too," Jane added.

"Again," Eric said.

Bradley continued watching as the helicopter continued burning on top of the military vehicles when another slight humming sound came from the distance. He looked forward up the main road looking through the dark black smoke to see a small black dot in the sky slowly coming towards him getting louder and slowly getting bigger.

"What's that?" Eric asked.

"That's a helicopter," Kate went, wiping her mouth.

"It sure is," Bradley replied. He looked on in disbelief as a US Naval Sea King helicopter slowly came into view from the horizon.

"Look," Eric went.

"I know," Bradley replied.

The group waved their arms as the huge warship hovered above. The black smoke from the burning helicopter below seeped to the ground as the Sea King helicopter slowly approached. The force from the blades blew the smoke and fires away as it landed in the middle of the street.

"Come on," Bradley yelled. "Let's get the fuck out of here."

"I agree," Eric said.

Bradley watched as Kevin, Max, Eric, Colin Kate and Jane ran down the metal stairs, to the bottom of the building, He followed them down, inhaling the thick black smoke as he ran into the street and the door of the helicopter was flung back.

"This way," a soldier yelled.

"Come on, go," Bradley said. He ran over to the helicopter feeling the strong gusts of wind coming from the blades Entering it, he looked at the military personnel inside.

"Are you ok, sir?" the soldier yelled over the engines. "Any one injured?"

"Yes, thanks," Bradley went. "No, I don't think any of us is injured apart from her arm."

"Good, can I have your name, please?" the soldier asked. "I'll get my friend to look at that."

"Bradley Harrison," Bradley yelled. He watched the soldier as he wrote the group's names down on an A four piece of paper.

"Right. What we're gonna do, is drop you off at the police station. It's about a five minute flight there. You can find your friends or relatives and escape the city from there," the soldier said.

"Ok. Are there any more of these things around?" Bradley asked.

The soldier looked out of the helicopter. "No, sir," he replied.

"So let's get out of here," Bradley said.

The helicopter took off, flying away from the scene. Bradley looked at the soldier as he stared out of the side of the craft looking down onto the city. "Have any of these things landed anywhere else?" Bradley asked over the engine sound.

"No, sir. It's just being reported that Manhattan is the only place that has been invaded," the soldier yelled.

"Suppose that's a good thing," Bradley said.

"Go and sit down, mate. You looked knackered," the soldier said.

"I will, thanks," Bradley replied. He slowly walked back, and sat down on a side seat. He looked down, out of the window, onto the burning city as the smoke from the burning apache motors blasted into the air. The helicopter pilot pushed the control lever forward, slowly moving away from the crash scene.

"What's the city like?" Bradley asked trying to get a conversation on the move.

"It's totally destroyed. I'm surprised you're still alive. I wasn't expecting to find anyone," the soldier said.

"I'm surprised myself. Luckily we came across a weapon store and managed to stock up," Bradley replied.

"Yeah, I can see that," the soldier said.

"How is the evacuation going?" Bradley asked.

"Not quick enough. People are turning up at the main police station in the hundreds and my people are having to expand the perimeter around the station," the solder went. "We're running out of room."

The young soldier reached into his pocket and pulled out a small map. He slowly unfolded it and showed it to Bradley.

"You see this route here? This is the only safe way out of the city. This road here leads to the Queensboro Bridge and we haven't got enough vehicles to evacuate them any quicker," the solder said.

Bradley looked at the map as Kate lay back in the seat feeling her heart start to slow down at last. He looked down onto the stricken city as they flew over the police station towards the landing zone. He felt the blades start to slow down as they got lower towards the ground. The huge white H stood out as the tanks and jeeps guarded the small landing zone. Bradley felt a sign of relief as the helicopter touched down on the road and the military tanks surrounded the area, ready to fire at the first sign of any alien. The side door swung back. The three solders stepped onto the road wielding their rifles. Bradley stepped down onto the road, too. He wiped the gun powder marks away from his head, as he felt the wind from the blades as they spun around.

'Cheers," Bradley yelled.

"No problem," the soldier yelled.

"Fly safe," Kevin wished him.

"We'll try," the soldier yelled in return.

The engines powered up. Bradley turned around and watched as the huge helicopter lifted off the ground and headed back into the city looking for any more survivors although the chances were very bleak. He slowly turned around and caught up with Kevin. He looked into his pouches and at all the empty magazines. "I thought we were never gonna get away," he said to Kevin. "But now we are here."

Kevin nodded gently at him as they continued walking up the small path towards the police station. "Can I ring my mum?" Kevin asked.

Bradley pulled his telephone out of his pocket. He stared down at it, looking at the dead signal. "No signal," he said.

"Oh dear," Kevin said. "I bet my mum is shitting herself."

"My mum may have said something to her," Bradley said.

"What do you mean?" Kevin asked.

"They probably all met down at the school today," Bradley said.

"Oh I see," Kevin said. "Can't wait till we hit that bar tonight."

"Ha," Bradley laughed. He looked over at the subway as people surrounded it while it was guarded by military personnel. The group slowly walked up to the steep steps of the station. They looked up at the huge NYPD logo above the entrance, casting its shadow down onto the ground and frightening people. Bradley looked in through the windows as the people sat on their chairs, trembling with fear.

"Come on, Colin," he said. "Let's go see Ms. Javies."

"Can't wait to see her face," Kevin said.

"If she is still here," Bradley went.

Colin didn't say a word. He kept dead quiet. The group walked through the swing doors into the station. Bradley looked around at the officers as they guarded the entrance to the offices, the fear of god in their eyes. He took a deep breath as Kate and Jane slowly walked into the office followed by Colin and Eric. He slowly walked in behind them and looked at Ms. Javies as she stared out of the window. Mr. Knightsbridge sat in the far corner, slumped in his seat, his pink silk tie hanging limply from his neck, not saying a word to anyone. Amelia was still not far from him. Some of the students sat next to one another. Ms. Javies slowly turned around, holding her half smoked cigarette. She dropped it on the floor and folded her arms as Bradley, Max, Kevin and Eric looked at her. "We're back," Bradley said. "And here is Colin."

"Oh, oh, my god," she said, trembling. "Is, is that you?"

"No, it's a figment of your imagination," Bradley said. "Jesus Christ!"

Kevin giggled. Ms. Javies slowly walked across the office as Mr. Knightsbridge looked up at them.

"Hello," Eric went.

"Bradley," she gasped again. "How are you?"

"Thank you. You finally noticed it's me!" Bradley replied folding his arms. "And I am fine. How are you?"

"I'm ok. Come on, sit down," she wept.

"Isn't she nice?" Bradley went, turning around. "So, Ms. J,who else is missing from our lovely group?"

"No one, thank god," Ms. Javies said, trembling.

Bradley looked at Kevin giggling as Mr. Knightsbridge got up slowly. "Hey, Mr. K, how are you?" Kevin asked. "How was your trip through Manhattan?"

"I, I am, I am good, thank you," he went. "Relieved."

"Well, I'm glad you're all ok," Bradley said to them. "Any chance of us getting out of here? I'll tell you all about our experience in New York." He took a shallow breath. "Oh, by the way, has our E M P course work got to be in next week?"

"No," Mr. Knightsbridge said. "You've already got an A."

"Oh, that is nice," Bradley went. "Now, how are we getting out of here?"

Ms. Javies trembled. "There is a bus on its way. You

are just in time," Ms. Javies replied, taking a puff of her newly lit cigarette.

Bradley slowly walked up to her as he folded his arms. He looked at her trembling muscles as the group looked at him walking up to her. He coughed out the light smoke as he pulled the half-puffed fag out of her mouth and slowly flicked it away. "Don't smoke. It's bad for you," Bradley went as Kevin giggled. He turned, looking at Colin. "Go on, go see her," he said.

Bradley turned around walking out of the office quickly. He looked over his shoulder as Kevin, Max and Eric followed him. He walked into the hallway and up the spiral stairs to the top floor of the building. He looked at the toilets and walked through the brown door. He walked up to the shiny white, silver basin, turned on the tap and felt the cool water splashing onto his hands.

"I thought we were never going to get away from those things," Bradley went.

"I'm still wondering if they are going to invade the rest of the earth," Kevin replied.

"Well, as long as we are away from them," Bradley said, "I don't give a fuck where they invade."

"Apart from Hawaii," Max said.

"Yeah, I suppose," Bradley said. "We can flee there if they come again."

"I don't think they will," Max said.

Kevin watched Bradley as he splashed the water onto his face washing away the grime from the gunpowder. He looked into the basin as the dirty water flushed down the plughole into the sewers which were most probably full of blood and human remains. Bradley wiped the last of the muck away from his face and walked out of the toilet back towards the stairs.

He looked at the middle-aged officer who walked up to the group. "Excuse me, gents," he went. "I need them."

"What?" Bradley went.

"I can't let you walk around here armed. I'm sorry," the officer went. "We need every weapon available for my officers who are weapon trained."

Bradley looked at Kevin as he unclipped the weapon belt, and handed the weapons to the officers.

"You seem very well organized," the officer remarked.

"Yep, we ran into this shop. Let's say," Bradley replied, "it was right up our street. Besides, it helps being a member of a gun club."

"Oh I see, boys," he went. "Thanks."

Kevin looked at Bradley as he handed his weapons over. Eric watched as they took his shotgun away. "I'll miss you my precious," he mourned. Bradley looked at Kevin and shook his head. He looked out of the front exit as a bus pulled up. The people slowly started boarding it, waiting to get away from the city.

Bradley watched as Mr. Knightsbridge slowly walked out of the office followed by his students and the bus filled up quickly with people. "We're not gonna get on this one," he said.

"Yip," Kevin went. "Next one."

Bradley queued for the next bus and watched as Mr. Knightsbridge and Amelia got onto the bus.

"One minute," the officer went.

Bradley looked over his shoulder as Ms. Javies stood by Kate and Jane. He giggled as the next bus turned up outside the entrance. Colin looked out of the door as people struggled to get a seat or a place. Bradley walked down the steps as people looked at the group quickly boarding the bus. "Come on," he mumbled.

He climbed up into the bus and sat down next to Kevin as he watched Kate and Jane sit down at the front with Ms. Javies who still kept her head down. Colin was not far behind. The two soldiers walked onto the bus as some people stood holding onto the rails. A soldier closed the doors as people struggled to stand up. Bradley lay back in his seat. He felt the hidden handgun push into his back. He smiled secretly as the bus pulled out of the parking bay onto the clear road ahead.

"What we doing when we get home?" Kevin asked.

"Well," Bradley said, "I'm getting pissed and laid."

Kevin looked at him. "Oh," he went. "Who with?"

"I don't care," Bradley said. "As long as she is free, I don't care."

"Ok," Kevin said. "What about tomorrow?"

Bradley looked ahead. "Tomorrow," he said, "I'm raiding my savings account if the bank is still there. I'm going to Barry's and buying as much ammo as I can. I still have a bad feeling about this."

"I agree," Kevin said. He lay back in the seat as the driver picked up speed. He stared out the window at all the smashed vehicles shoved at the side of the road where the military vehicles had moved them out the way.

"I still don't know how we are still alive," Kevin went.

"Well, all those martial art and shooting lessons paid off," Bradley replied. "Just think of the story we could tell the paparazzi."

"Init?" Max replied. "And the cash…"

"Don't you mean pepperoni?" Eric said.

Max giggled. "No," he said.

The coach continued along the road towards the Queensboro Bridge. It would not be long now till they arrived in Queens. The soldier looked out of the dirty window and looked down the road at the cars piled up everywhere. He looked to his left to see a slight gleam coming towards the bus. It was closing in very quick.

"Holy shit!" he went.

The other soldier looked out as well. "INCOMING," he yelled.

Bradley jumped. "Oh, now what?" he mumbled. He looked up as the gleam slammed into the side of the bus. The people screamed as the bus lost control. Bradley felt the left wheel flatten into the road. The sparks flew out of the wheel rim as Bradley grabbed the old fabric on the front of the old seat. The screams continued as the standing passengers fell onto one another and onto the floor. Mobile telephones flew everywhere as Bradley slowly opened his eyes. He looked up at all the collapsed people as they all looked at one another.

"What happened?" one person asked.

"We got hit by something," another passenger replied.

Bradley shook his head as he pulled the hidden handgun out from behind his trousers. He held onto it as Kevin looked at him. "I thought you had to…" Kevin said.

"Emergencies," Bradley replied. "And it's a good job I did." He looked forward as the two dead soldiers fell out of the coach and two aliens climbed in wielding their weapons.

"Nobody move," one ordered.

"Ok," Bradley mumbled. He lowered the handgun as he didn't have a clear shot of the cabin.

"Who shall we take here?" the alien went. "Hmm… which one?"

The two aliens looked at Kate, Jane and Ms. Javies as they huddled together, trembling.

"No," Bradley said quietly. He jumped out of his seat as the aliens pulled Kate, Jane and Ms. Javies away from the bus.

"Eric, Max, Kev, come on," he went. He held onto his firearm as he jumped over the people on the floor of the bus.

"Wait," Colin yelled.

Bradley didn't hear Colin tell him to wait. He stumbled out of the bus and landed on the ground.

"Ouch," he groaned. "Fuck it."

He groaned some more with pain as his hands slammed into the asphalt ground. He slowly lifted his head and looked at his hands as the tiny bits of grit fell to the ground followed by the tiny streams of blood. He let his breath out as he looked up. He saw Kate, Jane and Ms. Javies being bundled into one of the parked military jeeps that the aliens had hijacked.

"Shit!" he gasped. "Come on." He opened fire on the green jeep as the aliens got in and started up the engine which roared to life.

Eric slowly walked up behind Bradley. "Look," he said.

Bradley swung his head and looked at the New York Police patrol car as it stood parked in the middle of the sidewalk with its doors open. He turned around and chucked the handgun through the air to the two men as they staggered off the burning bus.

"Here," he yelled. "Take this. Someone will be here in a minute."

"Wait, what about you?" the man yelled.

"Don't worry about us," Bradley yelled. "Just get out of here."

"What's your name?" the man yelled.

Bradley didn't answer them. He ran over to the police car, pulling the door open even more. He looked in at the keys still in the ignition, ready to be used. The aliens pulled away from the crash scene in the military jeep and Kate, Jane and Ms. Javies yelled for help. The floor rumbled as the jeep moved off. Bradley got in and started up the engine.

"Come, come," he yelled. "In, in, in."

Colin jumped in unnoticed. Eric got in as Bradley slammed the car into reverse.

"Hang on," Eric yelled. "Seatbelt."

"No time," Bradley replied.

Bradley slammed the accelerator down, twisted the wheel, and skidded the car around. Eric fell onto Max as Kevin, slipping his seat belt on, looked down the road. Colin didn't say a word as he sat quietly in the back seat. Bradley slipped into drive. He rammed the accelerator down and screeched along the road. He switched on the blue and red lights.

"Cool. A police chase," Colin said.

Bradley looked into the mirror to see Colin. "What?" he said. "How did you get in here?"

"Just got in," Colin replied.

"Great!" Bradley said. "Stuck with you again!" He looked at the jeep again. The two aliens looked into their rear view mirror to see the NYPD car slowly catching up with them, red and blue lights on and off.

"Shit!" one went.

Kate and Jane didn't know what they were saying. They sat in the back, trembling, and Ms. Javies didn't say a word. Kate watched as one of the aliens pulled out a small radio form his pouch. She listened in as the alien slowly crawled over her towards the two rear windows. It kicked through the glass on the top. Bradley watched as it clambered onto the machine gun positioned on the top of the old vehicle.

"Oh no," Kevin went.

Bradley saw the alien swing the heavy weapon around, ripping the lever back and looking at the white patrol car.

"Oh yes," Bradley said. He swerved the car out of the way as a rain of bullets was fired from the weapon. He looked up the road as the military jeep swung to the right. The smoke from the dark black tire sprayed out as Bradley followed close behind. He was getting bored of the sirens now but kept them running. He looked up to see Times Square slowly coming into view. He saw the advertisement boards still flashing. No one was walking around, crossing the road or heading in any direction. The hot dog stands were toppled over on their sides. The alien on the machine gun stopped. He looked over his shoulder and slowly turned the weapon around. The gold clock of Times Square came into view. The alien opened fire onto the digital board as it looked out onto the square. The bullets slammed into the huge board. Sparks rained down as the hinges holding it in place shattered. The huge board slowly fell to the ground.

"Oh shit!" Bradley yelled. He watched the military jeep turn left on the side roads as the board continued falling towards the ground. The sky above them went dark as they sped under the plunging board. Bradley closed his eyes as they just about cleared it. He looked over his shoulder at the board as it ignited into flames.

"That was close," Eric went.

"Too close," Colin exclaimed.

"Shut up, Colin," Eric went.

"No, you shut up," Colin yelled.

Bradley took a deep breath. "Both of you shut up," he yelled. He couldn't take his eyes off the burning board as it ignited into more flames. He had to take his mind off it. He shook his head and looked down the road. "Is everyone ok?" he asked. "No one injured?"

"We're fine," Max replied.

"Right," he went. "Let's get these bastards." He rammed the accelerator down to full again. He sped along and caught up with the jeep. He watched as the alien spun the machine gun around again, looking at him through the scope.

"Kevin," Bradley went. "Take him out."

"What with?" Kevin asked.

"Agh," Bradley went. He reached over and pulled down the dashboard. Bradley looked around the new squad car. "There we are," he said.

Bradley handed Kevin a handgun. Kevin wound the window down and slowly leant out of it. He looked through the scope and opened fire at the alien on the back of the jeep as he struggled to reload his out of date weapon.

"Come on. Take him out, Kevin," Bradley cried.

"I'm trying," Kevin yelled. "Give me a second."

Kevin aimed. He slowly pulled the trigger and launched the bullet through the air. The golden capsule flew through the air and slammed into the alien. Bradley watched as the small being rolled off the jeep onto the ground.

"Yeah!" Kevin yelled.

Bradley looked up as the green jeep turned onto the highway leading up and around Manhattan. He stared at the huge concrete pillars hold the bridge up.

"There, there, there," Kevin yelled.

Bradley skidded the car onto the highway. He looked ahead at the green military jeep as Kevin held onto his handgun, Bradley looked at his hands trembling as he grasped the weapon and looked dead out at the car. "Hey," he went.

Kevin turned his head to the left looking at Bradley as he continued holding on to the handgun.

"It's ok," Bradley went. "We'll be out of here soon."

"Yeah," Kevin went. "We almost were."

"Agh," Bradley went. "Never mind." He started to catch up with the jeep as the alien clambered onto the heavy machine gun again. It swung it around pointing it towards the police cruiser.

"Oh, shit! Here we go again," Bradley went. He swerved the car to the left, trying to dodge the bullets as they pierced the metal work. Eric, Max and Colin ducked down as the ricocheting echoed around the car.

"Shoot back, shoot back, shoot, shoot" Bradley yelled.

Kevin wound the window down and leaned out of it. He stared through the scope taking pot shots at the alien on the weapon as the last of the golden bullets launched out of it.

"Shit!" The alien went. It clambered back into the jeep

and sat down. It looked over its shoulder at Kate and Jane as they huddled up against one another. "Look at you," it went.

Kate and Jane didn't reply. Ms. Javies still stayed quiet in the back seat as they looked forward out the front of the jeep to see one of the city's trucks. Kate, Jane and Ms. Javies stared at the double deck vehicle as it carried one of the new city trams on it. Bradley looked at the front and back tram as they were poised over the end of each floor of the vehicle, the carriages behind them. They were most probably being taken away back to the depot.

"Jesus Christ!" Ms. Javies groaned.

The jeep swung to the left as Bradley stayed close behind. He looked forward, his eyes open wide with fear as he looked into the mirror as he saw the Empire State Building. He looked at the tall, huge building as it stood out in the middle of Manhattan Island. The sun peeped out in the distance as it slowly started to go down below the horizon. Bradley looked forward again at the tall truck as it hauled the trams along the highway. The sirens wailed as the green military jeep was now out of sight.

"Shit!" Bradley went. "Where are they?"

Bradley looked up at the truck and caught a glimpse of one of the aliens as it stepped through the tram on the bottom floor of the truck.

"What are they doing?" Kevin asked.

Bradley stayed quiet as Kevin held onto the sidearm. He looked up as one of the aliens shot out the front glass window of the tram cab. It swiped its sidearm pointing down onto the car, the green rays fired out of the weapon slamming into the asphalt road.

"Shit!" Bradley yelled, ducking behind the steering wheel.

"Shoot, back, shoot back, shoot, shoot," Bradley yelled.

Kevin wound the window down and crawled out,

holding onto the sidearm. He stared through the sights and squeezed the old weapon trigger in. The golden bullets fired out of the weapon. The tiny grains of dust blew into his face as Bradley kept behind the truck weaving the car from left to right trying get note of the jeep. "Where are they?" he mumbled. He looked up again as the two aliens shot out the metal chain holding the tram onto the bottom deck of the truck. "Ohhhh shit!" he went.

He hit the brakes hard as the front two carriages of the tram rolled out onto the road. The strong metal wheels turned up the asphalt road as it dangled over the back of the truck. Bradley struggled to keep away from it.

"Jesus! Fuck!" Kevin yelled.

Bradley watched the front of the truck start to swerve in and out of the smashed up cars causing the tram to sway all over the place. The front cab slammed into the side of the car forcing it over to the right.

"Ohhhh god!" Colin yelled.

Eric looked down at Colin. "Don't worry, mate," he went.

Bradley looked at Kevin as he continued dodging the loose tram as it scraped along the highway road. The tiny bits of asphalt kicked up onto the wind screen. The alien at the front of the huge truck shot down at the huge clamps holding the tram in place. Bradley slammed the brakes on, skidding the car to the right, grasping onto the wheel as the tram rolled off the bottom of the truck into the streets.

"Shitting hell!" Kevin went.

Bradley looked forward again as the top of the loader started to lower, the back cab pointed at Bradley.

"Oh, here we go again," Kevin went.

Bradley looked up at the truck. The two aliens clambered through towards the middle carriages. They looked at the huge rubber joints as they held the carriages close together. One alien pointed its ray gun down onto the carriage joints as the last of the sun's light beamed in through the window of the once new tram. The bolts burnt away as Bradley tried to see what the aliens were doing. He saw the flames from the rays as they continued shooting down onto the bolts of the vehicle. The rusty chain fell away front the front of the tram as the rubber started to tear.

"Ohhhh, shit!" Kevin went.

"OHHHHHH, Yes," Bradley yelled.

The rubber tore, the front of the tram rolled off the truck, onto the highway. Bradley swung the car to the left. He felt the back screech as he looked into the rear view mirror as the new tram rolled along the highway.

"OWWWWWWWWWWWWWWWWWWWWW," Kevin yelled, leaning out of the window and watching the front of the tram disappear into the distance of the long highway. "Shitting hell!" he went.

Bradley focused ahead at the back of the truck as the next carriage rolled off the truck onto the highway. It tumbled onto the road, glass shattering everywhere. Bradley sped past the carriage looking up at the truck as the top was still lowered. He swung the cars to the left catching a glimpse of the jeep. But it what was further ahead that caught his attention. He saw a road block that had been set up by the aliens. "I've got an idea," he said, looking ahead as the green jeep was let through the blockade. "Ok, Kevin, how many rounds you got left?"

Kevin looked down at his weapon. "Three," he said.

"Ok, take three single slow shots at the cab" Bradley said. "Distract him."

"Got it," Kevin went.

Kevin leaned out of the window and took pot shots at the cab. As the alien ducked down it lost sight of the road block.

"Hold on boys," Bradley went. "We're going flying." He eased the accelerator, falling behind the transport vehicle. The alien looked up again and saw the road block close to him.

"Holy shit!" it yelled and slammed the brakes on.

Bradley saw the bright red lights come on. He rammed the accelerator down. Smoke bellowed out from the wheels as the truck came to a stop. The alien looked into the rear view mirror as Bradley held onto the steering wheel. The car travelled through the air, flying over the road block. Kevin looked down as the two front wheels slammed back down onto the asphalt highway. The suspension bounced back up as Eric's seat belt locked, stopping him from flying forward.

"Phew!" Kevin said, looking at Bradley.

"I bet you never thought of that, did you?" asked Bradley.

"No, I didn't," Kevin admitted.

Bradley watched the green jeep swing off the highway. He pulled of the highway himself, pulling the car around onto the road below. He looked at the empty streets, as he sped south, back towards Manhattan. He looked up again as the car started to jolt. He looked down at the fuel gauge seeing the needle go into the red. "Shit!" he went. He looked up as the green jeep swung to the right into a car park. "Hang on," he said and ripped the handbrake up, swinging the car into the empty car park. Old plastic and paper bags were blowing everywhere in the light breeze.

"There," Kevin went.

Bradley watched as Kate, Jane and Ms Javies were bundled into the outdoor shopping centre. The automatic doors sealed closed as the engine on the patrol car cut out.

"Shit!" Bradley went.

The car rolled to a stop by the green jeep. He slowly got out looking at the automatic doors as the sparks rained down from the sensor. "Shit!" he said again.

He looked into the dull, dark shopping centre. The only

light seen was that of the sparks.

"We going on?" Kevin asked.

"What do you think?" Bradley said. He stared up at the shopping centre name as the smoke hissed out of the patrol car engine. He walked back over to the driver's seat, reached in and pulled out the radio. "Anyone near the Ravensgate Centre, get here. It may be your last chance out of the city," he said and chucked the radio back into the car as he reached into his inside pocket.

He flicked out his baton as the rest of the group did the same. Bradley looked at them as he crept up to the automatic glass doors and then looked over his shoulder into the car park. Not a soul was in sight. "Let's go then," he said.

He looked through the glass doors as the sensors had stopped sparking. He slipped his baton into his pocket and grabbed hold of the door. He slowly slid the tight doors open. "Come on," he said and shimmied through, looking down all the empty aisles. Not a soul or alien was in sight. "Kate," he whispered.

He watched as Max and Kevin entered the shop holding onto their flick out truncheons.

"Where are they?" Kevin went.

Bradley scanned the empty store, looking at the open freezers and the frozen food sprawled everywhere. Just then he heard a scuffle. Bradley looked over his shoulder to see Eric stuck between the two glass doors. Colin was looking at him. "Oh, for god's sake, get him out," Bradley whispered pointing his baton at Eric.

"Come on Eric," Kevin went.

Bradley looked down all the long aisles of the huge building. "Ok," he said, turning to the group. "Kevin, you're with me. Max, Colin, Eric, you three go that way."

"Understood," Max went.

Bradley slowly crept down the aisles of the shopping

centre holding onto the rubber material. "Kate?" Bradley went. "Jane?"

Kevin looked over his shoulder. He felt the freezing cold air from the freezers blow onto him as he stepped on the broken glass on the floor. The crack echoed around and he froze in his tracks, looking at Bradley. "Sorry," he mumbled.

Bradley shook his head smiling as he continued walking forward and grasped the baton. He heard a faint scream coming from somewhere further in the store. "This way," he whispered.

Bradley and Kevin crept along through the aisles and stopped to see Max and Eric on the other side. Bradley signalled the two along as Kevin stuck behind him. They turned the corner only to see Kate, Jane and Ms. Javies kneeling down on the floor, looking at one another.

"Shit!" Bradley went. He ran over to Kate and Jane holding on to the baton as Kevin, Colin, Max and Eric followed close behind. He dived down to the floor. "Hey, you ok?" he gasped.

Kate didn't say a word as she trembled with fear.

"Hey," he said, "Can you hear me?"

Kate slowly looked to her right as Bradley knelt beside her. There was a sudden sound of clicking coming from all around him. He slowly stood up and closed his eyes. He turned around and saw the whole group completely surrounded by the alien invaders. "Shit!" he went.

He dropped his weapon and looked up as one of the aliens slowly walked up to him holding onto its sidearm. He felt his heart pounding in his chest as the rubber suit squeaked as it walked closer to him. Bradley's adrenaline rushed through his system as the alien stopped and looked at him. The alien swiped his sidearm, whipping it over his face. Bradley fell back onto the floor and looked up at the alien as the pain shot through his face.

"Please," Kate yelled. "What do you want?"

The alien looked down at Bradley as he slowly leaned back up again, the red mark bruising the side of his face as the pain started to die away. Bradley spat the phlegm out of his throat as he sat down and looked at the alien.

"What do we do with them?" one alien asked.

The first alien looked down at the small group.

"Take this three," it ordered, "but kill the rest."

Kate, Jane and Ms. Javies all looked at one another as Bradley looked up at the alien. The sweat ran down his head as the two girls and teacher were carted away.

"Take them back to the ship," the alien went.

"To the ship?" Eric mumbled.

"Yes, we have a ship," the alien replied.

Bradley looked up at the alien as these were probably the last few minutes he has left on the planet.

"Any last words?" the alien went.

Bradley looked up at the alien. "Yes," he said.

"What?" the alien asked.

Bradley jumped up and head butted him. The alien tumbled back onto the floor, looking at Bradley as it swiped its weapon from the side pouch. The power built up in it as Kate, Jane and Ms Javies were led out the back door. Bradley looked at Kate as she was being led away, when the floor slowly started to rumble. The alien looked down at him as the vibrations in the floor increased. Bradley slowly got up and moved next to Eric as a sudden crash was heard coming from one of the side entrances. He looked at the huge shelves of food as they started tumbling into one another like dominoes. "Move," Bradley yelled.

He grabbed hold of Eric by the scruff of his t-shirt collar and pulled him out the way of the tumbling freezers. Bradley and Eric looked up as one of the NYPD SWAT vans skidded into the centre and the back finished skidding around as the back doors swung open. Two young Chinese men jumped out holding onto old AK47 assault rifles. They ripped of their face masks and looked at Bradley.

"Move your arses," one yelled.

Bradley got up quickly picking up the flick out baton. "Come on move," he yelled. "Move, move."

"Hey," a voice went.

Bradley swung his head to the left. He jumped up grabbing onto the AK47 assault rifle. "Cheers!" he yelled. "Get that van out of here. It's our only transport."

"Got it," the man yelled.

Bradley held onto the weapon as the round magazine clipped into place below the weapon. The two back wheels spun, the fridges collapsed onto one another blocking his way to the exit. He looked down at the timer on the bomb. He only had fifty five seconds.

"Shit!" he went. "EVERYBODY OUT."

Bradley looked around as the aliens jumped out from all corners. He opened fire on them as Kevin led Max, Eric and Colin out. Bradley watched as the last bullet fired out of the weapon. "Shit!" he mumbled.

He watched as one of the aliens swiped his shiny sword. He flicked his baton out, clinging to the rubber end. "Come on, then," he yelled.

The alien sped towards Bradley who swung the baton around and slammed it into the shiny sword as his heart pounded. The alien tumbled to the floor. Bradley looked at the timer as it continued ticking. He spun around and ran through the shop, looking for Kate and Jane.

"Kate?" he yelled. "Jane?"

He looked around. "Shit!" he cried. "Where the fuck are they?"

He had only about thirty seconds left. He swung his head to the left and looked down one of the aisles at the huge glass window. That was the way he had to go. He sprinted along the aisles, looking into the freezers stacked with food. He felt his heart pound as the timer hit zero. The semtex bomb erupted. Bradley felt the floor vibrating as the fireball ripped up the aisles. He looked to see a small crack starting to form in the huge glass window. He threw the flick out baton through the air, and watched as the weapon careened through the warming air and the metal bolt slammed into the window, cracking it. Bradley took a shallow breath as he arrived at the window. He closed his eyes and dove through the window. He slammed into the concrete pavement, picking up the baton at the same time. He ran through the car park as the force from the eruption threw him forward into the cool afternoon air.

*   *   *   *

"Bradley," Kevin yelled.

Bradley opened his eyes a few seconds later as he was picked up off the ground.

"Shit, man! You ok?" Kevin asked.

Bradley didn't answer. He looked around the car park.

"Where's …?" he asked.

"Sorry," Max said. "They've gone."

"SHIT! FUCK! NO!" he yelled.

"Come on," Kevin said.

Bradley was helped over to the SWAT van.

"Bradley," a man yelled.

"WHAT?" Bradley yelled back.

"We can help you," the young Chinese went.

"Like how?" Bradley asked.

"Listen, come with us" the man went. "Let's get out of here first."

Bradley kicked the stone away in anger as he walked up to the van. He clambered up the metal steps and sat down on a seat in the back of the van. The young man pulled the doors shut as the driver stared up the engine.

"How did you know we were here?" Kevin asked.

"Radio. You put a call out for help," he said. "Name's Cheng and this is Garcious."

Bradley looked out of the rear window as they slowly drove along through the empty car park and the burning building got smaller and smaller.

"How did you boys survive?" Cheng asked.

"Trial and error," Kevin replied.

"A lot of error," Bradley said.

The van continued along through the streets, heading south towards Chinatown. The smoke from the burning shopping centre slowly disappeared.

16

Lieutenant Kipling walked down the concrete steps to the crowded police station, looking at the group of frightened people as they staggered along, escorted by his troops.

"What happened?" he asked holding onto his rifle.

There was a short silence.

"Down there, about half a mile away," a soldier said, "a couple of the things broke through one of the barricades and attacked the bus. They kidnapped a few of the people. We believe they are two girls and a teacher. They were shortly followed by a group of lads who went in pursuit of them."

Kipling didn't say a word at first.

"Right," he then said. "Damn brave! Where did they go?"

The rest of his sentence seemed to be stuck in his mouth.

"The aliens got into one of our jeeps and the boys got into a NYPD car," the soldier said. "I think they are dead."

Kipling took a few seconds to think. "I want no vehicles leaving the city until we know it's secure," he commanded. "All coaches, buses, trucks - anything are to be escorted from now on."

"But, sir, that will slow us down," the soldier said. "The area is struggling enough as it is."

"We'll hurry it up," Kipling said.

The two soldiers ran off in different directions.

"Jesus Christ!" Kipling said to himself walking back to the police station. He took another deep breath looking out of the window at all the frightened people as they stood waiting for vehicles to come and take them out of the stricken city.

"Sir," a soldier went.

Kipling slowly turned around, looking at one of his men.

"There's a call for you," the man said.

"Who is it?" Kipling asked.

"Don't know. Sorry, sir," the soldier replied.

Kipling nodded and slowly walked up the stairs towards one of the back rooms. He looked down the spiral stairs as he slowly opened the old white door and walked in. He closed the door, took his hat off and looked at the small screen as it stood on the table. The screen slowly came on. Lieutenant Kipling looked in disbelief to see President Green, sitting in his office in The White House, pop up on it.

"Mr. President, Sir," he gasped.

"Thank you, Lieutenant Kipling," President Green said. "Bring me up to speed on the situation there, please."

Kipling had to think. "Erm," he mumbled. "Very intense here, sir. We just had a failed evacuation. We lost two men and a small group of people. We have had to cancel all vehicles out of the city until we can arrange for more armed escorts to the Queensboro Bridge."

"Have any of the aliens broken out of the zone?" Green asked, putting his pen to his mouth.

"No, not that I am aware of," Kipling said. "All bridges in and out of the Manhattan area have been destroyed. The only way out is via the Queensboro Bridge."

Green didn't say a word for a moment. "Ok," he then said. "I'm sorry to say this but I have ordered the annihilation of Manhattan Island at eighteen hundred hours tonight."

Kipling looked at his watch. "That only gives us three hours," he said. "We won't have time."

"I'm sorry, but I cannot risk the lives of any more people" President Green said. "If there are any more of these things around I just cannot risk it. Take care, soldier."

President Green switched off the TV. Kipling looked into it and then took one last look at his watch. "God have mercy on our souls," he said.

He shook his head knowing he had not got a minute to spare. He walked out through the police station and passed all the frightened people who looked up at him as he simply walked by in his uniform. "Come on," he yelled. "Let's get these people moving."

*   *   *   *

President Green swiveled around in his chair. He placed his face in his hands and then looked at three men dressed in military uniforms. "I've just seen New York," he said. "Are the B 52s ready?"

"Yes, they are, sir," the USAF general said.

"Get them in the air and tell them to keep well out of sight," President Green ordered.

"When are we annihilating Manhattan?" the general asked.

"Eighteen hundred hours," Green replied.

"Why so early?" the general asked.

"Because if these aliens break out of the quarantine zone we could have more problems," President Green said.

"I understand, sir," the general replied.

There was a short break. President Green was running out of questions to ask.

*   *   *   *

The three B-52 jets lined up on the runway at Edwards Air Force Base. The huge atomic engines roared to life one after the other as they stood parked on the runway, ready to head towards Manhattan. The pilots pushed the throttles forward, powering the engines up and picking up the grit on the runway as they sped along. The long wingspans gently lifted up as they went faster and faster. The three jets slowly turned towards the north east and headed towards the State of New York.

17

Kate opened her eyes and looked around to see Central Park as the two aliens pulled up by the entrance. She looked out of the window as the two aliens got out of the car and walked towards the two rear doors to get them. Ms. Javies trembled as the cool evening breeze from outside blew into the car as the door was pulled open.

"Out," the alien ordered.

Kate, Jane and Ms. Javies slowly got out of the car and stood in the middle of the road as the two aliens then ordered them into the park. Kate stumbled over the twigs on the ground as they snapped beneath her feat. The two aliens guided them through the park towards the shrubs and bushes. Kate looked through them to see a small opening.

"Don't move," one alien ordered.

Kate, Jane and Ms. Javies all looked at one another wondering what the hell was going on. The aliens' eyes glittered as they focused on the group of three. Kate gasped as she looked down at her body starting to glow a light green.

"What the…?" Ms. Javies went.

The group slowly started to shrink in size, one after the other.

"What happened?" Kate asked.

"You are now less than an eighth of your size," one alien said.

Kate looked up into the sky, as the huge leaves started

to fall off the trees, casting a huge black shadow over them.

"Move," the alien said.

The aliens made sure the girls and Ms. Javies entered a cave. Kate looked into the cave. She couldn't see anything as it was too dark. The three of them slowly entered into the cave, when a light came into view ahead.

"What's that?" Jane asked.

The aliens continued walking with the girls as the Armazoid ship came into view. Kate stopped and looked at the huge ship parked right underneath Central Park.

"Look at the size of it!" Ms. Javies gasped.

"I know," one alien said. "It's a big one, isn't it?"

The group progressed down the short ramp towards the bridge leading over to the ship. Two alien guards turned off the electric laser beams as Kate and Jane, followed by Ms. Javies, slowly walked across to it. The two aliens walked up to a small box on the side of the large elevator that would take them down into the ship.

"Put this on," an alien ordered.

The two girls and Ms. Javies jumped as the aliens forced the helmet and masks on them.

"What's this?" Kate asked.

"So you won't be overcome by carbon monoxide, dear," the alien said.

The two girls felt the heavy helmet stick to their heads and Ms. Javies didn't know what to say or think as they walked to the huge elevator. The aliens pushed the tiny buttons down on the control box. Kate jumped as the huge lift went on. The screeching of the brakes echoed around them as the huge lift slowly started to descend down into the depth of the huge ship. Kate stood trembling, not knowing what she was about to experience.

The lift slowed down and stopped on arriving at the lower level. The huge shutters slowly started to open. Kate watched as the light from the other side of the shutter entered the lift. The lights gleamed as the waiting aliens looked at them. Kate, Jane and Ms. Javies walked off the elevator, looking at the parked alien transport vehicles.

"What's it like up there?" one alien asked.

"Dead," another alien replied. "I think we have slaughtered half of these people."

"Still don't know why we didn't roll the tanks out," the first alien said.

"Hmmm," the other alien said. "Why were they sent up there, anyway?"

"It was to disable half the land so we could send that signal back home without being attacked."

Kate, Jane and Ms. Javies got into the vehicle and sat down on the shiny grey seats. Kate tried to keep her emotions to herself as the alien got into the driver's seat and started up the engine. The vehicle stared to drift along the shiny floor.

"Where are you taking us?" Kate asked.

The alien driver didn't answer as they continued along through the ship. After a little while Kate felt the vehicle slowly come to a stop. She looked out of the shiny clean window into the ship. The alien got out of his seat and headed towards the door. He swung it open, pulling out his sidearm and looking at the two girls and Ms. Javies. "Move," he ordered.

Kate quickly stepped down onto the shiny ground followed by Jane and Ms. Javies and they walked along a narrow aisle. The small group headed towards a set of shiny doors. Jane turned around and looked up at the heavy machine weapon post as an alien stood behind it, ready to open fire on any one or thing that would try to escape. Kate looked around as they walked into the holding block. She looked at all the small cells with frightened people in them. 'Their masks are off so it must be ok to breathe inside,' she thought. "What are you doing to these people?" she asked.

"Just move," the alien demanded.

Kate followed Jane and Ms. Javies across the silver floor towards their holding cell. The shiny blue door hissed open. Kate, Jane and Ms. Javies slowly walked in. They sat down as the door was sealed shut. The machine on the roof extracted all the carbon monoxide, allowing the girls to take off their masks. Kate threw her mask onto the floor as the alien walked away from the cell.

"We are so screwed," Jane went. She put her head into her arms as she leaned down, trying not to vomit.

"Calm down," Kate went. "We'll get out of here."

Ms. Javies still continued to stay quiet. Kate slowly got up and walked over to the cell door. She looked out at the guarding aliens as they walked around. She slowly turned her head and looked into the other cells and at the people trembling with fear in them.

"We're screwed," she said quietly.

18

Mr. Knightsbridge watched as the bus pulled out of Queensboro Bridge. He looked out of the window at the military personnel as they stood guarding the entrance to the Queens command centre with Manhattan in the background. He looked at Amelia as the bus pulled into the quiet street by the river. He looked out of the window onto the skyline of the city and he looked out of the back window for Ms. Javies' bus to appear. Followed by Amelia, he slowly got up and walked down the narrow aisle of the bus. He stepped down onto the road and looked out over the river at two tanks pointing their turrets over the city skyline.

"You ok?" Amelia whispered.

Mr. Knightsbridge let his breath out. "Yeah, I'm fine. Let's just get the rest of us here and get the hell out of here." He sat down on the wooden bench and looked out over the city skyline.

A young soldier holding a rifle stepped up to the bus. "Hey," he said "Is there a Mr. Knightsbridge here?"

"He's over there," a student said.

The soldier ran over to the couple as they sat by the river and watched him. The soldier said something to Mr. Knightsbridge who bent over and felt his stomach turning as, helped by the soldier, he and Amelia slowly walked back to the bus. He climbed into the bus with Amelia and the driver started up the engines ready to drive to the station. The doors shut as the driver pulled out of the waiting bay. He looked out of the window as he sped along the roads. Terrified people were running out of their houses, packing their vehicles, ready to leave for a long time. The bus turned the corner. The train station came into view. A long line of trains was lined up, ready to take the people out and away. Mr. Knightsbridge slowly got up and walked down the aisle of the long new bus. "Ok people," he quietly said. "Let's go home."

The people slowly got up one after the other. The bus was quiet as they walked down the stairs onto the tarmac and queued up, ready to board the huge train. Mr. Knightsbridge fretted about what to say to his pupils as they got onto the train.

The doors sealed closed as the whole train was crammed with people. The driver started up the engines, ready to roll out of the station to the next evacuation zone. Outside, cars sped along the highway in one direction- out of the city- as the military tanks continued to roll in the other direction, prepared for a fight. The train rolled along the tracks heading away from New York City. The long skyline slowly disappeared from sight as Mr. Knightsbridge lay back in his seat and closed his eyes.

19

Bradley looked out of the window of the NYPD SWAT van as it pulled up into Chinatown. The area was completely deserted. There were no aliens or people walking around. A noodle stand was still stocked with food.

"What are we doing here?" Colin asked.

"Yeah, what are we doing here?" Eric asked.

Bradley didn't answer as he was too busy looking around. He had no weapons to defend himself with, only the flick out baton. He reached in and pulled it out of his pocket as the breeze blew through his hair. He flicked it open as he looked at the streets and the warehouses behind the buildings and cafes around the city.

"This way," Cheng said.

Bradley followed, expecting some aliens to jump out of no where. Kevin looked at the set expression on Bradley's face. He knew that he was thinking of Kate and Jane but not caring about Ms. Javies. The group stopped. They turned up a small side alley. Bradley tried to block the strong smell of burning Chinese food from his nose but it continued to linger. The group walked up the alleyway, Rivers of blood told the story of how people had tried to escape.

"In here," Cheng said.

The group walked through an open gate. Bradley waited for the group to go through. He watched as Kevin ran through and caught up with the group. Bradley closed the

gate and closed his eyes as the long squeak from the rusty
hinges and bolts screamed out at him. Looking down at it,
he pulled the bolt across. Kevin turned around as the back
metal door opened and Cheng banged onto it. Kevin ran
through the seating area trying not to tread on the empty
cans left by the workers of the huge building.

"Brad," Kevin whispered.

Bradley continued looking down at the bolt.

"Brad," Kevin said again.

"Who...? What...? Where...?" Bradley asked, shaking
his head.

"You ok?" Kevin asked.

Bradley released his breath. "Yeah, I'm ok," he said in a
dull voice. He got up and walked through the seating area
with Kevin. They approached the dirty metal back door.
Bradley slowly pushed it closed as Cheng held on to his
AK47 assault rifle. Kevin watched as he slowly pushed the
door closed, locking it into place. The sounds from the
outside slowly disappeared as they turned around and
headed into the building. Bradley looked into the empty
offices of the building as they continued heading along the
dark corridors. Windows were boarded up with wood and
only tiny bits of light got through them, lighting the area
around. The group reached the top of the stairs. Cheng
looked ahead to see Marco standing in the middle of his
office, peeping through a tiny hole in the wood used to
board up his office window. He was looking out onto the
city, and at the aliens in the distance walking around the
once great city.

"Marco," Cheng said.

Marco slowly turned around. Bradley looked at the aged
man.

"Good to see you again," Marco said. "Thought I'd lost
you man."

"We're all fine," Cheng said. "This is Bradley, Kevin,

Max and Eric."

"Hello," Eric said.

Marco looked at the young group. "Where did you find these people?" he asked.

"We were driving along the main street looking around for people, when a call came over the radio about being at the Ravensgate shopping center. So we headed there and found them," Cheng replied.

"Why were you there?" Marco asked.

Bradley took a deep breath. "Our friends have been kidnapped by them things," Bradley said.

"What?" Marco went.

"Yes, they have," Bradley said again. "And we want them back."

"How do we get them back?" Eric asked.

Bradley turned around. "We find one of those things, drag him in here, and kick the shit out of him until he spills," said Bradley, his voice raised.

"Don't be stupid," Colin said.

"Didn't one of them mumble something about going back to their ship?" Kevin asked.

Bradley stopped. "Yes," he said. "Yes, they did."

Kevin looked at Bradley.

"We grab one of them things, find out where their ship is and in we go," Bradley yelled.

"Hang on, hang on," Marco said. "We don't know what these things are capable of or even if we have the fire power to take them on."

"We will," Bradley said. "We have survived all day"

"I'm up for it," Kevin said.

"Me, too," Max went.

"And me," Eric jumped in.

"Ok, Brad, if that's what you want. I've always wanted another kick at the enemy," Marco said.

"What?" Eric asked, looking at him.

Marco stood up straight. "General Marco Bentley," he snapped. "I was in Vietnam once."

"Great," Bradley said. "Just what we need."

"Follow me," Marco ordered.

Bradley looked at Marco. He could see he was revving up for the attack on the Armazoids. He followed him through the corridors to two wooden doors. Marco pushed them open and walked to a huge balcony looking down into the warehouse. Bradley walked down the metal steps to the warehouse. He looked at all the stacked up crates and boxes.

"What do you do here?" Eric asked.

"Business," Marco said.

"What sort of business?" he asked.

"Just some very good business," Marco replied. "And if we survive this I think I am going to be doing a lot more business."

Bradley looked around at all the frightened men as they stood gently puffing on their cigarettes. There were black marks on their feet where they had stamped tobacco into the ground umpteen times earlier.

Marco looked at the different men of various ages. "Listen up," Marco yelled. "We have a problem."

Bradley looked at the two young black men who stepped forward. "This is Bradley," Marco said.

The young black men walked over to Bradley. "How are you?" one went. "The name's Carl, but call me CJ."

Bradley shook CJ's hand.

"This is AJ," CJ said. "Best friend."

AJ stood quietly. He kept a steady eye over his shoulder at his handgun on the ground.

"Ok," Marco said. "Bradley here has had two of his friends kidnapped and he wants them back."

The group looked at Marco without reacting.

"What?" Bradley gasped. "I thought you lot have been desperate for a kick at this lot."

"No, he has," CJ said.

"Of course," Marco joked. "Reminds me of 'Nam."

"What friends?" CJ asked.

"Two girls," Bradley said. "Plus a teacher. We were being evacuated by bus when the vehicle came under attack."

"Jesus," CJ said.

"Yes," Bradley said. "Who is with me?"

The warehouse went quiet.

"Well, we can't sit around here waiting to die," a Chinese man said. "I'm in."

"Thanks," Bradley said. "Anyone else?"

The large group of men slowly walked forward. Bradley admired the courage of all the men as they stood ready for orders.

"Ok," Bradley said. "In a few minutes I'm going out with a few men to capture one of these things. I'm bringing him back and we are going to kick the shit out of him until he tells us the whereabouts of their ship."

"I like that," AJ said. "Can I come? CH lost his girl and his ma when these things invaded."

"Ok," he said. No weapons."

Bradley flicked out his baton. "Oh, I'm going to enjoy this," he said.

Bradley walked with CJ and AJ through the warehouse towards the front exit. He pushed the wooden door open and looked at the armed guard as he stood by the door peeking through the wooden boards looking for any aliens that may attack. Bradley slowly pushed the front door open. He walked with CJ and AJ into the car park. He watched all the empty burger and coke cans rolling around on the ground.

"Come on," Bradley whispered.

CJ and AJ followed Bradley along the empty road, keeping their eyes peeled.

"Where the hell are they?" Bradley said "Ten minutes ago there were hundreds of them."

He turned out of the Chinatown road and looked up the narrow sidewalk to see two aliens slowly walking up it, the weapons in their side pouches ready to be used.

"Come on," he went.

Bradley crept up the sidewalk with the two men, keeping a constant look out over his back in case there were any behind. He stopped as the alien on the right slowly turned his head to the left. He swung around and looked at Bradley as he held his baton up ready to swing it at one of them. CJ and AJ close behind with their silenced weapons, ready to shoot. Bradley watched as the alien yelled a bit and the other snarled but he swung his baton around, slamming it into the alien on the left. "Take him out," Bradley said.

CJ walked up to the alien as he lay on the ground. He slowly raised his handgun and pulled the trigger. The bullet slammed into the alien's head. Bradley looked up as the other alien started running away from them. "Oh, no, you don't," he said.

He ran along the sidewalk chasing after the alien. He caught up with him and rugby tackled him to the ground. The alien put up a fight. "Get up you little shite," Bradley yelled at him. He picked the alien up with one hand.

"Don't hurt me," the alien said, trembling.

"Shut up," Bradley said.

AJ and CJ helped Bradley drag the alien through the streets, back towards the entrance of the warehouse. It struggled to get away.

"Get off me," it yelled.

Bradley and the two men dragged it through the car park, kicking the tiny pieces of rubbish away. As Bradley pushed the alien through, Marco walked up to the door and slowly opened it, handgun at the ready. He slowly closed the door after making sure no other aliens were watching. He closed the door and sealed the metal bar across.

"Stay here," he ordered the guard. "First sign of any movement, get me."

"Yes, boss," the man replied, nodding as he looked out of the window onto the warehouse car park. Bradley watched as Marco walked in. He looked at the alien as he sat down on the wooden chair set out by the men, ready for the interrogation.

"Look at this piece of shit," he went.

"Please don't hurt me," the alien cried.

"Ok, we won't hurt you," Bradley said, "if you tell us everything we want to know."

"Ok, ok," the alien said. "My name's Arkalon."

"Well, that's a start," Bradley said. "The fist question is- why are you here?"

Arkalon took a short breath. "Ok," he went. "We were assigned to investigate a planet, not known to you. We believe they are building weapons of mass destruction, capable of blowing this planet out of its orbit round the sun"

"Ok," Bradley said. "So why are you here?"

"A few months ago, one of our ships was sent to scout the planet. It managed to get some intel, but it didn't return to our ship," Arkalon said. "This craft that was sent to gather information was lost and we managed to trace a signal from it to this planet here."

"So why all the bangs and killings?" Eric asked.

"We don't negotiate with our enemies," Arkalon said.

"Us enemies?" Eric yelled. "You fucking…"

"Eric, take a walk," Bradley demanded.

Eric slowly walked off. "Enemies!" he grumbled.

"So that is why we are here" Arkalon said. "We're looking for our ship."

"Have your people communicated with ours?" Bradley asked.

"I don't know about that," he replied, "but you will have a problem."

"Surprise me," Bradley went.

"When we landed, our antenna dish was damaged. Before long many more of our people will be here," Arkalon said.

"Jesus," Kevin said.

"So that means the complete earth could be invaded?" Max asked.

"Yes," Arkalon said.

Then the direction of the conversation changed abruptly. "Two of your people kidnapped three people of ours. Where are they?" Kevin asked.

"In the holding cells back at our ship," Arkalon replied.

"That's where we go," Bradley said.

"How?" Arkalon asked.

Bradley took a shallow breath. "With you. We're getting them back, and every single one of these men is behind me," Bradley said.

"Oh," Arkalon went. "What about me? They will kill me."

"That's your problem," Bradley said.

Arkalon didn't answer as Bradley turned around and looked at Marco. "Marco," he said, "Guns- and I mean lots of them."

"Follow me, boy," Marco said.

He led Bradley through the warehouse. Bradley stared up at all the crates one on top of the other. Marco picked up an old black crowbar. He ripped off the wooden lid of a box and looked at the M16 machine guns piled up in the crate. He stared at the small launcher below it.

"JESUS CHRIST!" Bradley gasped. "My favorite gun!"

"Well," Marco said, "help yourself."

Kevin walked over and looked into some other crates as Marco ripped them open. "MP 5," he said. "My favorite gun!"

"Yep," Marco said. "Sixteen hundred a piece; three thousand a piece soon."

Kevin reached in and pulled a weapon out of the case.

"Take this," Marco said, handing Bradley a utility vest with pouches for the extra magazines. Bradley started loading them as the rest of the group armed up, readying for the assault on the ship.

"We need a plan of their ship," Kevin said. "Do you think…?"

"He will," Bradley said. "Trust me on that."

"When haven't I trusted you?" Kevin joked.

"Ha," Bradley laughed. He walked away, holding onto the M16 as he loaded the last few grenades into the pouches and tightened up the straps. He felt the strong material biting against his skin. Max walked up to Eric as he pulled the pump action shot gun out of the crate. He held onto the shells, loading them into the tiny pouch.

"You be careful with that, Eric," Max said. "I know what you're like."

"I will," Eric replied. "But what do you mean?"

"Remember that day at the shooting range? You put the shot gun shells in back to front."

"Oh, I remember," Eric said. "What a laugh that day was!"

"It wasn't," Max joked. "I think Barry nearly had a triple heart bypass."

"A triple what?" Eric asked

Bradley looked over. "Max, don't," he said.

He sat down in front of Arkalon. "We need a plan of your ship," he said.

Arkalon reached into his pocket and pulled out a tiny object that appeared to be a disk. He handed it to Bradley.

"What's this?" Bradley asked.

"It's a map of our ship," he replied. "If you push that small button it will show you the whole ship."

Bradley put the small disk down on the table. He watched as the hologram of the ship popped up.

"Jesus, look at the size of it!" Marco went.

Bradley didn't answer. He and Marco sat down at the table as the rest of the group continued to arm up.

Max looked over his shoulder as Marco and Bradley planned the attack on the ship. He looked at the green holographic image of the ship. He wondered if he was going home that night. He shook his head knowing he had to stick by Bradley. He turned to Bradley.

"You ok?" he asked.

"Fine," Bradley replied, taking a deep breath. "Ok," he said. "Listen up carefully."

The group looked at Marco and Bradley.

"This is the Android, hemorrhoid or whatever it is called. It is currently parked underneath Central Park. Have no idea how it got down there but our friend here is willing to take us to it. The ship has a main elevator here. This is where we will be entering. We shall remain on the second floor as a few of Marco's sharp shooters take out the awaiting aliens," Bradley said, wiping his forehead. "When the first lot has been taken out we shall move on and take out the rest. Marco will stand by the elevator. Behind these crates he will be out of sight." He paused and took a deep breath.

"Why is Marco staying there?" a voice went.

"Because when we get the girls out we may need to get the elevator back quickly so he can keep an eye on it," Bradley replied. "There are a few parked vehicles at the elevator entrance. My friend here is going to drive. He will take us along this corridor to this part of the ship."

"What's that?" CJ asked.

"That is just behind the cell block."

Kevin stared onto the hologram as Bradley pointed at the holding cells.

"But that's away from the cell entrance/" Kevin said.

"It's our only option. The main entrance is heavily guarded/" Bradley replied. "We enter through a small ventilation shaft here as Max and a few others stay in the vehicle keeping an eye. This will take us right above the cells."

Bradley stopped for a second breath. "And now the assault/" he said. "We remove the shaft entrance. When no one is looking we drop this flash grenade into the block and slide down the copper wire we are taking with us."

Kevin stepped forward. He took a closer look at the ship.

"When we enter the cell block, I and who ever is with me will take out any guards/" Bradley said. "Eric, Kevin, you two pull back here taking out any aliens that burst in, while I and somebody else busts the girls out."

"What about Ms. Javies?" Colin asked.

"We'll worry about her when we get to her" Bradley replied. "Oh yeah. Colin, can you use a gun?"

"No" Colin said.

"Good boy" Bradley replied. "Max, give Colin a one to one on firearms lesson please."

Bradley looked at the men lined up as Max took Colin aside. "Any questions before I go on?" he asked.

The men stood silent. "Ok" he said. "Once we are out, we rendezvous back at the vehicle here with Max, and then we head back to the elevator. Then you lot get the hell out of there."

"What about the ship?" Max asked. "And where after that?"

"We get back to the bus. We drive as fast as we can to wherever they are evacuating and we get out of this city, because to be honest I don't think they are going to continue the evacuation."

"Why?" Kevin asked.

"Look at the state of that evac zone. They got through them soldiers. How the hell are they going to evacuate the rest of that police station and the rest of the people? There are hundreds there," Bradley said. "I personally think there will be a mushroom cloud soon."

"True," Max said. "That most probably will be true."

"Shall we move?" Bradley said.

"Right. Mount up," Marco yelled. "Where's my girl?"

Bradley turned around as Marco walked away from the group. "What girl?" Eric asked,

"Have no idea," Bradley went.

"Is he married?" Eric asked.

"Him married?" CJ said. "Was married."

"Yep," Marco yelled. "Married for ten damn years. Worst time of my life."

"What about Vietnam?" CJ asked.

"That was the second worst time of my life."

Marco walked into the back office moving his desk out of the way. He felt his hand tremble as his weapon dangled by his side. The small grenades were in the utility belt. Bradley watched as he walked out of his office holding a heavy machine gun. The long line of golden bullets dangled by his side when he had locked them into place.

"What the...?" Bradley went.

"Right. Let's see who goes for me with my bitch," Marco went. "Oh yeah, I've just thought of something." He walked over to a set of un-opened crates.

Bradley walked up behind him. "What're these?" he asked.

Marco pulled out what appeared to be a parachute.

"A parachute?" Bradley queried.

"Not just a parachute," Marco replied. "Look."

Bradley looked at it.

"A parachute, floating devices, and a pocket for the radio," Marco said, "Also an extra strap in case you have to mount up with someone."

Max watched as one of the Chinese men pulled out a box of radios.

"I'm line one," Marco said.

"I'm line one too," Bradley said. "We can stay in contact. Use the ear pieces as well."

Bradley looked at the small kit. "Wait. What's this?" he asked.

"Binoculars," Marco said strapping it to his body. "Sold about hundred of these babies so far."

"Who to?" Bradley asked.

"Just some people I know."

Bradley took up his radio as the alien called out to him. "Remember what I said about the carbon monoxide" Arkalon said.

"Yes," Bradley said.

"What's that?" Marco went. "What did shit face say?"

"They breathe out carbon monoxide. It will kill us." Bradley said, "if we have too much."

"Masks," Marco yelled. "And all of you take five extra each in your bags, in case."

Bradley looked at the gas mask as he tuned the radio up. "Testing, one two three," he said over it.

The men nodded as they tested theirs one after the other.

"I can't hear anyone," Eric went.

Marco slowly walked over to Eric. He looked down onto the radio at the on button. He turned the small knob on.

"Now try," he went.

"Oh yeah," Eric went.

"You sure about him?" Marco asked Bradley.

"Yeah, he's alright," Bradley replied. He laughed gently as he turned, thinking it may be a way to settle his nerves. Bradley looked over his shoulder to see CJ walk over again.

"I'm with you all the way," CJ said. "I was due to propose to my girl when we would be on holiday in the Bahamas next week. All they were doing today was some shopping for it. I want your girls back as well. I'm all the way with you."

"Thanks," Bradley went.

"Right. There's a bus outside. We can take that," Marco went. "Been there for ages. I think the driver did a runner."

One of the Chinese walked out to get it. Bradley held his M16 as he prepared to leave the warehouse and venture out into the city. He walked up to the back exit and looked out of the boarded up windows to see the bus reversing. "Come on," he went.

He led the group over to the bus still keeping his eyes peeled for anyone or anything. The old doors hissed open. Bradley walked on down to the back of the bus where he usually sat, and tried to put the invasion out of his head as he took the time to get his energy back into his system. The rest of the group got onto the bus. He had never felt this tired before, even after a day of working out. Now he had to go to an alien ship, which had been shrunk in size, underneath Central Park. 'What a day!' he thought.

Kevin walked down to Bradley at the back of the bus. "Hey," he went.

Bradley nodded, trying not to say anything, still trying to preserve his remaining energy. Kevin looked down the bus as Marco held onto his heavy machine gun, his shiny golden bullets wrapped around his body.

"Ok boys," he yelled. "Ready for a bit of action?"

"Oh yes, we are," a voice went.

"Right. Away driver," Marco went.

The driver started up the engine. He slowly pulled

towards the exit. He looked both ways along the street. - No one or thing in sight. He hauled the wheel to the right, heading towards the outer road which led towards the center of the city. The main police station only being about four miles away, he didn't want to go anywhere near it unless they got tied up in something. The roads continued to stay quiet. There was not a police or military vehicle in sight. They were probably at the main police station trying to get out of the city. Bradley lay back in his seat; hand on his head as his energy started to build up again. Something caught his eye as they passed a small side road. "Stop," he yelled.

The driver put the brakes on. Bradley jumped up and ran down the aisle, followed by Kevin.

"What's up?" Kevin asked.

Bradley steeped off the bus and ran along as Marco got up, grasping his heavy machine, ready to use it at the first sign of any conflict. Bradley turned the corner thinking what he has just seen could not be true. He stopped and looked ahead as Kevin came up behind him. They both stepped forward and stared at a New York News helicopter smashed into the ground but still standing on its legs, blades dangling down and hisses of smoke popping out from the engine. Bradley slowly walked up to it, looking into the smashed cockpit door window. All the electrical gauges fizzled where they had slammed into the ground.

"Anyone there?" Kevin asked.

"No," Bradley replied. He turned around slowly walking through the streets and back towards the bus.

"Wait," a female voice came from the wreckage.

Bradley turned around to see a young lady news reporter followed by her young, black camera man.

"Hi," she went. "Sorry to startle you."

"Hi," Kevin said, smiling at her.

"Oh, thank god there are people still alive," she said. "I

thought everyone was dead in this part of the island."

"Quickly," Bradley said. "Move before the things hear us."

Kevin helped the cameraman back towards the bus, while Bradley stopped to look at the crashed military jeep. He pulled the metal door open and looked at the back seat. "Oh, nice," he said.

Kevin walked up to him. Bradley pulled out a couple of small unused rocket launchers.

"We'll take these," he said. "May come in handy." He handed the three launchers to Kevin.

"Give them to a few on the bus," Bradley said.

"Come on," Kevin said. "Let's get the hell out of here."

The young reporter got onto the bus. The group of men looked at the young girl as she stood in her light pink suit and skirt. "Nice legs," a voice went.

Bradley helped the reporter along the bus to the back seats. She sat down onto the old tatty material and looked at Bradley. "So where you people been?" she asked.

"Around," Bradley replied.

"I see you are all armed and ready for a fight," she said. "Where are you going? To the evacuation zone?"

"No," Bradley said.

Laura was shocked. "No?" she gasped.

"We are on our way to Central Park with him," Bradley said.

"Emm, why?" she asked.

"Two of our friends were taken from us a short while ago and we want them back," Bradley said in a stern voice. "So your friend had better get his camera ready because you people are going to get the story of a life time."

"Ok," Laura quietly said. "If we must."

20

The driver swung the bus around the corner. He looked at the outer edge of Central Park. Not a living soul was in sight. Bradley looked at Kevin with a smirk on his face. "Here we go," he said in a quiet voice. He got out of his seat as the bus pulled up into a parking space and walked alongside the bus as Marco got up, still clinging on to his heavy machine gun. He stepped down onto the road. The ground below him felt different. No one was around; no one bumped into one you as they rushed to their destinations. Bradley watched as the group stepped out of the bus yet keeping by it, trying to stay out of sight in case any aliens came after them. He turned and looked over at the café he had been in only a few hours earlier. He stared at all the tables and chairs over turned from when people had fled when the aliens first started to appear out of the park. Kevin looked over at Bradley who slowly started walking over to the café, and pulling out his silenced handgun, walked into the café. He pushed the small wooden door open, trying not to slip on the split coffee beans on the ground. The small beans crunched under his feet and he felt his hands burning as he clung to the weapon. He caught a glimpse of a small shadow in the rear room. He pulled out his handgun and put the silencer onto it in case any more of the aliens were nearby. He slowly crept towards the shadow, ready to pull the trigger if an alien was lying in wait to attack him. He took a deep breath as the door slowly closed with the breeze. He lifted his leg up and kicking it open, charged in.

"Don't shoot," a voice yelled.

Bradley looked through the scope at Demmio, the waiter who had served him earlier that morning.

"You," Bradley said. He slipped his handgun back into his side pouch.

Demmio slowly got up and looked at Bradley. "Hey, good to see you again" he went.

"Yeah," Bradley said. "What happened? Why aren't you at the police station?"

Demmio slowly got up and brushed the dirt off his old white apron. "It all happened so fast," he said. "One minute I was serving somebody a coffee and the next these things came out of the park. It was horrible."

Bradley walked back through the café with Demmio. He crunched over the split coffee beans. "This the first time you been out since then?" Bradley asked.

"Yes," Demmio said. He felt the evening sun burn down on his face. He winced as the smell of burning lingered in his nose.

"You'll get used to that," Bradley said.

Bradley and Demmio walked over to Marco.

"Hey" Marco said. "Who's this?"

Bradley turned and looked at Demmio. "This is Demmio," he said.

"Hi, Demmio. You tagging along with us?" Marco asked.

"Yeah. Come on, let's get out of here to that evacuation zone," Demmio urged.

"We're not going to the evac zone," Marco said.

"What?" Demmio asked in a shocked voice.

"Not you either," Marco said.

Bradley took a deep breath, and looked over his shoulder as a small crisp packet blew over his head with the breeze. "A short while ago we were being evacuated by bus from the central police station," Bradley said.

"Yes?" Demmio said.

"But as we were going along the road some of these aliens attacked our bus, kidnapping a few of our friends including Ms. Javies," Bradley said.

"Ms. Javies?" Demmio repeated in a shocked voice.

"Yes, she was taken as well," Kevin interrupted.

"Ok, what are you doing?" Demmio asked.

Marco walked over to him. "We are going in," he said.

"How?" Demmio asked.

"With the help of our friend here," Bradley said indicating the alien Marco was holding on to.

"Who? Him?" Demmio went.

"Yes, him," Bradley said. "He has co-operated so far."

"Good," Demmio said. "Let's get the hell in there." He stormed over to the bus and boarded it, looking down at the crate of weapons. He picked up the MP5 and utility vest, loading it with magazines. He looked up at the sky as the evening started to show. Slowly stepping down of the bus, he looked at the group. "Ready when you are," he said.

Bradley smiled as Marco slowly walked towards the entrance to Central Park. Marco led the way as he held onto his heavy machine gun, scanning the area around him.

"Right. Where is this ship?" he asked.

"Em, it's over here," Arkalon said.

Bradley followed Marco through the empty park. No animals were swimming on the lake or kids chucking stones into the pond. Arkalon walked up the tiny, invisible path towards a small cave entrance in the muddy ground.

"It's in there," he said.

Bradley grabbed the alien forcing his head against the ground.

"Hang on, hang on," Arkalon shrieked.

"Get up," Bradley rasped.

Arkalon got up.

"Where is your ship?" Bradley asked.

"It's in there but I will need everyone to stand here by me," Arkalon said.

"Ok," Bradley went, letting go of Arkalon. The group of men walked up to the alien. Bradley looked down at Arkalon as his eyes gleamed. He felt confused, as he was about to enter a world where no human being had ever known to have been before. The alien's eyes stopped glittering. Bradley's heart started to pound as his body started to glow a light green.

"Oh my god!" Laura went. "Get the cam ready."

The whole group went a light green, Bradley looked up into the sky as the tree seemed to be getting taller and the ground got closer. He shook his head as the green glow disappeared from the group.

"What happened?" Eric said.

"We is shrunk," Kevin said.

"How did you do that?" Bradley asked the alien.

"We just can," he said.

Laura looked at Ben, her cameraman. "Camera," she went

and slowly rolled the microphone up to her mouth. "This is Laura Welshman reporting from Central Park. You are not going to believe what we have to say to you viewers," she said.

Bradley turned around and looked at Laura as she spoke into the camera. He pulled out his handgun from his pocket and looked at the entrance to the cave. "Come on," he went.

Marco followed Bradley towards the huge entrance. He stared upwards, not seeing the top of it. "This must be some ship" he said.

Bradley turned on the handgun flashlight. He looked down on the ground, looking for any large sized rats or spiders which they would have to deal with. The group continued descending down into the cave. When the ledge was seen,

he said to Marco, "Look."

The group slowed and, knelt down. Bradley pulled out the small pair of binoculars. He zoomed in and looked ahead. He strained his eyes to see the top of the huge ship. But he couldn't see the other side. "Hmm," he went.

Marco looked as well. "There are a few guarding it," he went.

"I remember something like this when I was in 'Nam," Aussie said. "I was patrolling when we came across a Vietcong camp. There was loads of the bastards," he went.

"We're not in 'Nam now," Marco said, "but I remember."

"They're mine," Aussie went.

"Aussie, wait," Bradley cautioned. "If they know we are here it would compromise us."

Bradley looked again to see a few aliens guarding a bridge leading over to the ship.

"There's a few," Marco said. "We can take them."

He slowly stood up and turned round looking at the two men with the silenced M16s. "You and you. Take 'em out," he ordered.

The two Chinese men crept forward wielding their weapons. They knelt down as Bradley turned the light of his weapon on. He listened to the bullets firing through the air, taking down the aliens.

"Got 'em," he went.

Trying not to slip on the dry ground, Bradley moved forward down towards the ship and approached the bridge. He stopped when he noticed a set of red beams zooming across and above it. "What's that?" he asked.

"That's electric," Arkalon replied. "If you go through them the alarm will go off inside the ship."

"Turn it off, then," Bradley demanded.

"I can't," Arkalon said.

"Why not?" Kevin asked.

"The control box is on the other side," Arkalon said pointing over at it.

"Oh," Kevin went.

"What do we do?" a voice from the group said.

Bradley looked over to the other side of the ship at the metal control box. He turned around and looked up at the rock bulging out behind him. "Marco," Bradley said.

"Yeah, boy?" Marco went.

"Where's that rope?" Bradley asked.

"Bradley, no," Kevin said.

"We've got to," he replied. "This planet depends on us."

He took the rope out the man's hand and tied a tiny knot in it, making it into a snare. He took a deep breath and walked up to the edge of the ship. He looked down into the deep dark edge between the ship and cliff.

Marco slowly walked up behind him. "Deep," he went.

"Damn, Marco," Bradley gasped. "I do wish you wouldn't do that."

"Keep your eyes open boy," he said. "Can't always be here to protect you."

Bradley stepped back. He started swinging the rope in the air. He chucked it through the air as Marco watched him. The noose fell into the depth. Bradley clung to it as he started winding it up again. "Shit!" he gasped.

He finished pulling it up as he looked over his shoulder towards the cave entrance. There was nothing in sight.

"And we try again," he said.

Bradley hauled the rope again over the edge towards the ship. The noose went over to the small power box. "Got it," he gasped. He pulled the rope tight and slowly walked back over to a rock jutting out of the ground. He wrapped it around the rock, tightening it into a tight knot, and then looked around the cave. The rope was tight. Bradley placed his M16 on the ground. He jumped up, and holding on to it, slowly lifted his legs up around the rope, looking down into the deep crater where the ship had landed. Bradley felt his arm muscles burning as they held his tall, thin body up on the rope.

"Won't be long," he said.

His hands burned as he approached the other side. Still watching the tiny grains of dirt falling down into the depth, Bradley released his legs landing on the deck of the ship. He stared down at the power box. He pushed the small, red button releasing the electric beams. "Got it," he went.

The red beams disappeared. Kevin picked up Bradley's M16 and ran across the bridge. He handed it over to him.

"Thank you," Bradley said as he put the M16 over his back. Marco ran over to the large elevator. He looked down at the digital screen as it showed the lower deck about a third of a mile down as Bradley came over. "Ok," he went. "Listen up."

The group looked at Bradley.

"Does anyone want to go and take a nervous piss or shit over the side?" he asked.

The men all shook their heads.

"Ok, you know what to do group alpha. Head along Corridor A with me. The rest stay with Marco," Bradley said.

"Gas masks," Marco ordered.

Bradley slipped the small, mask over his face and switched on the radio. "Testing," he said.

The group all heard Bradley's voice.

"For god's sake do not take them off," Bradley insisted. "A few whiffs of carbon monoxide and you're history."

"What's monoxide?" Eric asked.

"Don't take your mask of at all," Bradley said to Eric.

The men shook their heads trying to get used to the

tight feeling over their faces. Bradley turned around and looked at the digital command box. He pushed the buttons in one after the other. The brakes clunked off one after the other. "Here we go," he whispered.

He felt a butterfly in his stomach as they slowly started to descend into the depth of the ship. The rollers slowly took the huge plate down into the ship. Kevin looked at Bradley as he stood holding on to his M16, magazines filled in each and every pocket of the utility vest. Bradley looked up as the top of the elevator shaft closed and sealed shut. "That's it," he went.

Laura looked into the camera. "You are not going to believe what we are currently doing," she said into the microphone. "We are slowly descending into the alien spacecraft."

The elevator continued dropping down into the depth of the ship. The huge plate started to slow down as it approached the shutter.

"Ready," Marco went.

Bradley swiped the silenced handgun from his side pouch. He walked over to Kevin as he held onto the MP5 machine gun. The shutter slowly started to roll up. Bradley knelt down as the inside of the ship came into view. The aliens swung around as they saw the group of armed people ready to raid the ship. Bradley looked through his handgun scope. He pulled the trigger and took the aliens down, one after the other before they even had a chance to fire back. Marco kept back. He grasped his heavy machine gun, desperate to open fire on the aliens.

"Yeah," Aussie yelled.

"Get them. Move," Bradley demanded. "And Aussie, be quiet." He looked around and stared down the long corridors as the lights shone down on them. There was an eerie silence around Bradley. He kept looking over his shoulder and down the long corridors as they passed in front of the large elevator.

"You guys ready?" Bradley asked, holding his silenced handgun.

Kevin, Max and Eric walked forward followed by Demmio, AJ and CJ and the rest of the group. Bradley looked over at the parked alien vehicle as Marco walked up to Bradley.

"Right, let's do this," Bradley said. "You lot stay out of sight over there, behind them crates."

"Got it, Brad," Marco said.

Marco turned around, walking over to the blue set of containers all stacked up one onto another. Bradley walked over to the long alien vehicle. He admired the shiny tracks as Arkalon, still trembling with fear, knowing what would happen to him if he got caught, stepped into the driver's seat. He turned on the engine as Bradley looked out of the window, and stared at the group as they hid behind the crates. The alien pushed the small accelerator down. He looked into the mirror as Bradley slowly walked up behind him, hiding behind his seat.

"Don't forget, one false move and I'll blow your shitting brains out," Bradley said, clenching his fist.

Arkalon pulled away from the elevator. Eric lay on the ground as Kevin crept down the aisle towards Bradley. "You ok?" he asked.

The light from the outside seemed to distract Bradley. "Yeah," he went.

"You ok?" Kevin asked again.

"Yeah, I'm fine," Bradley replied.

The vehicle slowly rolled along the shiny floor passing the other vehicles. Arkalon looked out of his window to see a set of lights coming toward them. "Hey," he went.

Bradley looked up. "What?" he said in an abrupt voice.

"I've got to let these people pass," Arkalon said.

"Why?" Bradley asked, grasping his M16.

"You'll see," Arkalon said.

The alien pulled over to the side. Bradley and the rest of the group slowly started to raise their heads and look out of the windows. The alien vehicle started vibrating.

"What the...?" Kevin went.

Bradley peeked up through the window. He watched in horror as a long line of alien military vehicles rolled by.

"What the hell are they?" Eric asked.

"I don't know," Bradley said. "They look like tanks."

"They are," Arkalon said.

"What?" Bradley asked.

"It's coming," Arkalon said.

"What?" Bradley yelled over the loud vibrations.

"You know, that signal which is being sent to our planet," Arkalon said. "They're planning to station the ship above the city, so they can send it."

"Shit!" Bradley went. "Come on."

The last of the alien vehicles rolled away towards the large elevator.

"I'd better warn Marco," Bradley said. He flicked on his radio. "Marco," he said over the radio.

"Yeah, Brad?" Marco replied.

"We have a problem," Bradley went.

"Surprise me," Marco said.

"You've got a large convoy heading your way. For Christ's sake stay out of sight," Bradley urged.

"Will do," Marco said. He turned and looked at his group. "Stay down, people," he ordered. "You heard the man."

A short while passed. Marco stood behind the blue containers by the elevator. He held on to his heavy machine gun, still trying to smell the napalm from Vietnam. The image of the trenches, the smell of the burning buildings as the shells from the machine guns flew over his head, still haunting him. He felt the ground starting to vibrate. He peeked between the sets of crates as the huge alien vehicles came into view. He stared at the long turrets as they came down the long corridor. "Jesus Christ!" Marco gasped. "There's enough fire power there to blow the shit out of this island."

The aliens opened the elevator up. The shutters slowly rolled open, allowing the vehicles to roll on. Marco watched as the vehicles lined up one after the other. Two aliens rolled their machine onto the elevator. They watched as the shutter came down, slowly locking into place. The brakes released one after the other. The huge elevator rolled to the top of the shaft carrying the few alien vehicles. The two aliens rolled off the elevator, running over the bridge onto the muddy ground. They sped through the cave heading towards the exit. Their tracks turned up the mud as they rolled out of the cave heading onto the pathway. The aliens looked around the empty park as their machine returned to their normal size. They glowed a light green as they headed off into the destroyed city.

21

Holding onto his M16 rifle, Officer Adam Jones looked through the glass door of the New York lawyer's office. It was where he and his fellow comrades had been hiding out the whole day. He turned around and walked back into the building. "How long now?" he asked.

"Calm down," Jack went.

"Calm down?" Adam went. "We have to get out of here."

"Adam, listen to me" Jack said. "Go and have a rest. The guys and I back here have been planning a way out."

"Well, let's go," Adam shrieked.

"Adam," Jake said, "go and sit down you have been on your feet all day."

Adam nodded and slowly walked through the building. He looked at the two soldiers as they stood at the rear of the building, holding their rifles. "You guys ok?" he asked.

"We're fine," one of them said.

Adam turned and walked over to the set of leather couches. He placed his M16 down on the brown leather and turned to look at the set of glasses on a small wooden table, probably set there for visitors. He reached over and picking up the glass jug, poured himself a glass of water. He glugged half of it down and thumped the glass back down on the table in front of him. He opened a glossy magazine, trying to take his mind of the attack. But something captured his attention. Adam looked at the glass. He stared down at it looking at the water rippling up from the bottom. He reached for his M16 and slowly picked it up. He got up and walking through the offices to the front entrance looked at Jack as he stood by the entrance to the building.

"I thought I said sit down," Jack said.

"Quiet," Adam smirked.

He walked through the glass door to the sidewalk. He looked around at all the smashed up cars as two US soldiers walked out. He looked down the road feeling the vibrations under his feat. Adam felt his heart pound as a long turret came into view from the side road. He didn't recognize the model as the shiny vehicle rolled out, heading towards the building. "What the…?" he said.

The two soldiers walked back into the building. They ran to their rocket launchers stationed at the back of the building. They reached down and, picking them up, headed back to the entrance. The two soldiers kneeled down on the ground, arming the launcher and looking through the scope at the alien vehicle. The rocket zoomed through the air and slammed into the vehicle. Adam squinted his eyes and looked through the smoke.

"Did you get it?" Jack asked.

Adam didn't say a word. The dark smoke started to disappear. The long turret of the alien tank came into view again.

"Holy shit!" the soldier went.

He reloaded his launcher and took another shot at the vehicle. The two aliens giggled as they lined the turret up with the building. Adam looked down the long black turret as it just stood pointing at him. The alien pushed the button in. The rocket fired from the launcher.

"SHIT!" Adam yelled as he ran back into the building. The huge fireball ripped through the glass and erupted in the building. The two aliens laughed as they pulled away from the burning building and headed towards the East Side of the island. They saw the Hudson River come into view as they slowed their vehicle down. The brakes hissed as they looked over onto the military camp. All of the vehicles were slowly driving around as soldiers patrolled the outer perimeter. The aliens looked at one another as they pointed their turret at the military camp.

A young soldier grasped his rifle and stood by the metal fence, continually looking over his shoulder towards Manhattan, waiting for the invasion to get worse. The alien in the vehicle pushed the fire button. The soldier turned round and looked into the air to see a yellow gleam coming from the direction of Manhattan. He squinted hes to see it was a rocket. "INCOMING! INCOMING!" he yelled.

The people ran out of their tents and looked on as the rocket dived into the compound. They started heading towards the exit. The rocket slammed into the compound and erupted. "MOVE! MOVE!" the soldier shrieked.

He helped the people away from the compound as the rain of rockets slammed down onto the base. The rocket launchers and tanks erupted into flames. The two aliens laughed as they turned around to regroup with the others back at Central Park.

*   *   *   *

Bradley looked out of the vehicle as Arkalon slowed down and stopped. "Here it is" Arkalon said.

Bradley looked up and down the ship for any aliens which could attack at any time. Holding on to his M16, he walked over to the wall of the ship and looked up at the lights as they beamed down onto the shiny floor. Arkalon reached into his pocket, pulling out a tiny screwdriver from his pocket and slowly started working on the shiny bolts of the vent. Kevin walked over.

"Remember what I said. They will be just below us. It's

too dangerous to go straight down and in. It is very heavily guarded," said Arkalon

"Got it," Bradley said.

Max walked over to Bradley. "Ready?" he said.

"Yes," Bradley said, looking down at the alien. "CJ, you, AJ and the rest stay in that, but for God's sake keep your heads down. "We'll be out in a minute."

"Got it," CJ said.

"And make sure they stay down as well," Bradley said again.

CJ ran back to the alien vehicle. He stepped onto it, ducking down and staying out of view. Bradley pushed the alien into the vents. He reached out, picked it up and placed it in the hole where it had been. Bradley struggled to turn around in the narrow tunnels. He slid along the shiny metal work, catching up with Kevin.

"What is this place?" he asked.

"Ventilation," Arkalon said. "It can be sealed off in the event of a fire."

Bradley, followed by Eric, continued crawling along.

"It's just here," Arkalon whispered.

Bradley stopped looking down through the shaft. He stared through the tiny slits onto the single cells lined up next to one another. He shook his head in disbelief when he saw many more people in the cells next to Kate, Jane and Ms. Javies. "We're gonna need more masks," he said, taking his bag off his back, slowly unzipping it and looking at the extra masks inside.

"I've got four," Max went.

"I've got six," Bradley replied.

"I've got two," Eric went.

"Might be enough," Bradley whispered. He took another look through the long slits down onto the cells.

"Must be air tight," Kevin said.

"Pass that thingy," Bradley said to Arkalon.

Bradley started unscrewing the ventilation shaft gently trying not to make a noise. He pulled the tiny metal plate out of the shaft and handed it to Kevin. He bent his head down and looked all around trying his best to keep out of view. Jane slowly stood up and walked over to the door. She blinked her eyes and looked over to see Bradley dangling his head down through the shaft. She opened her eyes wide again. Bradley gently shook his head as one of the guards walked over to Jane. "What?" he said in a harsh tone.

Jane tried not to look up at the ventilation shaft but her face and eyes kept rolling towards it. Bradley pulled his head back in and re-placed the metal plate just as the alien looked up and did not see a thing.

"Sit down and shut up, you little tart," the alien went.

Jane sat down, wondering if she had really seen Bradley or if it was a mirage.

Bradley looked around again from the shaft as the guards walked around. He knew there was no way he could take them all out with a single weapon. "We've got to go to full," he went.

"Well, let's go," Kevin said.

Bradley nodded. "Right Kevin," he said. "You're with me. We and the others will take out what we can, as Max and Eric guard the main entrance."

"Got it," Max said.

"Me, too," Eric said.

The other men waited, ready to go into the cellblock.

"Flash," Bradley went.

Max chucked Bradley a small flash grenade.

"Tie that to that," Bradley demanded.

Max tied the small roll of copper wire to a tiny hole in the top of the shaft. He tied it right round, and slowly unrolled it.

"Ok, you lot ready?" Bradley asked,

"Ready," Eric said first.

Bradley shook his head in shock.

"Ok. On my mark. Kevin, you're with me. Eric, Max you two guard the main entrance in case any more of them appear. The rest of you keep taking them down," Bradley instructed.

"Got it," Max said.

"You with me," Bradley said to Arkalon. He grabbed the roll of copper wire and placed his hands around the tiny hole, ready to drop it down to the ground.

"Go," he whispered.

He ripped the steel plate away, putting it onto the ground of the shaft and ripping the grenade pin out. The aliens looked up as the tiny grenade bounced along the floor. "Cover your eyes," Bradley said turning away.

The small grenade erupted. The aliens fell back onto the ground from shock as the bright white light blinded them.

"GO, GO, GO," Bradley yelled.

Bradley grabbed hold of the wire. He slid down, feeling his hands burning as he landed on the ground. The aliens were barely able to see Bradley holding onto his M16 machine gun. He pulled the trigger, taking them down as they reached for their weapons.

"MOVE, MOVE," Bradley yelled. Kevin slid down followed by Arkalon, Max, Eric and Demmio.

"Kevin, me," Bradley ordered. He sprinted over to the cell holding Kate and Jane. Kate and Jane quickly got up and looked at Bradley and Kevin as they stood there in their gas masks.

"Hi, how are you?" Bradley said. "Long time."

"Get us out," Kate yelled.

"Erm, yes, we will," Kevin went.

Bradley pulled out the gas masks. "Where's the control room?" he asked.

"This way," Arkalon went.

Kevin stood at the door. "For God's sake, do not open this door until I say so," he yelled.

"We know," Jane yelled.

Bradley ran into the control room as the sirens and alarms wailed. He looked up at Max and Eric as they knelt down away from the door, ready to attack the incoming aliens.

"I can't wait. I can't wait to get at 'em," Eric stuttered.

Max looked down at his shotgun. "Em, Eric," he said, "it's not loaded."

"What?" Eric said, looking down at the Winchester. "Oh yeah." He started putting shells into the weapon as he flicked on his radio. "Hey, Marco, why didn't you load my gun?" he asked.

"Do you really think I would give you a loaded weapon?"

Marco joked. He looked up as the metal doors slowly started to open.

"Get ready," Max went.

Demmio ran up to the cell with Ms. Javies in it.

"Oh, Demmio," she gasped.

"I'm here for you," he said.

"Demmio, don't open that door until I say so," Kevin yelled.

"Got it," Demmio replied, holding on to his handgun as he looked at Ms. Javies.

"When I get you out of here I'm taking you to my home in Brazil," he yelled.

Ms. Javies smiled as Bradley ran into the control room of the ship. He looked down at the digital screen. He looked at all the images of the cells on it.

"Ok, there's Kate and Jane. Them first," Bradley said.

"Ok, on three. One, two, three," Kevin yelled.

Kate and Jane ran out as Kevin helped them put their gas masks on.

"Who's next?" Kevin yelled.

"Dragon," Bradley yelled.

Kevin, followed by Demmio, ran over to Ms. Javies.

"Ready on three," he yelled.

Bradley released Ms. Javies. Demmio placed the mask over her face. "Just for a while," he went.

"Ouch! This is disgusting," Ms. Javies moaned.

Max and Eric took down the attacking aliens as they ran into the prison block. Kevin ran over to a young American Chinese soldier and freed him from the cell.

"Thanks. Name's Lieutenant Jefferson," he said.

"Cool," Kevin said.

Jefferson ran over to a small room and picked up his rifle and ammunition.

"Ready, when you are," he said.

"Come on," Max yelled to Bradley.

"Which way we going back?" Eric asked.

"Main," Bradley yelled.

Bradley and Kevin supplied masks to the frightened group. He looked at a young black girl and her mother. "You ok?" he asked.

"We're fine," the girl replied. "Just not used to a gas mask."

"You'll be fine," Bradley said. "Keep close."

He led the way to the main entrance of the cell block. As he approached the main door, however, blue rays suddenly rained down on it.

"Shit! Get down," Kevin said, pulling Bradley back.

Bradley peeked out and saw a heavy ray gun firing down on them. "Oh, don't worry about that," he went. He loaded a grenade into his launcher and slowly started to creep out from behind the door, looking through the scope at the ray gun. He pulled the trigger of his weapon, launching the small grenade into the air. The alien watched as the small metal capsule landed next to him. Bradley ducked back behind the door as the flames erupted. "MOVE," he yelled.

Kevin followed Bradley out of the cell. A long line of people were headed down the corridor.

"Bradley," CJ went over the radio. "We got contact."

Bradley didn't answer. He looked at Kevin as they started sprinting along the corridors back towards the alien vehicle. He ran up the small ramp heading towards the vehicle. He looked ahead to see a group of aliens attacking the vehicles.

"Fire," he yelled, taking down the attacking aliens. "Move, move," he yelled.

The group of frightened people got on the long, alien vehicle as Bradley. He felt the floor suddenly start to vibrate. He turned had and looked down the corridor he had just run from. To his dismay he saw more of the alien vehicles progressing towards them. "Oh shit!" he moaned. "Not again!" He turned around and ran up to the alien vehicle.

"Come on, move," he yelled.

He stepped into the vehicle, almost slipping on the shiny floor. Arkalon sealed the doors shut and rammed the accelerator down to full. CJ turned around, looking at the group. His heart started to pound as he looked towards the back of the vehicle. He saw Marsha, his girlfriend and his mum both standing at the back, looking at him.

"CJ," Marsha said.

CJ ran down the vehicle towards them. He grabbed Marsha and pulled her to his chest. The tracks of the vehicle spun as the other alien vehicles caught up with them. Bradley looked down at all the frightened people as he walked along the alien vehicle towards the back. He had no choice. He grasped his M16 and shot through the back window. The glass shattered everywhere on the back seat. He looked through the scope at the vehicles as they closed in on them. He pulled the trigger, firing at the vehicles as they started to ram them. "Shit!" he gasped.

Bradley reloaded one of the grenades onto his launcher. He looked into the white eyes of the chasing aliens. He smiled and placed his fingers on the small trigger. The grenade fired through the air slamming into the chasing vehicles. Bradley watched as they rolled over with the explosion. "Yeah," he yelled. He turned around and walked down to the front of the vehicle. "You lot ok?" he asked.

"Yeah," Kevin replied.

Bradley looked forward again out of the front window. "Oh shit," he yelled. "Turn right." He looked forward to see a road block of alien vehicles. Arkalon swung their vehicle round to the right. Bradley grabbed onto the metal pole as the force pushed him around, towards the door. The alien rammed the accelerator down to full as the corridors behind slowly disappeared from sight.

"We've lost 'em," Kevin said.

Bradley felt relieved as they speed along through the empty corridors of the ship.

"How far are we now from the elevator?" he asked Arkalon.

"About two miles," Arkalon replied.

"Cool. Not far then," Bradley said.

Arkalon put the brakes on, slowly turning a corner.

"What's this place?" Bradley asked.

"It's a storage facility," the alien said. "Everything from weapons to food is stored here."

Bradley looked at the green crates as they were moved around by the huge cranes above them. He let his breath out looking out the broken window at the back of the vehicle, something caught his eye. He slowly looked up through an open skylight in the roof of the vehicle and there, to his horror, he saw one of the green containers dangling above their vehicle.

"Oh shit!" he gasped in a quiet voice, looking around. He looked up again at the green container as it dangled in the breeze. He looked up through the small binoculars as the tiny grappling claws came undone. "Oh shit, move," he ordered.

Arkalon slammed the accelerator down a moment before the huge, green container thundered down from the air and slammed into the ground, exploding as it did so.

"Come on, move," Bradley yelled at Arkalon.

"I'm going as fast as I can," Arkalon yelled.

Bradley watched as the containers landed in front of the alien vehicle.

"Jesus, these guys are serious," Kevin said. He turned around and looked at Ms. Javies as she stood with her head against the back of the seat.

"You ok, Ms.?" he asked.

"Fine," she said in a dull voice.

Bradley stared forward out of the window as they came to the other side of the compound. "Phew! We're clear," he said.

"Not far now," Arkalon went.

The alien pulled out of the exit into the compound.

"It's just down this way here… about two miles," Arkalon said.

Bradley looked out of the glass window as he flicked on his radio. "Marco, it's Brad. We're coming up to you in about four minutes," he said over the radio.

"Ok, Bradley. We're ok. What the…?" Marco said and things went deadly quiet for a second. "What the hell? Jesus Christ! Open fire! Give it all you've got."

Bradley and the rest of the group listened through their radio as the shooting got worse at the other end.

"Marco," Bradley went.

There was no response.

"Shit!" Bradley gasped. "Come on, move."

"I'm trying," Arkalon wept.

Bradley scanned the way ahead. Something caught his eye. He looked more closely to see a small gleam coming towards him. "What the hell?" he said, squinting his eyes. He saw a small alien rocket.

"Holy shit!" he yelled. "Incoming."

He reached over and grabbed the wheel. He swung the vehicle to the right trying to get the rocket to slam into the side or miss them. The rocket slammed into the side of the vehicle. He felt this body being thrown to one side as the vehicle was thrown aside.

"Shit!" Eric yelled.

The alien vehicle skimmed on its roof. The screeching that could be heard from inside slowly came to a stop. The smell of burned parts still hung around the inside of the vehicle. CJ grabbed onto Marsha and his mum as the vehicle came to a stop.

Bradley slowly opened his eyes and looked around the overturned vehicle. "Ouch!" he moaned, rubbing his back.

"Quick thinking, Bradley," Kevin said, slowly getting up and walking along the roof of the vehicle. He stared down at the frightened people as they slowly started to come around. "Anyone hurt?" he yelled.

There was a dead silence. Nobody said a word. They were all most probably in shock. AJ opened his eyes and looked out of the window of the vehicle to see two aliens slowly advancing towards them. "Oh shit!" he yelled.

Bradley turned around, knelt down and looked out of the window. He saw the aliens armed to the teeth and slowly walking towards them. They stopped and stared at the overturned vehicle as smoke started to come out of the engine. Bradley looked through the scope of his M16 at the two aliens. He felt the ground start to vibrate. He looked over his shoulder to see the aliens from the road block catching up with them. "Oh double shit!" he went. He took the two aliens in front down and headed towards the other side of the vehicle. He looked through the scope as Eric walked down towards them.

"I'll get these people out," Eric said.

"Good. We'll hold them off. Be careful. I think Marco is still under attack," Bradley said as he flicked on his radio.

"Marco?" he went. "Marco?"

The radio was dead.

"Shit!" Eric gasped.

"Come on, go" Bradley went. He shot out the glass in the window and looked through the scope at the oncoming vehicles as they got closer and closer. He took a peek over his shoulder looking at Eric as he helped the stricken people out of the vehicle.

"Eric," Bradley yelled.

"Yeah?" Eric said looking in through the window.

"When you approach that turning to the elevator stay back until I and the rest get there," Bradley said. "Do you understand?"

"Yes, understood," Eric replied.

"Ok, on my go," Bradley said.

The vehicles got closer. "GO" he yelled. Bradley watched as Eric crawled away from the vehicle. "Em, Eric," Bradley said.

Eric turned back and knelt down.

"You've forgotten something," Bradley said.

Eric looked to his right as the rest of the alien vehicles got closer and closer. He looked to see his shotgun. "Oh shit!" he went.

Bradley shook his head, looking back through the M16 scope onto the vehicles as they pulled up. "Don't fire till I give the word," Bradley said.

The aliens stepped out of their vehicles and headed

towards Bradley. He placed his hand on the trigger ready to open fire. The aliens got closer and closer. "Fire. Fire at will," he yelled.

The group opened fire onto the aliens as they shot from their vehicle.

"Max," Bradley yelled. "You take them three back to Eric. Kevin and I will follow."

"Got it," Max said.

Max crawled out of the overturned vehicle. He grasped his weapon while running with the three men as AJ and CJ continued firing onto the aliens and vehicles.

Bradley looked around as Eric and the group had disappeared. "Come on, go," he ordered. "CJ, go be with your mum."

Kevin and Bradley slowly started crawling out of the vehicle running along the shiny corridor towards the elevator. Bradley walked up to Eric. "You ok?" he asked.

"Yeah," Eric replied. "Never felt better."

Bradley reloaded his M16 and slowly started creeping along the wall so he could see the elevator. He peeked his head around the corner. He looked at the ground and saw loads of dead aliens sprawled all over the place. "Shit!" he went.

A few of the vehicles stood static in the middle of the corridor. Bradley slowly walked over the dead aliens looking at their green slimy blood as it coagulated on the ground.

"Marco?" Bradley whispered. "Marco?" he called while advancing forward towards the elevator shutter. "Marco," he whispered again "Where the fucking hell are you?" He slowly crept up to the blue container holding onto the M16.

Marco jumped up from behind the blue container. "Aggggh," he yelled. "Who wants a piece of me? You lot want to try it? You Viet cong bastards…"

Bradley fell back. "Marco it's me," he yelled

Marco stopped and looked at Bradley as he stood holding his M16. "Hey Brad," he went.

Bradley was relieved. "Marco, you shit," he went. "Ha, ha," he laughed

"Let's see them, then," Marco yelled. "Who's the others?" he asked.

Bradley turned around looking at Kate, Jane and MS. Javies. "Just a few extra we found," Bradley said.

Marco held onto his heavy machine gun. Bradley turned around, looking against the shiny wall, and saw the shadows of the aliens running towards them.

"Oh, shit, come on," Bradley yelled. He ran over to the elevator control box and selected the top floor. "Ready," he went. He listened in as the shutter stared to roll up. Marco held onto his machine gun ready to open fire at anything. Bradley ran through the shutter as it was opening. He made sure Kate and Jane, followed by the other people he had just rescued, got on. Marco turned around and opened fire on the aliens as they ran towards the elevator. "Come on. Close," Bradley yelled.

The shutter slowly started to go down. Bradley continued firing as it locked into place. The brakes clunked off. Aussie stood staring. Bradley felt relieved as the huge plate slowly started to roll up towards the top of the shaft. Laura spoke into her camera. The aliens outside armed up their rocket launcher looking at the large generator as it operated the hydraulics to the lift. They looked through the scope and slowly stepped back. The rocket launched from the launcher whistled through the air and slammed into the generator. Flames erupted from the machine. Bradley fell back onto the ground as the lift slowly rolled to a stop.

"What the…?" Marco went.

The elevator stopped suddenly. The brakes clinked off one after the other. The huge plate suddenly started dropping quickly. "WHAT THE…?" Marco yelled.

The girls screamed as the emergency brakes came on, skidding along the metal box to a stop. "Is everyone ok?" Marco yelled, getting up. He looked down the side of the huge plate to see light smoke starting to come up. "Shit! What happened?" Bradley asked.

"They blew the generator," Arkalon said.

"What? How do we get out?" Bradley gasped.

Arkalon looked around. "Follow me," he said. He ran across the plate into the far corner. He bent down and slowly lifted a small metal slab. "We go down," he said.

"Down? Don't you mean up?" Max went.

"It's a quicker way, trust me," Arkalon said.

Bradley shrugged his shoulders and walked over to the slab. He looked down the long ladder.

"Down the hatch," Eric went.

Bradley, followed by the rest of the group, slowly started to climb down the ladder.

"How far?" Bradley asked

"Not far at all," Arkalon replied.

Bradley continued climbing down looking through the dense smoke from the fire. "Christ," he went. Suddenly he stopped. He had heard some shuddering. He looked up at the huge elevator seeing it slowly starting to drop. "Holy shit!" he went. "How far?"

"It's just down here. It's a small shaft. We squeeze through," Arkalon went.

Bradley quickly started to lower a ladder.

"There it is," Arkalon went.

Bradley lowered the ladder down past the shaft. "Go on, go," he went. He and Arkalon watched as the group made its way into the shaft.

"Come on, Kevin," Bradley yelled. "That thing is going to drop."

Bradley pushed the people into the shaft as Kevin led them along through the tunnel. He looked up to see a middle-aged man dressed in a new suit. "Go," he said.

Bradley crawled into the tunnel. He turned around looking up at the lift as the brakes couldn't hold it any longer. "Shit," he yelled. "Come on."

The man tried to crawl in. Bradley peeked down at him as his trouser got stuck between the ladder and wall. Bradley struggled to pull as the lift started to drop. The man looked up as the lift thundered down the tracks towards the shaft. Let go," he yelled.

Bradley let go as the elevator slammed into the man, Bradley squinted his eyes closed as the sound of the screaming man echoed down the shaft and slowly faded away. He peeked his head out and looked down as the huge fireball rassed up the shaft. The intense heat burned his face as he pulled into the small escape shaft. "Come on, move," he ordered.

He crawled along the small tunnel catching up with the group. "Bloody hell, it's hot," he moaned.

Kevin, followed by Marco, ran to the left. "There," Arkalon went.

Kevin looked through the shaft. He scanned the area for any aliens that could attack. "Clear," he whispered. He removed the tiny plate and dropped into the corridor. "Now where?" he whispered to the alien.

"This way," he replied.

Kevin turned around as the rest of the group came down the ventilation shaft. "Where is Bradley?" he asked walking up to it. "Bradley?" he yelled.

"I'm here," Bradley yelled. "I'd get back if I were you."

Kevin stepped back as Bradley slid down the long tube, head first. "Stand clear," he yelled. He was flung out of the tunnel, and landed on the ground. "Lovely," he went. "Let's move."

He followed Arkalon along the quiet set of corridors. "Where now?" he asked.

"This way," Arkalon yelled.

Bradley ran along the corridor and skidded to a stop looking at a set of steps leading down to what appeared to be a monorail station.

"This way," Arkalon yelled again.

Bradley ran halfway down the stairs. He slowed down and crept on to the empty platform.

"Where's the ticket machine?" Eric asked.

"It's free," Arkalon went.

Bradley looked up the tunnel, while looking at the overhead rail. He watched as a large group of people stood on the platform. He caught a glimpse of the light coming in from the tunnel. "Hide," he said.

He ran down the platform towards the end, spun around and lay down on the ground. He looked at the long line of lights as the monorail train rolled into the station. "Don't fire yet," Bradley said over the radio.

"Got it," Marco went.

Bradley looked through the scope at the alien as he sat in the driver's seat of the monorail. He gently placed his finger on the trigger, ready to pull it. Then he pulled the trigger, launching the bullets through the air as the aliens stepped off the monorail onto the platform. Marco opened fire on them as Bradley ran along the platform boarding the monorail. He turned left and ran up towards the cab, kicking the door open. He pulled the alien out of the seat chucked him to the ground and stared at all the multi colored lights as the power stick stood on idle. "Piece of cake" Bradley went. He turned around and walked to one of the open doors. "Come on" he yelled through the mask.

Marco ran onto the monorail followed by the armed men and survivors as Bradley looked over his shoulder at the group as they sat down on the shiny white chairs.

"Ready?" Bradley asked, looking over at the stairs. He saw the aliens charging down the stairs towards him.

"Shit!" Bradley said. "Time to go."

Bradley pushed the power lever to full. The long monorail quickly rolled out of the station heading off into the tunnel. He lay back in the seat, feeling his legs coming back to life after the long run he had just had from the burning elevator. "Is everyone ok?" he yelled.

Kevin walked into the cab and looked at Bradley. "We're ok," he quietly replied.

"How far do we go?" Bradley asked Arkalon.

"Not this stop. It's the next," he replied.

Bradley sped along the tracks. He gave it full power, feeling the g-force pushing him back into the seat as the lights lit up the tunnel ahead. The monorail approached the first station. Bradley jumped on seeing the platform full of aliens.

"Shit!" he gasped and zoomed the monorail through the station, heading back into the tunnels as the rays bounced off the vehicle. Bradley turned around looking at Kevin as he stood with his feet up on the entrance to the cab. "Stand by for the next one" he yelled.

Kevin stood up, holding onto his MP5 as they approached the next station. The monorail turned the small corner and slowly rolled into the station. Bradley looked around to see no one or thing around. He gently applied the brakes and rolled towards the stairs of the platform. He looked up and opened his eyes with fear as he saw one of the heavy alien machine guns poised at the top of the stairs, ready to blow them away. "Holy shit! Get down" he yelled.

The alien opened fire on the top of the monorail. The rays burnt through the clips holding it to the overhead line and it erupted into flames. Bradley felt the front carriage start to drop down. "Kevin, move," Bradley yelled.

Kevin ran down the carriage of the monorail as the nose dropped down into the ditch below the station. Smoke poured up from beneath, filling the station. Kevin pulled his body up onto the next carriage. It all happened very quickly.

Bradley slowly started to open his eyes. He stared down at the control panel of the monorail, as the lights switched off one after the other. The control stick was sticking into his stomach. He slowly moved his body away from it. "Ouch, damn it!" he moaned.

"Bradley?" Kevin yelled down.

"Ok," he went. "Still alive."

He slowly stood up and brushed the muck off his clothes looking up at Kevin as he leaned over.

"Come on," Kevin said. "I'll help you up."

Bradley slowly placed his foot onto the control box. He hauled his body off the shiny floor as Kevin reached down, put his arm out to help him and pulled him up. Bradley stood up, shook his head, and walked down the monorail, looking out of the windows.

"Stay down," Kevin said.

Bradley knelt down. "Bring me up to speed," he asked.

"That," Kevin went. "We can't get past it."

"Here, Brad," Max said.

Bradley turned around looking at Max as he crawled closer towards him.

"Can't we jump off here, head back along the tunnel and get off at the next station?" Max asked.

"No," Bradley replied, looking up at the alien machine gun as he rubbed his head. "Those things are probably on their way up it now to us and we won't have the time. Any one got a launcher?"

"I do," Marco yelled.

"We'll need a distraction," Kevin suggested. "I'll go," he said.

Bradley reloaded his M16 and looked up at the alien as he took shots at the monorail. "I see what you mean," he said.

"Give me the launcher," a Chinese man said.

Marco handed the man the launcher. He armed it, ready to open fire onto the machine ray gun.

"Ready? When it's distracted, fire," Bradley instructed.

"Got it," he replied.

Bradley ran down the monorail to the front. He shot out the window, wiping the sweat of his forehead. He looked through the scope at the weapon. He pulled the trigger and shot at the metal case. The bullets bounced off it one after the other as the alien turned and pointed the weapon down at him.

"Shit!" he yelled. "Fire!"

The young Chinese dove out, looking through the launcher scope at the weapon. He pushed the red button in as the alien swung the weapon back around. He pulled the trigger, firing the rays into the man. Bradley watched as he fell back onto the floor as the rocket whistled through the air and slammed into the weapon.

"COME ON," Marco yelled.

Bradley ran off the monorail, onto the platform holding his M16, kneeling down on the ground and scanning the exit for any of the aliens that could come out of nowhere. Marco knelt down and looked at the Chinese man he had only known for a short while. "He's dead," he went.

"Rest in peace" Kevin said remorsefully

Bradley shook his head, turning around as Kate and Jane walked down the platform; Colin was close behind as well, staying quiet. Bradley and Kevin ran up the stairs, looking both ways, checking to see that the coast was clear. "Move up," Bradley said.

The group ran up the stairs. "This way," Arkalon called.

Bradley ran along the corridor as Kevin ran behind, making sure they all stayed together. Bradley slowly raised his fist and stopped the group. He raised his M16 and slowly crept along the wall of the ship. The way ahead didn't feel right. Bradley peeked around the corner to see the other elevator with another one of the alien vehicles there. "Move," he yelled. He ran up to the huge vehicle. "Jump on, people," he ordered.

Then he suddenly stopped. He felt the huge ship suddenly start to move. "What's that?" he asked.

"They're starting up," Arkalon said. "Not long now."

"What do you mean?" Bradley asked.

"They are preparing to move the ship," Arkalon replied.

"Let's get out of here," Max said immediately.

"I agree," Jane replied.

"Me, too," Colin said.

Bradley ran off the vehicle over to the control box. He selected the top floor, rubbing his hands. The huge shutter slowly started to roll up into the open position. Bradley looked down at his hands as he started to glow green.

"We're resizing," Arkalon went.

CJ turned to look at Marsha. "Won't be long," he said to comfort her.

"Saves you a job," Kevin went.

Arkalon slowly moved the vehicle onto the metal plate as Bradley stepped down through the open door. He turned round watching the huge plate slowly start to close. The ship slowly disappeared behind the huge shutter.

"Bye, bye," Colin said, "fucking place."

"For once I agree," Max said.

The brakes clunked off one after the other. Bradley sat down in the seat next to Lieutenant Jefferson. "Was this in the job description?" he asked.

"Yes, it was," he replied. "But I never thought I'd live to see this."

Bradley laughed. "I might sign up after this."

"I think we are going to need all the help we are going to get," Jefferson replied, "if any more of these people come."

"They won't," Bradley said. "They won't."

The elevator came to the top of the shaft. Bradley looked around the top of the huge ship. "Where is the edge?" he asked.

"This way," Arkalon ordered.

The group looked along the top of the huge ship. "Come on, come on," Bradley mumbled.

Arkalon put the brakes on, slowing down as they came to the ridge. Bradley stepped down from the vehicle ripping the mask of his face. "Oh, that's nice, fresh air," he said. He looked over the edge of the ship, down on to the city. "Where would you say we are?" he asked.

Kevin scanned the ground below him, trying not to stumble. "Careful," Bradley went.

"I'd say we are about a mile from that cop shop; maybe a bit more," Kevin replied.

"Good," Bradley replied, "Right. I need some more M16 ammo."

"What are you doing?" Kevin asked. "Why can't we jump now?"

Jefferson ran over. "How do we get down?" he asked.

Bradley looked around. He stared at the skyline of the city to see a small Black Hawk helicopter flying towards the city. He swung his head around looking at Jefferson's assault vest. He looked at the small, yellow canister in the vest. "Thank you," he said reaching in and pulling the flare out. He kneeled down and looked over his shoulder as the group stood quietly on the top of the ship. Bradley looked at Kevin as he ripped the white cord out of the yellow canister.

The young helicopter pilot looked over at the top of the ship. He looked at the green smoke blowing up into the air. "Look," he went, turning towards the ship. He looked down onto the ship to see the group on the top. "We're going in," he said.

Bradley smiled as the helicopter flew towards the ship.

"Right, who's going in this?" Kevin asked.

"Em," Bradley replied. "Kate, Jane and Ms. Javies are jumping the rest on that."

"I'll take Marsha," CJ yelled. "Mum can go with someone."

"I'm ok with that" Bradley said. "Can I have any spare M 16 rounds, please?"

"Right," Kevin replied. "Wait. What about you? Why do you want more ammo?"

"I'm going back," Bradley said.

"WHAT?" Kevin freaked.

"Do you remember what shit face said in the warehouse?" Bradley asked.

"Oh god," Kevin said.

"Yes," Bradley replied. "So I'm going back with my friend here."

"I'm coming," Kevin said.

"No, you can't," Bradley replied. "You need to get Demmio, Kate, Jane and Ms. J down to the ground because we all can't fit in that thing," Bradley said, raising his voice.

"Look, let me come. Demmio can take them down," Kevin replied, trying to persuade Bradley.

"No," Bradley replied. "Go, get them down and get to that cop shop and, for god's sake, stay off the main streets."

"Ok," Kevin replied in a subdued voice. He turned around as Max and Eric walked over.

"Are we off, then?" Eric asked.

"Not all of us," Kevin said.

"Why? Who's staying?" Max asked.

Kevin looked at Bradley.

"Bradley?" Max said. "Why are you staying?"

"In a short while these people are going to relay our

location to their home planet. If that signal is sent we would
be invaded by more of these people and I'm not having
that," Bradley said, folding his arms.

"There will be other ships out there," Eric said.

"Even if there are any more out there looking for us. At
least with the signal cut, it will buy us some more time,"
Bradley replied, "to prepare ourselves." He nodded his head
as the black hawk touched down on the deck. Jefferson
helped the stricken people onto the old machine.

"How many are left?" Kevin asked.

"Just me, Jane, Ms. J and Demmio," Kate yelled, "Plus
Marsha and CJ's mum."

"Cool," Bradley said. "Right. Who's taking Jane and
Kate?"

"I can," a voice said.

Kate looked at one of the kits attached to the man.

"What is that?" she queried.

"It's a parachute," he replied.

"A what?" she yelled.

"A parachute. You're going to drop." Bradley smiled at
her.

"Oh, no, I'm not," she went.

"Oh yes, you are," Bradley said. "It's the only way."

"Aren't there escape chutes?" Eric asked.

"No, Eric," Max said. "That's in an aircraft."

Bradley turned around as Jefferson waved the helicopter
off the stand. He watched as the helicopter flew over them.
He looked up at the frightened people as they looked out of
the open door.

"What's that?" Eric asked.

Bradley squinted in the sunlight to see a small, blue
light traveling through the sky. Kate shut her eyes as the
blue rocket slammed into the Black Hawk. Bradley watched
in dread as the helicopter spun out of control and slammed
into the skyscraper, slowly falling down the side.

"Bollocks!" Marco yelled.

Bradley shook his head looking at Eric, Max and Kevin.

"Right," he went, looking around at the men. "Let's try to work out how to get the rest down. There are no more kits left. This means that some of you are going to have to help someone down."

"How?" Cheng asked.

"Simple," Bradley said. "You drop with somebody who you know you can hold onto."

"Like him," Cheng said, pointing to Colin.

"Yes, like him," Bradley said.

"I'll take Ms. J," Demmio yelled. "I'll be ok."

Bradley nodded as the group started taking off parachutes and handing them to the single droppers. He looked at Kevin and the rest of his group. "Come here, boys," he went. He placed his arms around the group, hugging them. "We've come this far. For god's sake, don't fuck up here."

"We'll be ok," Eric said.

Bradley kept his feelings to himself, struggling to hold them in. "Sorry if I've been a pit picky," he said.

Kevin looked up at Bradley. "Bradley, you haven't been picky" Kevin said. "If it wasn't for you, we'd be dead."

"Me, too," Eric went. "Don't even know what it means but I second it."

Bradley let the small group go. He looked at Kate and Jane as they stood by Marco. He watched as Kate suddenly started to run over. She leapt into Bradley's arms. She placed her lips on his as Kevin watched in amazement. Eric smiled as she let Bradley go.

"Right," Bradley said. "I'll see you boys later."

"What?" Kate said.

"Oh, you don't. No, you don't," Bradley said.

"What?" Kate said. "I don't know what he's talking about."

"I'll tell you later," Bradley said.

CJ turned and looked at Marsha. "I'm not dropping, either" CJ said.

"WHAT?" his mum gasped.

"I have to go," CJ said. He reached into his pocket. His mum watched as he kneeled down on the deck of the ship. "Marsha," he quietly said. Bradley looked over as he held onto the M16. CJ slowly opened a small ring box. Marsha placed her hands over her cheeks and looked down at the engagement ring.

"I'm sorry. This is the wrong place, but I was going to ask you when we would have been away next week. However, I think that has been canceled for now," CJ said. There was a short pause. CJ tried to steady his nerves. "Marsha," CJ said slowly. "Will you make me the happiest man in the world? Will you marry me?" he asked.

Marsha nodded as she wiped a few tears away from her eyes. "Yes," she wept. "Yes, I will."

CJ slowly pulled the silver engagement ring out and put it on Marsha's finger. He looked up at his mum.

"Oh my god!" she gasped. "My little boy's getting married." The group started clapping as CJ and Marsha kissed.

"Right. I've got to go," CJ finally said. He looked at Marsha and his mum as they both had solo parachutes on. "For fuck's sake be safe," he yelled.

"Right," Bradley yelled. "CJ, AJ, you're with me."

"I'm ready," AJ yelled.

"Me, too," Jefferson yelled.

Marco looked over at Bradley. "Marco," Bradley went.

"Yeah boy?" he yelled.

"You take Eric. He is quite small," Bradley ordered. "Then Kate and Jane have a chute each for themselves."

"What about Colin?" Max asked.

"He is with me," a voice yelled.

"And Ms. J is with Demmio," Bradley asked?

"I got her," Demmio said.

The group prepared for the drop.

"Who's taking Aussie?" Marco asked. He looked at Aussie as he stood there, looking dazed.

"He can go by himself," Kevin went as he handed Aussie the chute.

"What's going on, now?" Eric asked.

Marco walked over to Eric. He reached out and grabbed him. "Come here, boy," he yelled. "You're coming with me."

"What?" Eric gasped. "What are we doing?"

"Get here," Marco ordered. "Stop chatting." Bradley watched as Marco held Eric to his body ready to jump.

"What are we doing?" Eric asked again. "Inform me."

He looked over the side of the ship as Marco hooked his arm around him. "Are we going to jump?" he asked

"No, Eric," Marco said, "We're going to fly."

"Argh, cool," Eric joked. "How far?"

"Not that far," Marco replied. He looked over at Aussie as he looked down onto Manhattan. "You ok, Aussie?" Marco yelled.

"Yeah," Aussie replied. "Just like Nam."

"God, not another one!" Eric said.

Bradley looked at the group as they prepared to drop. "Right. I'm off," Bradley went.

"Take it easy," Kevin said. "Oh, and I want you back. I think its Downtown Haven tonight."

"Too fucking right," Bradley said. "Get to the police station and wait there or, if you can, Queensboro Bridge."

He got into the alien vehicle, followed by CJ, AJ and Jefferson. He started up the engine as Arkalon stood holding onto the pole.

"Right," he said. "Let's get this done."

Bradley started up the engine to the vehicle. He

slammed the accelerator down as Kevin turned around and watched it disappear along the top of the ship. He turned around again and looked at Jane as she looked over the edge of the ship down onto the city, trembling with fear.

"You guys ready?" Kevin yelled.

"Ready when you are," Marco yelled.

Kate looked down as Jane stood trembling, almost being sick.

"Are you two ok?" Kevin asked, placing his hand on Jane's arm.

"I, I, I am fine," she wept.

"Ready," Marco yelled. "On three. One, two... three."

Marco and the rest of the group leaped off the top of the ship. Eric yelled as Marco reached under his arm and pulled the rip cord. Kevin listened to Marsha as she yelled at the top of her voice while ripping out her parachute cord. Kevin looked over the side of the ship as the red parachutes all opened up one after the other. Jane stood looking down at the ground as Kevin looked at her. "I knew you wouldn't," he said.

"How did you know?" she wept.

"I just knew," Kevin said. "Remember gym class a few years ago? You were too scared to jump of that vaulting box."

Jane burst out crying.

"Right. You're gonna jump," Kevin ordered. "Remember -rip this cord out and it will release the chute and before you know it, you will be down on the ground."

Jane nodded as she wiped the tears away from her face.

"Ready?" Kevin said.

Jane shook her head.

"Ready- on three. You can do this, Jane," Kevin yelled. "And when we get back to Haven it's us and Bradley in the bar."

Jane gently nodded.

"Ok, ready," he yelled in her ear. "One, two…"

Kevin pushed Jane off the top of the ship. He heard her scream as her chute opened out.

"Ha, ha," Kevin laughed. "I'm a bastard, aren't I?" He looked at the chutes as they floated to the ground. He took a deep breath, and leapt off the side, pulling the ripcord. He felt his body slow down as the chute opened up. Slowly he descended to the ground. He felt the cool air blowing into his face as the ground got closer and closer. "Oh, I love this," he said as he pulled his legs in, ready to land on the street. The smell of the burning vehicles came to his nose again. He looked down at the group as they stood by the entrance to an alleyway looking around for any aliens. Cars had been slammed in all directions by the alien tanks.

Marco watched as Kevin landed onto the ground rolling in the grass. "Ouch!" he moaned.

"Come on, boy," Marco yelled.

Kevin unplugged the chute from his kit.

"You ok, Kev boy?" Marco asked.

"Yeah. Wicked! Must do that again sometime," he laughed.

Jane ran over to Kevin. She opened her hand and slapped him on the face. "Three, he says," she yelled. "We'll jump on three."

"I'm sorry," Kevin went.

"You could have killed me," Jane yelled.

"But you survived, didn't you?" Kevin said. "Told you, you could do it."

Marco looked up at the ship through his binoculars. He saw something moving. "What the…?" he said quietly. He stared up through the lenses as a small cannon rolled out from underneath the ship. It seemed to be pointing down towards the ground. He felt his heart pound wondering what the hell it was going to do. He heard Kevin and Jane as they continued squabbling about the jump down.

"Guys," Marco went.

Neither Kevin nor Jane heard him. Marco looked at the ground as he held on to his binoculars. "GUYS," he yelled.

"WHAT?" Jane and Kevin said simultaneously. They both looked at Marco and then up at the ship.

"What is it?" Kevin asked, pulling the small set of binoculars out of the survival kit. He zoomed the lenses and looked up at the ship. "What the fuck!" he exclaimed. He looked up at the cannon and saw a light blue light building up on it.

"Oh, hell no," Marco went.

"Oh hell, yes," Kevin replied. He put the binoculars back into his pouch as the cannon fired down towards the ground.

"Come on," Marco yelled.

They looked at the long beam as it slammed into the ground by the group. It slowly started traveling towards them.

"Come on," he yelled.

Kevin pushed Jane along as the intense heat from the ray burnt them.

"Shit, shit and double shit!" Kevin went.

Marco ran ahead as the blue ray continued to follow them up the alleyway. Kevin passed Ms. Javies as she ran along the alleyway with Demmio. The ray incinerated anything in its path. The small grey dustbins melted down to the ground. Ms. Javies stumbled over as the ray honed in on her. Demmio looked at her as she lay on the floor and looked back as she felt the heat burn the back of her neck. Demmio ran over to her. "Come on," he said, picking her up. He yelled in pain as the raging heat burned his back but he hauled Ms. Javies along the alley.

Kevin looked up as Demmio hugged her. "Demmio, will you marry me?" Ms. Javies asked.

"I'd love to," he replied.

Ms. Javies looked at the burn on his back. "Ouch," she went.

The group came to a stop halfway down the dirty alley. He watched as the energy disappeared back into the ship.

"Ok, take five," Marco yelled.

Kevin leant against the wall. "You ok?" Marco asked.

"Yeah," Kevin replied. "How about you?" he asked Demmio.

Demmio looked up at him. "It's just a burn. I'll be ok. I've had worse."

Ms. Javies looked at Demmio. "I love you," she went quietly.

Kevin rolled his eyes. "Come on," he went.

The group continued along the dirty alleyway, looking up every now and them at the underneath of the ship in case any more of the spikes reappeared.

Bradley kept the accelerator down to max as he sped along the corridors.

"It's here," Arkalon said.

Bradley skidded the brakes to a stop. CJ watched as he stepped off the vehicle holding his M16 machine gun and followed by Jefferson. The small C4 charges dangled by his side as he approached the set of green doors. "Open them," he ordered.

Arkalon ran up to the door as Bradley knelt down, ready to go in.

"Right, let's get these planted. Blow it and get the fuck out of here," AJ said.

"I agree," Jefferson went.

Bradley watched as the two green doors slowly started to roll open.

"Move," Bradley ordered. He advanced through the opening doors holding his M16 machine gun, knowing he hadn't many rounds left to use. He walked forward opening his eyes. There, in front of him, stood a huge generator, electricity surging round it as the large satellite looking dish stood on top of it folded up, but ready to open and transmit.

"This is it?" Bradley asked.

"Yes," Arkalon replied. "Yes, that's it."

Bradley dove to the floor as some rays were shot at him. He kept way out of sight of the firing rays.

"Bradley," Circo said. "How nice to meet you!"

"Yeah, nice to meet you, too," Bradley yelled. "Could have been a lot easier the other way."

"Tell me," Circo said. "What brings you to this ship then?"

"We know why you're here," Bradley yelled. "You believed that other planet, was developing weapons of mass destruction and you think one of your crafts have crash landed here."

"Correct," Circo said.

"Why didn't you come here in peace? We may have been able to help you," Bradley yelled,

"We Armazoids don't work like that," Circo said.

"Ha," Bradley said. "So is that who you are?"

"What was that?" Circo yelled.

"Nothing," Bradley replied, struggling to yell through the gas mask. He slowly looked over at CJ, Jefferson and AJ as they stood hiding in the corner by the entrance to the room.

"So when you transmitting? "Bradley yelled.

"Any minute now," Circo yelled. "And then this dump of a planet will be ours."

Bradley signaled to the group. He held three fingers out slowly counting them down to one as he reached for the small C4 charges. "Fire," he yelled.

The group dived out from the entrance and opened fire onto the aliens as they stood pointing their weapons down at them. Bradley coughed as he set the M16 to full automatic fire. He pulled the trigger and fired rounds from the weapon. He snuck beside the control box looking at a small set of steps leading along the side of the satellite generator. "Aha," he went, reloading the weapon.

He reached into his pocket and pulled out the charges as Jefferson, AJ and CJ fired onto the shooing aliens. Circo watched them on the camera as Bradley slipped down the side, laying small charges ready to blow the shit out of the machine. He laid the last charge and slowly walked up the stairs, keeping his head down while reaching into his pocket and pulling the detonator out. He took one last look around as one of the aliens shot down at him. He dove to the ground, dropping the small detonator. "Oh shitting hell," he shrieked.

Circo looked at Bradley as he struggled to pull it out of the tiny cracks in the floor. He pushed the small button down as he looked through the control room cameras at the front of the ship.

Bradley watched as the huge brakes clinked and clanked off. The huge metal plate slowly raised the satellite dish towards the top of the ship. "Shit!" he gasped. "Come on." He struggled with his fingers in trying to get the detonator as CJ, AJ and Jefferson fired onto the shooting aliens.

Bradley looked up as the dish slowly got to the top of the ship. The huge fans started to open up, pointing into the air, ready to transmit the signal back to Armazoid billions of light years away. Bradley wrenched his fingers through the sharp metal slits as he tried to reach for the detonator. He struggled with all his might as Jefferson, followed by CJ and AJ, ran over. The alien looked through his scope as AJ ran towards Bradley. He pulled the trigger and fired the ray through the air. The ray slammed into AJ's back.

"NOOOOOOOOO," CJ yelled.

AJ fell onto the floor, blood running from his body. The whiteness of his eyes gleamed as his body fell to the floor.

"Got it," Bradley yelled, pulling the detonator out.

He looked up as the satellite reached the top of the ship and he pushed the small button down. The huge antenna slowly started to unfold. The group looked up as huge explosions rocketed through the shaft. The brakes on the satellite's metal lift exploded. CJ grieved over AJ as he lay on the ground dead, and as he looked up at the explosions and the fire raining down on the group. Bradley took another look up to see the huge elevator dropping down. The green doors were sealed shut.

"Oh shit, now, where?" Bradley asked.

"This way," the alien said, running down a small staircase underneath the elevator.

"CJ," Bradley went.

CJ stood looking at AJ. "I knew him all my life," he quietly said.

"CJ!" Bradley shrieked.

CJ turned around and ran over to Bradley as the huge satellite dish thundered down the shaft. Fire raged from all corners. Bradley felt the intense heat as they ran along the shiny corridor away from the fireball. He heard the elevator slam into the ground and peeked over his shoulder as the fireball chased them along the maintenance tunnel. He looked ahead again to see a set of open doors.

"Quickly," Arkalon yelled.

Bradley ran through the door. Arkalon turned around, pushing the tiny buttons on the door. The doors slowly closed as the fireball slammed into it. CJ gained his breath back. He clenched his fist as Jefferson leant against the wall.

"Shit! Fuck! Shit!" CJ yelled.

"CJ," Bradley went.

CJ slowly turned and looked at Bradley. "I'm sorry," he said remorsefully, nodding at Bradley.

"Let's get the fuck out of here," Bradley said.

CJ nodded. Bradley looked at Jefferson. "You ok?" he

asked.

"Yeah. Loving it," Jefferson replied.

"Come on," Bradley went. "Let's try and get out of here."

The three Armazoids walked through the small door at the back of the ship. They stared forward at their three ships all lined up on the launch pad, ready to be launched from the top of the ship. They stared at the long, white noses and stumpy backs and the cockpit doors all open and ready for them to board. They walked over the metal plate and stepped into their spacecraft. The huge metal plate slowly lifted the Aramazoid space fighters up into the air from the bottom of the ship. The Armazoids looked up as the set of metal doors opened, allowing it up on to the deck of the huge ship as it hovered above Manhattan. The engines powered up to the maximum. The craft launched off the deck flying out over the Hudson River. They turned to the right, looking out into the distance to see the three B-52 Bombers slowly flying towards the city and descending ready to fly underneath the ship and blow the Armazoids away for good.

"Let's go," one Armazoid pilot said.

The three crafts flew closer to the group of B-52s as they looked out onto the huge dirty river and ocean. The group of B-52 pilots stared as the alien space fighters got closer and closer to them. "What the hell is that?" one said

The Armazoid crafts flew in front of the B-52s. They pointed their ray guns at them, pulling on their triggers. The blue rays zapped out from the cannons, incinerating the three B-52s. The onlookers on the ground looked up as the huge black aircrafts slowly started floating down from the sky, the jet fuel still burning in the cool, evening mid air. The three space fighters slowly turned around and headed back towards Manhattan. They looked out to their left to see some USAF fighter craft flying towards the ship. The three slowly turned the craft to the left as they flew over the top of the mother ship. They looked at the small craft as they got closer and closer to them.

"Let's get 'em," one Armazoid said.

The group armed up their lasers, looking at the group of crafts flying closer to them. "Right. Let's whip their human asses," another Armazoid said.

The three F16s flew up over the Armazoid crafts towards the mother ship. Their rockets fired out, slamming into the ship. The rockets bounced off the heavy amour and did no damage whatsoever.

"Holy shit!" one of the USAF pilots said.

The Armazoids flew behind the F16s and pulled their triggers, firing at them. The F16s tumbled down from the sky in flames.

Kevin continued running along the alleyway. Marco was way ahead with his boys. Demmio and Ms. Javies were most probably ahead as well, nearer the main police station. Kevin skidded to a stop. He stared up into the air as one of the Armazoid space fighters hovered above the alleyway. He admired the shiny paintwork as the Armazoid looked down on him. His eyes opened wide with fear as the fumes from the engine blew all the garbage around the dirty alleyway.

"Oh fuck!" Kevin said. "MOVE." He pushed Colin along the alleyway as the blue rays kept coming out of the cannon on the Armazoid space fighter. Kevin kept forward as the concrete from the buildings on either side tumbled down onto the ground leaving a horrible mist of dust. He coughed as he helped Colin along. As they slowly turned the corner they looked down the road at people running in all directions from the alien tanks and vehicles as they rolled closer towards the police station. The US Soldiers ran up the road ready to guard the main police station. Kevin heard a sudden scream. He turned to see a young

Chinese girl, most probably a student, slowly walk back towards one of the street lamp posts. Kevin swiped his Mp5 and looked through the scope. "Hey," he went.

The Armazoid turned and looked at Kevin who pulled his trigger, firing the shiny round out through the air. The bullet slammed into the alien's head and he watched as it slowly fell to the ground.

"Thank you," the girl softly said.

"No problem," Kevin said. "Now come on, follow my people that way."

Kevin ran up past Jane. "Jane, come on," he said as Marco, followed by his group, still ran along.

"Eric, Max, Kate, go," he ordered.

The group ran down the road as he waited for Jane who slowly started running behind Kevin. The aliens advanced up the road a lot quicker than he had thought. Kevin heard a scream and skidded to a stop, looking around to see Jane lying on the floor looking back at the aliens as they got closer. "Shit!" he gasped. "Go."

Demmio slowed down as Ms. Javies ran ahead with the other frightened people. Kevin ran forward. He looked at Jane as she held on to her ankle.

"It's my ankle," she wept.

"It's ok," he went.

Kevin picked Jane up and threw her over his shoulder. He resumed running along the road.

"I've been wanting to ask you something for a long time," Jane said.

"Oh, yeah? What's that?" Kevin asked.

It took Jane a few seconds to get her confidence up. "Will you go out with me when we get home?" she asked "I've always liked you."

Kevin panted for breath as he hauled her along the road dodging the aliens' rays and zaps.

"I'd love to," Kevin replied. "I was going to ask you,

anyway."

"Really?" Jane said.

"No" Kevin joked. He ran along the road as the chasing alien looked through his weapon scope. It laughed at Kevin as he carried Jane on his back. It laughed again and slowly pulled its trigger. The blue ray flew through the sky as Max turned around and looked at Kevin. The ray slammed into Kevin's back. Kevin came to a sudden stop in the middle of the road. He felt the pain fly up through his back. Jane fell to the ground. She looked at the still body of Kevin as she slowly got up and stood by the lamp post. His blood rang down his t-shirt and onto the ground.

"NOOOO," Eric yelled, pumping his shotgun.

Jane crawled to the side. She looked into the empty shop as the Armazoids fired onto the rest of group.

"SHIT!" Max yelled. He dropped to the floor hiding behind two garbage bins on the side of the street. He lay down on the ground and looked from under the old bin at Kevin as he lay in the middle of the road. His blood was running into the gutters.

"Shit!" Max said again. "He's losing blood."

The group looked at one another.

"Leave him," a voice went.

"NO," Max yelled. "He wouldn't have left us."

He took a second to think as the rays continued slamming into the bin. He looked at Kevin. "Right," he went. "Cover me."

"Wait," Eric said.

Max turned and looked at Eric who handed him a small yellow canister. "Thanks," he said. Then he turned back and looked at Eric. "I thought..." he said.

"I know. I just remembered I had one," Eric replied.

Max took a deep breath. He ripped the shiny pin from the smoke grenade allowing his MP5 to dangle by his side. "Ready," he said.

The group nodded. Max threw the grenade out towards Kevin. Kevin saw the smoke grenade land next to him and his eyes slowly started to close. The dense black smoke poured from the small canister filling the area around him and Jane.

"We'll cover you. On my go," Eric said. "GO."

Max leapt over the bin running into the smoke. Eric and the group fired onto the Armazoids as they shot at him through the smoke. Max felt the dense smoke entering his lungs. He coughed as Jane continued holding onto the lamp post.

"Come on," Max went. "Move."

Jane got up and slowly limped towards the group back at the bins. Max looked down on Kevin, his eyes still open.

"Sa.. sa… save Jane," Kevin mumbled. His blood still ran down into the storm drain.

"Oh no, you don't," Max went. He leant down and looked at Kevin. He took hold of his arm and started to lift him off the blood stained floor. He accidentally dropped him to the rays from the Armazoid weapons.

"Shit!" he went.

Jane arrived at the bins and ducked down behind them. She looked through the opening at the smoke as it slowly started to fade away. Eric stared into the smoke as the shooting stopped. He squinted his eyes as the ship continued to hover above them. Eric stared again into the smoke. A dim shadow slowly became visible. He smiled as Max ran out of the smoke, Kevin across his back.

"YES," Eric said.

"Come on. Go," Max yelled.

Jane smiled as they joined her at the bins.

"Come on," Eric said.

Eric put his arm around Jane helping her along the road as Max struggled with Kevin. Two US Marines arrived at that moment. "You guys ok?" one asked.

"No," Max said. "My friend has been shot."

"Shit!" one marine said.

The two marines helped Max carry Kevin along to a waiting ambulance. The two paramedics looked at Kevin as the blood ran out onto the soldiers' uniforms. They placed him on a stretcher and put him into the back of the ambulance as it stood stationed on the sidewalk. His blood continued running out from his back, on to the stretcher.

"He's losing too much blood," a medic said.

Max and Eric watched as the shooting started again. The medics placed plastic patches onto his chest, connecting the machine to him. They shocked his body time and time again. The heart monitor showed a straight line. The medic pounded down on Kevin's chest as the machine continued to stay monophonic.

"No," Max went. "No."

The medics gently shook their heads looking at one another.

Max wiped a few tears away from his face. Marco walked over to the group. "You boys ok?" he asked and looked into the back of the vehicle.

"Oh, what the...?" he yelled. He looked at Kevin as he lay in the back of the ambulance. "Shitting hell!" he said.

The shooting and firing were forgotten as Max and Eric stared at Kevin's dead body. The alien tanks rolled along the road heading down towards the main police station. The Armazoid space fighters still attacked the oncoming USAF jets. The frightened civilians ran up the stairs, struggling to find a room to be safe in. Max and Eric reloaded their weapons as the tanks came into view.

"Get ready for the worst, mate," Max said.

"I already am," Eric replied. "I am."

Bradley looked up as they came to the end of the maintenance tunnel. He looked through a small vent leading up into a small room.

"Ready?" he yelled. He clenched his fist and kicked the small tunnel cover off its hinges. He peeked his head out and looked around the empty room.

"What is this place?" CJ asked, jumping out.

"I don't know," Bradley quietly said. He slowly walked around what appeared to be a control room. He admired all the futuristic computers as the electricity surged through them. He looked down onto a large digital screen on the top of a table. He realized he was looking down at the huge digital screen of the ship. He slowly turned his head and looked at a small computer in the far corner of the room. He sat down and looked at the screen some more.

"What the hell is that?" he asked. He clicked on the digital mouse next to him and pulled up what appeared to be a view of a US army satellite poised above the planet.

"Jefferson" Bradley went. Jefferson ran over to Bradley holding his rifle. "What do you make of this?" he asked.

Jefferson looked at the digital screen. "I have no idea" he replied.

"Click on that icon there," Arkalon said.

Bradley clicked on the tiny black icon at the bottom of the screen. The picture of the satellite slowly got bigger as the speakers next to the screen opened up from behind the monitor.

"This is ZAPPY," a voice came from the speakers. "Zappy was invented by the United States Government as an alternate weapon of mass destruction but on a lower basis. Zappy doesn't let out any harmful form of radiation. It emits an electromagnetic pulse crippling anything with an electric circuit involved with it. Zappy can be charged to destroy a certain area of a map or location."

"Wow!" Bradley went. "Never knew of that!"

"If it's the US Government's, God knows what they have," Jefferson said.

"Area fifty one," Bradley said, looking over his

shoulder.

"No comment," Jefferson replied.

"Oh, go on. You can tell me," Bradley said.

"No. Classified." Jefferson said.

Bradley got up and walked away from the desk. He came to a stop, slowly turned around and looked at Arkalon as he stood looking at the digital computers. He looked at the small electric filter on his back as the light bleeped on and off. "That's it," he went. "That's it."

"What's it?" CJ asked.

"You know - that thingy," he said.

"Yes," CJ replied.

"Well, remember when we were back at the warehouse before we set off for here?" Bradley went.

"Yes," CJ said again.

"Well, if our Zappy could just send a wee shock over our dearly beloved Manhattan city" he said, "our visitors will no longer exist."

CJ turned to look at the alien as he stood looking at the computer screen. "Let's do it," he went.

"Wait. Will it work?" Jefferson asked.

"We have no choice," Bradley said.

There was a small pause. "How do we operate it?" CJ asked.

Bradley froze in his tracks. "Ah," he went. "Now that's going to take some thinking."

Arkalon slowly walked over to him. "You can use the computer," he said.

"What?" Bradley asked.

"The computer," Arkalon said. "We can control anything from here."

Bradley was shocked. "Holy shit! All this time your people had access to our weapons of mass destruction?" Bradley gasped.

"I'm afraid so," Arkalon said.

"Well, let's do this," Bradley went. He sat down at the computer and rolled the mouse over to the satellite. The machine beeped.

"As easy as that!" CJ went.

"Yes," Bradley groaned. He pulled up the map of Manhattan on the computer screen. "Shock of a life time!" he went, dragging the mouse over Manhattan. "Enough?" he asked CJ.

"Yep, that will do them," he replied.

Bradley clicked the mouse down. The timer was set,

"Six minutes!" CJ gasped.

"Yep, that's gives Kevin and the rest enough time to hold them back," he went, flicking on his radio.

*   *   *   *

Eric kneeled down by the police patrol car as the alien vehicles got closer and closer.

"Kevin?" Bradley could be heard over their radios.

Eric looked at Max. The shooting started again as the vehicles and aliens got closer to them.

"For fuck's sake, Kevin! For god's sake, you dildo, answer," Bradley went again.

Eric gently shook his head as Max flicked on his radio.

"Kevin's tied up right now," Max said.

"Well, where is he?" Bradley demanded.

"He is helping Kate," Eric replied.

Bradley didn't have any time to argue. "Ok, listen very carefully," he said.

Max looked up the road as the alien tanks stopped. He turned around looking down the long road and he could barely see the police station. The two alien tank drivers reloaded their launchers one after the other. They pushed a button down, firing the rocket from the cannon towards the US army tank.

"INCOMING, INCOMING, move, move," Max yelled.

Marco headed back as the tanks were tossed up into the air from the huge explosion. The fire rained down onto the streets. The apache helicopter flew low firing onto the vehicles. Max felt the turbulence from the blades as they blasted down on to them.

"Max, Max," Bradley yelled over the radio. "Oh, fuck me not again." He swung his head and looked at Jefferson.

"Let's get out of here," CJ said.

"But where to?" Bradley asked.

"There is a vehicle docking bay about half a mile from here," Arkalon said. "You could…"

"Cool," Bradley said. "Let's see if this works."

Zappy was positioned just out over Manhattan. The huge blades on the new dish slowly started to open as it pointed down onto the earth, ready to sweep along over the island. The disks at the back begun to spin, one after the other, powering up the pulse as the new machine continued opening up.

Eric and Max lay in the middle of the street. Eric pulled the trigger on his shot gun. The last shell fired out and slammed into one of the Armazoids as the vehicles slowly rolled towards the station.

"I'm out," Eric said.

"Me too," Max said.

Max and Eric looked at Marco as the last of the golden bullets fired out of his weapon.

"I'm out, too," he said.

It seemed that everyone was out of ammunition as they lay on the ground outside the police station. Eric closed his eyes wondering what death would be like. He just wanted to die quickly and get it over with. Zappy finished powering up. The huge force of electricity fired out of the satellite over Manhattan. The satellite slowly banked in orbit, sending the pulse over Manhattan. Eric looked over his shoulder seeing something coming down the road behind the police station.

"What the…?" Max went.

The EMP swept over Eric and the group over the Armazoids. Eric was shocked. He looked at the aliens as they fell to the floor one after the other. The space fighters fell from the sky one after the other, slamming into buildings. "Get down," he yelled.

The area was quiet. Max slowly got up, flicked out his baton and walked over to one of the dead aliens as he lay in the middle of the street. He kneeled down and looked at the Armazoid as its eyes slowly shut. "It's dead," he went. "It's dead. WE WON!"

Eric dropped his shot gun on the ground and looked at all the frightened people as they stared out in the streets at the dead aliens.

* * * *

Bradley looked up at the digital screen as Zappy fired its pulse over Manhattan. "Done," he went.

"How do we know it's killed them?" CJ asked.

"Don't know, pulse would have fried the radios" Bradley replied. "Right, I think it's time to flee."

"Good. Let's go," CJ replied.

Bradley loaded the last magazine into his M16 and loaded one of the grenades into the launcher. "Right," he went. "Let's get the fuck out of here."

He followed Arkalon towards the rear exit. He pushed the small red button that opened the shiny, silver doors. He held his weapon up and slowly sneaked down the shiny stairs. He kept slowly creeping along the shiny wall. He peeked his head around the corner and looked in disbelief at one of the alien tanks with a group of armed aliens, ready to attack.

"Shit!" he gasped. "It just gets better."

"What's up?" Jefferson asked.

Bradley stopped for a few seconds. "Ok," he went. "There's one of them tanks there, plus some of them things, so any one got a smoke grenade?"

Everyone in the group shook their heads.

"Ok," Bradley went. "Is there a rear exit?"

"No," Arkalon went. "Well, there is, but it's too far."

Jefferson stepped forward. "Ok," he went. "On my go. Go."

He cocked his rifle back ready to open fire.

"What?" Bradley yelled. "You'll be killed."

"I'll take the risk," Jefferson replied.

Bradley didn't answer as Jefferson crept along the wall.

"Ok," Jefferson yelled. "GO!"

Bradley and CJ ran out of the small turning as Jefferson rolled out. He opened fire on the tanks and aliens as Bradley sprinted up the shiny way. Bradley and CJ heard an explosion. He knew Jefferson was dead.

"Come on," he went. He looked at Arkalon as he ran in front of them. The floor started to vibrate as the alien tank rolled in hot pursuit of them.

"Shit! Move!" Bradley yelled. He struggled to keep moving as his leg muscles started to burn. But he felt his legs run over something on the floor of the ship. He looked down to see a set of runners in the ground.

"What's that?" he asked

"It's a set of shutters," Arkalon replied. "Look."

Bradley looked over to see a set of controls. He slowly ran over to them, and activated them. He watched as the huge doors slowly started to roll closed as the alien tank came into view. "Come on. Close," he went.

The shutters sealed shut.

"Should buy us some time," CJ said.

Bradley took a second to breathe before they moved on.

But something happened. Bradley and CJ heard a voice.

"Bradley," Circo said.

Bradley looked around.

"You've got this far. Now you are finished, and your friend and he," Circo went.

"Where are you?" Bradley yelled.

Circo didn't answer. Bradley heard a funny sound coming from the wall. He looked up to see a small flap open up on the side of the wall. Bradley and CJ's eyes opened in fear as they watched a black heavy machine gun slowly point down at them.

"Oh, fuck!" Bradley went. He watched as the blue power surged up behind it, ready to shoot down on him. "Come on," he went.

He grabbed Arkalon. The blue rays fired out the back of the weapon. Bradley grabbed the alien, pulling him to the floor. He watched as CJ was hit by the rays and fell to the ground, bleeding out from the burns.

"Go, go!" CJ mumbled. "Tell Marsha, I, I"

Bradley watched as CJ's eyes slowly closed. "Now I'm pissed," he went. He pulled out his M16. He looked at the small grenade as it sat ready to be launched. He placed his finger on the trigger, ready to open fire. He spun around as the weapon turned and pointed at him. He pulled the trigger, firing the grenade at the weapon. It slammed into the long black canister igniting it. "Ha," he went.

He turned around. He knew he had to get to that bay and get the hell out of the ship. But that horrible noise happened again. He looked up, watching another machine gun come out of the side of the walls. "What?" he moaned.

Bradley pulled Arkalon along, reloading his grenade into the launcher. He spun around, firing at it as the constant threat of weapons came out of the wall. He sprinted along the corridors. He reloaded the last grenade into the launcher and took out one of the chasing machine guns.

"In here," Arkalon yelled, opening a set of silver doors. Bradley bundled himself in with the rays slamming into the door as it sealed shut. Bradley slowly got up. He dropped his M16 onto the ground as it was now empty.

"What is this place?" he asked.

"This is the weapon storage room," Arkalon said.

"Wicked," Bradley went. He looked around at all the missiles lined up and ready to be used. He felt in his pocket for one of the tiny C4 charges Marco had given him.

"I wonder…" he went.

He reached down and pulled out the charge from his pocket. He kneeled down looking over his shoulder as he knew he only had a short time within which to leave the ship. He switched on the charges ready to blow the hell out of the rockets, and hopefully bring the craft down out of the sky. He suddenly jumped as an alarm wailed.

"What's that?" he asked.

"It's the ship," Arkalon said. "They are leaving the planet."

"Come on," Bradley said. He and Arkalon ran over to the large open elevator.

"This is it," Arkalon went.

Bradley looked at the huge silver plate. "Listen," Bradley went. "Thanks."

"No problem," Arkalon went. "You scared the shit out of me."

"Cool," Bradley said. "Well, thanks."

Bradley smiled at Arkalon as he walked onto the huge plate looking at all the stacked up missiles in the weapon storage unit.

"Blow you bastards," he went.

The brakes clunked off one after the other. He leant against the power box as the lift slowly started to lower down into the depth of the ship. He looked up and rubbed his face. He felt the lift shunt to a quick stop. The silver shutter slowly opened, allowing him to get out. He walked into the huge bay and looked at all the parked alien vehicles.

"Right. Let's leave this heap of shit," he said to himself.

He walked into the centre of the bay and looked around at the huge shutter leading to the outside of the ship. He continued looking around, making sure none of the aliens were hiding and waiting to get at him. But he did see something. He looked at a set of stairs leading up to the control room.

"Lovely," he went, slowly starting to walk towards the entrance as he was out of energy.

"NOT SO FAST," Circo went.

Bradley knelt down on the floor. The lights around the huge bay were switched on. Bradley looked around to hundreds of the aliens surrounding him.

"So, Bradley," Circo went. "Were you planning to escape?"

"Yes, I was," Bradley said.

"Well done," Circo said. "Was."

Bradley took a look at the control room as he knew he had to get to that lever to get out of there. He slowly moved his leg. He felt the flare gun rub against his leg- the one he had picked up from the weapon shop earlier on. He smiled, looking around at the aliens as they slowly advanced towards him.

"Don't make any sudden movements," one alien said.

Bradley looked at his watch. He knew he only had a couple of minutes left before the C4 blew and the whole ship went up in flames. He took a deep breath. He dropped to the floor and, reaching down to his leg, swiped the flare gun. He pointed it up into the air, pulling the trigger. He squinted his eyes closed and heading towards the control room stairs. The flash exploded, blinding all the aliens.

Bradley dove towards the stairs as the aliens struggled to get their vision back so they could kill him. He ran up the shiny silver stairs into the control room. He looked down at the red lever. He pulled it back and watched the huge door slowly start to roll down. He waited a few seconds for it to get down a bit further. He watched as the group of aliens ran up the stairs towards the control room. He reached into his pocket and pulled out the baton. He watched two aliens charge at him. He swung the baton, smashing it on the heads of the aliens. "Nice try," he went.

He looked out the door to the control room, seeing the huge shutter partly open. He ran down the stairs diving behind one of the alien vehicles as the aliens continued to fire at him.

"Shit!" he gasped.

Bradley looked to his left quickly as he felt the craft engines powering up. The intense roar roared through the ship as the shutter started to close. He knew he had only one chance to get out of the place. He looked under the vehicle so see one of the armed aliens holding a launcher ready to blow the crap out of him. He leapt out from under the vehicle and threw the baton through the air. The long metal rod twisted through the air and slammed into the alien. The alien fell on its left side, firing the rocket as Bradley leapt up and jumped onto the closing shutters. The aliens fired onto him as the shutter continued to close. One alien in the group looked through his scope and pointed the weapon at Bradley. It pulled the trigger and launched the ray through the air. The purple ray slammed into the back of Bradley's foot.

"Agggh," Bradley yelled.

He managed to keep himself going as the huge atomic motors on the bottom of the ship pushed the craft up. He made it to the top of the shutter. He looked down onto the ocean and Manhattan as blood drained out of his foot. He took a deep breath and threw himself from the shutter as the craft pointed upwards, heading away from earth towards outer space. He stared down at his watch as the cold air blew onto his face. He turned around and looked at the huge ship as it slowly started to disappear from sight. He looked down at his watch as he fell towards earth. The wind rustled through the air as the timer hit zero. He turned around and looked at the ship.

The countdown reached zero. The spacecraft shot out of the earth. The small C4 charge bleeped quickly. The explosion ripped along the through the ship blasting open all doors. The walls ripped into one another. The aliens on the ship looked down the long aisles at the huge flow of fire racing toward them. The huge craft blew up in flames as it left the atmosphere. Bradley looked at the huge ball of fire as tiny scraps of metal floated down past him. He turned around and looked down towards the ground as the Hudson River came into view. He looked down at the red cord on the chute. He placed his hand on it and grasping his hand ripped the cord halfway out. The chute didn't open.

"Oh no," Bradley went. "Oh fuck!"

He continued tumbling towards the ground. He pushed the small metal cord back in as the huge river got bigger and bigger.

"Come on," Bradley yelled. He ripped the cord on the chute again. The small parachute opened, pulling the large one out. He slowed down floating towards the river. He braced himself for a wet landing.

Manhattan was quiet. Smoke was still rising from the ground. Bradley closed his eyes as he slammed into the water. He looked over at Manhattan as the balloons on the side of the pack inflated after he pulled the small toggle. He listened to the canisters hissing as the blue bands slowly came out the side. He let his head drop into the cool water of the Hudson. He looked down as the small empty handgun slowly slipped out of his pocket landing in the river. Small air bubbles rose to the top as the weapon slowly sank. But the day was almost over. The sun slowly started descending on the horizon as the clear evening sky started to darken. Bradley looked at the tiny stars many millions of galaxies away. It had always been a dream of his to go and see one. But now it no longer was. He wanted to keep way away from them. The small waves rocked Bradley about. He slowly leaned up, feeling very drained by the lack of blood in his system now. He felt the wound stinging as he slowly started pulling himself to the pier a short way ahead.

*   *   *   *

Bradley climbed onto the wooden pier coughing up the sea water from his lungs. He slowly got up and walked around, looking around at some of the aliens as they lay dead in the middle of the roads and streets. He reached into his small pouch and pulled out a small bandage. He wrapped it around his legs, trying to stop the blood from seeping out of the wound. He looked down as the clean, white bandage helped and the blood stopped running from the wound. The road slowly started to vibrate again. He swung his head and looked down the road, thinking the alien tanks were still rolling. But it was a sight he would never forget. Bradley looked to see three US Army tanks, escorted by a few jeeps, rolling towards him. He placed his hand out as a jeep pulled up next to him.

"Hop on," the soldier said.

Bradley smirked as he got onto the jeep. He didn't say anything about the wound on the back of his leg. He just wanted to make sure the group was ok. The jeep sped along the dead roads bypassing all the dead aliens and alien vehicles as they stood parked in the middle of the streets.

The jeep made a left turn and pulled up at the police station. With the evacuation of the city on, Bradley walked up the concrete steps and looked at the people boarding the long line of buses waiting to take them away. These people were most probably never coming back to New York. He walked through the open glass doors. People looked at him completely covered in dirt and soot, and drenched to the skin. He started to dry off a bit as he walked through to the back offices. He looked through the glass window at Kate, Jane, and Ms. Javies as they sat down looking at one another. Bradley opened the door and slowly walked in, trying not to make them jump. He tried not to limp as the blood was starting to run through the bandage now. Kate slowly turned her head to the left wondering who it was who had come in. She caught a glimpse of Bradley and slowly turned her head away. She blinked her eyes slowly and turned back again to look at Bradley.

"Oh my god," she quietly went.

Kate jumped up and Jane looked at him as well.

"Bradley!" Kate went. She fell into Bradley. He groaned with pain as he hugged Kate. Jane, Eric and Max walked in as well and they all hugged each other after their horrific day.

"What a day!" Bradley went.

Ms. Javies looked at Bradley. "B… B…" Ms. Javies mumbled. "Bradley."

Bradley couldn't even look at Ms. Javies.

"You guys ok?" Bradley asked.

"Just about," Kate replied. "Better now we know you're ok."

There was a short break.

"You ok, dork?" Bradley said.

"I'm ok," Eric replied.

"Not you, Eric," Bradley said. "Him."

Bradley looked over at Colin.

"Oh, I'm fine," Colin said.

"You did good in that ship," Bradley replied.

"Thanks," Eric replied.

"And you Max," Bradley said. "You kicked the shit out of some of them."

"Ha," Max went.

"And you Demmio," Bradley said. "You were good as well. All that national service paid off."

"Cheers, mate," Demmio went.

"Love you guys," Bradley went.

"Bradley," Kate went. "You saved all our lives. If you hadn't been with us we would all be dead."

"Ha," Bradley went. "Of course. Anyway, I want to hug Kevin. Where's he?"

Kate looked at Jane as the group went quiet.

Bradley looked down at Kate. "What's up?" he asked, slowly starting to sway from side to side. The blood slowly ran down the back of this leg. He felt the tiny droplets running down it and into his wet shoes. He looked at the group as they looked at him.

"Bradley, listen," Kate went quietly.

Bradley looked down at Kate as she continued to hold him.

"Kevin, er…" she quietly said. "Kevin was killed a short while ago."

Bradley couldn't believe his ears. "No," he went "No, no, no."

Bradley looked over at Ms. Javies sitting down in a chair in the corner. He slowly leaned forward placing his head in his hands. More blood began to seep from the wound on his leg. "Aggh," he moaned.

"What?" Kate went.

Bradley fell back on the floor. She looked at the long line of blood as it started to seep from under the wet trousers.

"Shit!" she gasped. "Can we get some help in here?"

Bradley lay on the cold floor of the station as the group looked down at him. He struggled to keep his eyes open as the two military doctors ran in. They looked down at Bradley as he lay on the floor.

"Come on," Kate yelled.

The two doctors loaded Bradley onto a stretcher to take him to the military medical centre that had been set up. Bradley still drifted in and out of consciousness wondering if he was going to Kevin. He slowly turned his head to the right and looked along the corridors as they wheeled him in. He felt the red dark blood building up on his leg. The stretcher slammed through the rubber door and skidded to a stop.

"What do we have?" a doctor asked.

"Injured male," the other doctor said. "Lost a lot of blood."

Time went by slowly. The doctor looked on as Bradley was linked up to a heart machine. Bradley heard the beeping as he struggled to keep his eyes open.

"We're losing him," he heard. There was a straight, long beep.

The remaining hours of the day went by. It didn't seem to stop. The stars twinkled down onto the city as the military helicopters circled above the city looking for any aliens who might still be around. Kate, Jane, Eric, Max, Marco and Demmio refused to leave the military medical zone in case Bradley woke up. The small white clock slowly ticked the seconds away as the night passed very slowly.

22

Bradley's eyes slowly opened. They burned with pain as he had been out for quite a while. The soft sheet on the hospital bed rubbed against his skin as he looked to see an open window. He slowly sat up and rubbed his face, looking at the drip attached to his body. He gently moved his wrist, feeling the silver pin make it twitch. A cool breeze came in through the window, blowing the curtain out of the way. Bradley slowly slipped on his slippers and getting up, walked over to it. He looked out onto the Hudson River. The current slowly moved along as the sun sparkled on it. No smoke was coming from the buildings, nor were there any military helicopters flying overhead.

"What happened?" he asked, turning around and seeing a doctor walking in through the door to the private cubicle.

"Aggh, Bradley, my friend," he went. "My name is Charlie. You gave us quite a scare"

Bradley didn't answer as he was still feeling down about what had happened to Kevin.

"Come on, lie down," the doctor went.

Bradley slowly got back onto the bed.

"How are you feeling?" Charlie asked, placing his hand on Bradley's pulse.

"Where're my friends?" Bradley asked.

"Oh, they're just outside, mate," Charlie answered and walked to the door. "You can come in now," he said.

Eric, Max, Kate and Jane walked in. "Hey guys,"

Bradley mumbled.

"You ok?" Eric asked.

"Yeah, just about," Bradley replied. "What a day to remember!"

"Tell me about it," Eric said. "So, you ok?"

"I'm fine," Bradley said. "I'm sorry about Kevin."

The group all looked at one another.

"What?" Eric went.

"I'm sorry about Kevin," he said again.

"Uh, Bradley," Jane went. "Kevin is outside."

"Oh, is he?" Bradley said.

There was a short pause.

"WHAT?" he then gasped.

"He is outside," Max said. "Don't you remember what happened?"

"Yes," Bradley said. "Kevin was saving her."

"Bradley, you ok?" Jane went.

"I'm fine," he replied.

"Bradley," Charlie said. "You have been in a coma for about five hours. You were involved in a bus crash before you even got to New York. You took off your seat belt and banged your head."

Bradley shook his head. "So New York hasn't been…………..never mind"

"Go and get Kevin," Charlie went.

Bradley had to struggle to keep himself awake. He couldn't get the whole day out of his head. Kevin slowly walked in and looked at Bradley. Bradley reached out and grabbed Kevin.

"I love you," Bradley went.

"Your mum and dad are here as well," Charlie said.

Just then Bradley's mum and dad walked in. "Bradley," his mum yelled.

"I'm ok," he went.

"Oh god, I was so worried," she replied.

Kate looked at Mr. and Mrs. Harrison as they walked in. "Shall we go?" she suggested.

"Yeah, come on," Kevin said. "Brad, I'll see you soon."

Bradley smiled and leaned back into the pillow. "The doctor says you will be out in a few days," his dad said. "So what's this dream you had?"

Bradley lay back in his bed. He looked out of the window at Manhattan Island, as the jets from the airport continued to fly overhead heading to places all over the world. The stars were hidden behind the wonderful clear blue sky. He took a deep breath and looked at his mum and dad as they looked down at him. How could it all happen on a field trip and would they believe the story he was about to tell?

Lightning Source UK Ltd.
Milton Keynes UK
UKOW031839030912

198434UK00013B/9/P

9 781616 673086